THE DUMMY LINE

by

BOBBY COLE

CONTEXT™

The Dummy Line

Inquiries should be addressed to:
Context Publishing Company, LLC.
161 Pembroke Circle
Madison, MS 39110
www.contextpublishing.com
The CONTEXT logo is a trademark of Context Publishing Co., LLC.

Library of Congress Control Number: 2007940584

ISBN-13: 978-0-9800171-0-6
ISBN-10: 0-9800171-0-6

Cover art and design by Steve Erickson and Kyle Jennings
Author photo by Austin Delano
Book design by Kyle Jennings

First Edition 2008

10 9 8 7 6 5 4 3 2 1

Manufactured in the United States of America

Dedication

To my mother and late father, who by their loving example, are still teaching me how to be a good parent and decent man.

And to my wonderful wife, Melissa, who is nothing like Morgan in this book, but who did give me a wonderful daughter, Jessi, who is very much like Katy.

The Dummy Line

Life changes — usually in the blink of an eye. One minute everything's fine, if not stagnant, then, it's not. But your character's not defined by what happens to you but by how you respond to those emotionally significant events. Who will you become when your life turns on a dime?

CHAPTER 1

Hurry up, Katy," Jake Crosby called out as he took a wet tennis ball from his aged Lab, Scout. "We won't have enough time to build a fire and roast marshmallows if we don't get going."

What am I thinking? he told himself. *You can't hurry a nine-year-old.*

Katy had really taken an interest in the outdoors. She loved to hunt and fish and found fun in the smallest things. She would giggle for hours playing with crappie minnows or crickets. Katy had killed her first deer at seven, making a perfect shot on a small buck. This qualified her as a full-fledged member of the hunting fraternity...or maybe sorority. Anyway, she loved to go with her dad, and Jake gladly modified his hunting habits to accommodate her. Introducing Katy to the sights and sounds of the woods was a pleasure — a blessing. Katy's motivation was to "outdo" the boys in her class. She relished this competition. And Jake did his part to make sure she was successful. By eight, she had caught several limits of rainbow trout and a boatload of bass, killed four deer, and been on several successful duck hunts. Jake was raising a tomboy, and he loved it. On this trip, he was hoping to call up a gobbling turkey. If it would walk up struttin' and drummin' and put on a show, Katy would be hooked. This weekend she was going to experience what turkey hunting was all about.

Katy finally jerked open the front door and ran outside carrying her camo travel bag, two Beanie Babies, and an arm full of books. She was a reader. Jake loved the way she looked—her ponytail threaded through the back of a baseball cap—a cute tomboy. Jake smiled.

"Let's go, Dad. Are *you* ready yet?" she teased. "Can we play pool when we get there?"

"Sure. Have you got everything…boots, head net, gloves?"

"Yes, sir." Katy replied politely but rolled her eyes.

Jake's wife, Morgan, walked out carrying Katy's lime-green sleeping bag and a pink pillow.

"Please make sure she goes to the bathroom. Last time she didn't," she said with a little worry mixed with sarcasm.

"Well, I asked her. She just didn't really like the facilities. It's not exactly the Hilton. But I'll make sure she goes. Don't you want to come?" he asked, already knowing the answer.

"No, I'm gonna rent a movie, curl up on the couch, and relax."

"We'll be home by lunchtime…and I'm bettin' we'll have a turkey. Don't worry about Katy. I'll take care of her. Tate's already there and he'll have the lights on and a fire built. She'll have a blast."

"When are you going to finish that flower bed in the backyard?" she asked, not caring if they killed a turkey. She hoped they didn't because she knew Jake would claim it was Katy's first and want to get it stuffed for display in the den. To Morgan, Jake's improvised "trophy room" already resembled a frozen zoo with all of his dead critters. The deer heads seemed to stare at her, the turkeys were hideously ugly, the ducks she could tolerate, but his full-mount bobcat made her sad. *Why shoot a cat?* She always wondered.

Morgan hated hunting season. She hated deer season. She hated duck season. And then, just when things seemed to settle back down, spring turkey season rolled around—which she hated even more. She didn't really hate the "sport"; it just took up so much time—Jake's time, time that he should spend earning more money or making home improvements. Turkey hunting was especially exhausting for Jake because of the early hours. Turkey hunters operate like a clandestine cult, waking at obscene hours, painting their faces, and driving all over the country in the dark. The result: very little yard work got accomplished in the spring when it was most needed. While the neighbors were busy trimming bushes and mulching, Jake was either gone or asleep on the couch recovering from an early-morning hunt. The reality was that their yard looked better than most. Jake somehow always found time to get it done. But Morgan couldn't recognize it. Every time she saw Jake lying on the couch, it was a huge source of resentment.

If he's going to do something worthless, at least he could play golf like every other stockbroker in the world. Maybe he could make some deals on the course or at the nineteenth hole, she thought wistfully.

Even after two years of dating and eleven years of marriage, Morgan had not totally given up on trying to change him—she had just gotten better at tolerating him. She grudgingly acknowledged that Jake was a somewhat decent provider, and even she had to admit that he was a great father—she'd give him that, even if she did find him boring.

Driven more by a desire to silence Morgan's nagging than any personal desire for riches, Jake had invested heavily in a few "sure-fire" stocks that surprised everyone, then became de-listed within weeks of his taking a position. His biggest concern now was dealing with the reality of being owned by the banks. House payments, car payments, truck payments, private school, horse-riding lessons; it never ended.

There always seemed to be more month than money.

Morgan had married Jake because she thought he was going places, big places—away from West Point, Mississippi, a small town in a rural county, with a total population less than ten thousand. Jake and Katy liked West Point, but Morgan longed for a big city with all the trappings.

Now she hung on because of Katy. And she rarely missed an opportunity to needle Jake about his failures, like taking a bath on Krispy Kreme stock. Jake had insisted that all his clients buy the Krispy Kreme initial public offering. He had grown up eating the hot glazed doughnuts and knew the world would love them, too. Jake had made his clients and his firm a lot of money on paper. A few of Jake's clients smartly took their profits while too many others followed Jake's lead and stared helplessly as the Atkins low-carb craze blistered the doughnut business. Jake continued to hold and hope that the downward spiral would stop. It didn't. He just loved those doughnuts and refused to sell. Jake and Morgan's portfolio took an enormous hit. He desperately needed something that would get red-hot fast. His firm was listed as book-running managers on two tech companies for June, and he couldn't wait. He was also eyeing a way to capitalize on the Dutch IPO of a company that converted used motor oil into low-grade diesel fuel. *One big score and she'll get off my ass*, he thought.

Jake saw Morgan was still waiting for an answer about the flower bed. He said, "Soon. I promise. I'll get to the flower bed." He planned on doing it. It just wasn't a priority…to him.

"Load up, Katy. Let's go."

"Bye, Mom. I love you."

"I love you, too."

"Bye!"

"Bye!"

"Bye!"

"Jeez, girls, we'll be back tomorrow."

"Bye, Mom."

"Bye, sweetheart."

"Come on, Katy. Let's go. I feel like we're going off to college."

"Well, Jake…what if something happened? This...this might be our last goodbye."

Jake really didn't know what to say to that…what could you say? He just cranked up and waved goodbye.

"We'll be home tomorrow. Love ya," he said routinely.

"You too."

"Bye, Mom."

"Bye."

Rolling down the driveway, Katy waved until she couldn't see her mother anymore. Turning forward, she said, "Mom doesn't know what she's missing."

"Well, I've invited her plenty of times. Grandpa didn't hunt, so she didn't grow up around it and doesn't understand that it's way more than killing. Fasten your seat belt, girlfriend."

Their first stop was the Piggly Wiggly. Jake needed Honey Buns for their breakfast, Cokes for him, and Dr Peppers for Katy. Marshmallows, Cheetos, and a bag of ice rounded out the shopping list. Katy pushed an empty buggy around the store as Jake loaded up on junk food to eat—nothing healthy like Brussels sprouts and asparagus for these hunters.

The hour-and-a-half drive to Sumter County, Alabama, passed quickly. Jake called to check on his mother and then dialed in the new classic country station. It reminded him of high school. *Willie Nelson, Don Williams, Alabama*, each classic song brought back a flood of good memories. When Conway Twitty came on singing "That's My Job," commonly called "The Daddy Song," he made Katy stop reading her book to listen to the words. Jake loved that old song.

During the last few miles of the drive, as Katy read by Book-light, he thought about how lucky he was to be in this hunting club. Supposedly, the land had not been turkey-hunted in ten years. Supposedly. The eight members only deer-hunted. Jake's friend Mick Johnson had talked the club president into letting them have the turkey-hunting rights. Jake thought his share of the rights was a bargain at two grand a year. *Morgan would have a stroke if she knew,* he thought. But she didn't and wouldn't. He always had a few secret side projects that financed his hunting habit.

To say that the camp's clubhouse was a work in progress was generous. It had started out as an old farmhouse but had so many rooms added on that you really couldn't tell what was what. Neon beer signs hung on every wall. An old pool table sat in the center of the main room. The half-dozen deer heads were cluttered with hats. Jake hated that; he thought the deer deserved more respect. But they weren't his, so he kept his opinions to himself. It was a classic Southern camp, complete with a fully stocked bar, satellite dish, and every Playmate and *Sports Illustrated* swimsuit calendar since 1987.

Jake had hauled his old Airstream camper out there so he wouldn't have to sleep on someone else's bed in a roomful of snoring. The old silver camper was clean and warm—a sanctuary—a pragmatic getaway from a wobbly career, a shaky marriage, and the sounds and smells of other hunters. Some of his best nights' sleep came huddled next to the electric space heater. The "Love Sub," as he liked to call it, was parked right next to the camp house and used its electricity. The camper blended perfectly into the landscape of old tractors, pickup trucks, and utility trailers. Jake admired the camp's John Deere 2040 tractor the way his professional colleagues lusted after a new Porsche.

Tate Newsom worked with Jake and was a member of the turkey club. Tate was going to leave work early in an effort to roost a bird for Saturday morning's hunt. Jake hoped Tate had a fire going. Just the three of them would be hunting tomorrow. Tate didn't hunt that often, but he was great around Katy; he had a gift for entertaining kids.

Through his many trips to the camp, Jake had learned the west Alabama cellular system and knew that his last chance to make a call was the ridge just past the big Waste Management landfill. With only two bars of service, he called home to report that they had made it, so Morgan wouldn't worry about Katy.

"Hello."

"We made it," Jake said into the static.

"Hello?"

"WE MADE IT…we are almost there," he yelled into the phone, holding it in front of his face, staring at the screen.

"Okay...Y'all have fun," he heard Morgan reply.

"We will."

"What?"

"I SAID, WE WILL." Jake wanted to throw his phone out the window.

"Okay," Morgan replied, clueless as to how annoyed Jake was getting. The call went dead.

Jake hated cell phones. They were nice when they worked, but you couldn't count on them when you were in rural Mississippi or Alabama. He cringed every time his rang. It was usually somebody wanting something, or telling him about something that wasn't going as planned, or it was Morgan doing both. Slinging the phone down, Jake let out a deep sigh and drove on.

It was almost 8:30 P.M. when he finally turned onto the last gravel road. Jake's headlights reflected brightly off the white reflective tape on the heavy metal gate. Slowing to a stop, Jake was surprised to find that the gate was locked.

Where in the world's Tate? he thought as he got out and fumbled with the protected lock.

Tate Newsom was newly wed to a girl twenty years younger and frequently didn't show up when expected. *Forty-five and twenty-five.* That thought always made Jake smile. Jake figured that Tate must have taken his bride to the country club for supper and would be here by 10 P.M. at the latest. He pulled through and closed the gate, leaving it unlocked for Tate.

CHAPTER 2

Tanner Tillman was a few months away from high school graduation. He had been the quarterback of the Sumter County High School football team and was headed to Auburn University to pursue a degree in forestry. Tanner drove a 1981 Jeep CJ-7 with big mud grips and a sound system that had cost more than the Jeep. He was what the locals called a "good kid." Levi's, cowboy boots, and button-down shirts were what he wore most days. He rarely got into trouble, and, because his grandfather had been an alcoholic, his mother was very strict about drinking. Like most good ol' boys from the South, Tanner dearly loved his momma and he didn't want to hurt her, so he never drank. His grades were mediocre at best because he spent most of his time bird-doggin' Elizabeth Beasley, a cheerleader and the runner-up for homecoming queen last October. They had been dating most of the school year. Their Senior Prom was a few weeks away. Tanner was making big plans that included a limo.

Elizabeth's father was a very successful accountant, so she had grown up with most of life's finer things. She planned to attend the University of Virginia at Charlottesville to study architecture, specializing in the design of modern antebellum-style homes. Elizabeth was the perfect daughter—involved in everything and careful about whom she dated and her reputation. She was an all-American girl. Her appearance was striking; consequently, every red-blooded male in the four surrounding counties knew of her. The good guys spent every penny they had on dinners, flowers, and movies, unsuccessfully trying to win her affections. The bad boys lurked in the dark hoping her bright yellow Volkswagen Beetle would break down somewhere remote. All the girls were simply jealous. Without knowing it, she was on everyone's radar screen. Her father joked about building a moat around the house to protect her. Elizabeth didn't realize he was serious.

It was Friday night, April 15. Elizabeth's father would be at the office late finishing up the tax returns for his clients who had waited until the very final minute. Her mother always helped organize and mail the returns. These were the only few days of the year she worked, and she mostly did it to see how much money the other families in the community earned.

After months of persistent hounding, Tanner had finally talked Elizabeth into going parking out on his family's land. Her parents would be working late. This might be the perfect time to stay out much later than normal. The relationship was becoming serious. They had dated exclusively for the last several months. Tanner was working her hard because he knew that once she went to college she would never return. He needed her to fall in love with him.

Elizabeth had no intention of going all the way with anyone, but she liked Tanner more than she publicly admitted and she was a little curious about a few things. A strict Catholic upbringing had guided her so far, and she didn't intend to stray off the path…very much. Tanner was Southern Baptist; at this stage in his life, however, he wasn't guided by much of anything except his hormones. Elizabeth was special and he didn't want to push too hard or too fast. He respected her. Tanner knew that he was in love.

Elizabeth insisted they go someplace safe. Tanner had the perfect spot. His family owned 160 acres out in the county. There was no way in the world anyone would catch them out there. Tanner tried to sell her on the idea of watching for shooting stars. She knew what he had in mind. His second-biggest concern was draining the Jeep's battery listening to the radio, but he'd solved that problem. He'd borrowed a battery from a seldom-used delivery truck at the lumberyard where he worked. No one would ever know. If his sound system drained the main battery he was prepared. Elizabeth would be impressed.

The date started with a forty-minute drive to Tuscaloosa, west Alabama's society hub and home of The University of Alabama. Most all of their dates started with a drive to Tuscaloosa, as there wasn't much recreation for teenagers in Sumter County. Tanner had the top up on his Jeep so it wouldn't be too cold and windy on the interstate. After dinner at Dreamland Bar-B-Que, they went on campus to Thomas Sewell Stadium, commonly called "The Joe," to watch Alabama and Auburn play baseball. Night games were perfect for dates. The temperature was pleasant, the crowd was fun, and there was plenty of time to talk. They loved to talk. There was so much going on in their lives. College decisions were bearing down on them. Each was deeply interested in the other yet secretly suspected that their relationship couldn't survive the distance. They both wished they could step back—let the world slow down. The young couple shared a Dr Pepper in a big plastic cup. Tanner loved sharing anything with Elizabeth.

After the ball game they quietly walked back to the parking lot. He was so nervous he forgot to open the door for her. Tanner usually had impeccable manners. She smiled, recognizing what was going on. She knew what was on his mind.

Once they were in the Jeep, Tanner wanted to ask her about parking...hoping she was still willing. So far he had played it pretty nonchalant, like he planned these events all the time. Inside he was a bundle of nerves.

Something in his back pocket started vibrating, making a thumping sound against the tight canvas seats. He had forgotten that she had stuck her cell phone in his back pocket on the way into the game so she wouldn't have to carry her purse. The vibration really startled Tanner. Elizabeth got so tickled and laughed so hard that Dr Pepper shot out of her nose.

"Is that your butt vibrating?" she asked and burst out laughing again.

Tanner blushed and handed her the phone.

Elizabeth pushed her hair behind her ear and cheerfully said, "Hello," while she smiled lovingly at Tanner.

"Yes, ma'am, it was a great game. Well, except Auburn won." She winked at Tanner. "It was 9–7. We will…I promise. We'll be careful. Y'all don't work too late. I love you, Mom. Bye."

"Checking on you?" he asked.

"More like checking on you, to make sure you hadn't kidnapped me," she said with a grin.

"So, still wanna see the stars tonight?" he asked, starting the Jeep and giving her his best smile.

"Sure it's safe?" she squinted her eyes at him.

"I swear it is." He replied making a cross sign over his heart.

"Let's go!" she exclaimed, smiling widely and then kissing him on the cheek.

Tanner drove holding Elizabeth's hand while they listened to her new Kenny Chesney CD. When they finally got to the gravel road, Tanner dropped the Jeep's top. The sky was clear, the temperature cool. No one to interrupt. The perfect setting for a few hours of stargazing.

CHAPTER 3

The camp house was about 150 yards past the gate and stood silent, surrounded by massive pine trees. Enveloped in total darkness, Jake swallowed hard and hurried to park so he could turn on some lights. The darkness confirmed that Tate hadn't made it. Tucked into the corner of the lot and off to the side of the main camp house was the Love Sub. He parked right in front of it and left the headlights on while he got out, unlocked the door, and found the switch, quickly flipping on the lights. Relief flooded him as much as the lights did the darkness of the camper.

Katy was right behind him, claiming the top bunk for herself and the Beanie Babies. Jake left her on the bed and went outside to unlock the camp house and turn on the floodlights. Safely navigating the sheer quantity of junk lying around outside required as much light as possible. There were old cookers, bald tires, and tree-stands, and the grass was almost knee deep. *I gotta tell Katy to stay on the path so she won't step on a rattlesnake,* he thought.

As each light turned on, Jake felt progressively better. He wasn't scared of the dark, but at times it got a little spooky. On the far side of Jake's camper was an abandoned mobile home. It had huge holes in the walls, exposing the insulation, and all the windows were broken. Katy imagined it was haunted. Even at thirty-eight, Jake preferred not to think about it. This whole place was creepy. The camp looked like a Hollywood version of a Ku Klux Klan meeting place, complete with Rebel flags and animal skulls.

Katy was in the upper bunk doing whatever nine-year-old girls and Beanie Babies do as Jake moved their stuff from the truck into the camper. After turning on the electric space heater to knock the chill out of the air, he organized their gear for the morning hunt. Boots, long johns, socks, and camo were all ready for action. The only items left in the truck were his shotgun and his hunting vest.

"Let's start a fire. We can play a few games of pool while it gets going," Jake suggested.

"Oh, yeah!" she excitedly replied and began climbing down from the bunk.

One of the things Jake really liked about this camp was the outside fire pit. It was so relaxing to sit around a fire when the air was cool. Jake loved the way it felt when his front side got warm and his backside was cool. He could sit for hours just watching the flames and periodically poking at the wood.

By placing a starter log with a few pieces of fatwood in the old ashes and stacking dry logs around it, he methodically built the fire. Then, to get it going as fast as possible, he soaked everything with lighter fluid. He dropped in a match. The fire flashed. He immediately felt the heat on his skin. Standing there for a few seconds, he watched the fire quickly overtake every inch of lighter fluid.

"Wow...that's a big fire!" exclaimed Katy.

"Let's play some pool. I'll keep an eye on it. We'll let it burn down some before we roast marshmallows. Did you get enough to eat? Are you hungry, thirsty?"

"I'm fine, Dad."

"Well, come on. Walk right behind me. This grass is so high you might trip over something. Let's have the World Championship Pool Tournament. Loser leaves town," Jake joked.

"You're in trouble, big boy, 'cause I'm gonna beat you like a redheaded stepchild!" Katy rambled, doing her best tough-girl imitation.

"Katy, where did you hear that?"

"From you! You say it all the time when you're working Scout at the river."

"Well, don't say that anymore. It's not nice. It's just an old-timey saying. Jeez, girl, you're gonna get me in trouble." Jake said, rolling his eyes. *I'm gonna have to watch what I say around her. She's a sponge.* Walking toward the camp house, he remembered something else that might get him in trouble.

"Hey, Katy, don't pay any attention to the pictures on the walls, and don't tell Mom, okay?" Jake knew that wouldn't have deterred him when he was her age, but Katy was the kind of kid who typically would do what you asked. On his last trip to the camp, he had covered up the really bad ones (or good ones depending upon your perspective). All that could be seen easily were a few Texas girls in bikinis.

Jake suspected that the guys who owned this club never brought out their wives or girlfriends, based on the sheer number of pinups on the walls. Or maybe they did and the women just didn't care. Morgan would have walked in, looked around, and run right back out. Her idea of roughing it was a Hilton. Throw in a few nudy pictures and it would hit the fan.

"Please go to the bathroom, Katy, while I rack up the balls."

"Aw, Dad."

"Please."

"The door doesn't lock."

"It's just me…and I'm not going to bust up in there while you're doing your business."

"Uhhhh…okay." She shrugged and plodded off as though she were doomed.

Once the balls were racked, Jake picked out a cue and stuck his head out the door to check on the fire. It was still roaring strong.

"It won't flush!" Katy hollered, sounding perplexed.

"You must have broken it, girlfriend."

"Dad, I'm serious."

"Sorry. I forgot to turn the water on. Hang on." Jake found the water key and a flashlight that worked for a few seconds if he shook it real hard. He walked to the far end of the lot, shook the light, found the water service, and hurriedly turned it on. Jake never wasted time in the dark.

"Try it now," he yelled as he stepped back inside.

"Thank you!" she responded over the flush.

Jake smiled. All this with the bathroom made him think of *Sanford and Son.* His dad really liked that TV show. He would belly-laugh when Fred flushed the toilet. A lot of things reminded him of his dad.

Katy came bounding out of the bathroom, and the World Pool Championship began. She loved to shoot pool and was slowly grasping the fundamentals. Jake was a patient teacher, refraining from comment when one of her striped balls disappeared each time he stepped out to check on the fire. After Katy had won two games, they decided to go roast marshmallows. They talked and enjoyed the fire. Katy asked a million questions about the stars, for which Jake knew only a few answers. She could tell when he was making something up, so he was careful. He loved his time with her. It was very relaxing.

Watching her eat marshmallows, Jake realized how open-minded she was to even consider spending a Friday night and the better part of a Saturday in a hunting camp. She had even passed up a birthday party at the skating rink to be here. She was so vibrant and full of life. He wanted to hold her—to protect her from all the pains of growing up.

Girls. They're so cool. Make that little girls, he thought. All his buddies warned him about the hound-from-hell teenage-girl years ahead. But maybe all this bonding they were doing now would help him…them…through the rough years that surely were ahead.

"Katy, listen…that's a whippoorwill…hear him? You can never count his whistles…you'll always fall asleep first. He can go all night."

"That's cool. What does he look like?" She asked stuffing a blackened marshmallow into her mouth.

"To tell you the truth, I don't think I've ever seen one. The legend is he's an Indian brave who lost his girlfriend on the Trail of Tears, and he's constantly whistling trying to find her," Jake said in a scary voice.

Katy stared at him, listening to the distant whippoorwill's somber song. She cocked her head a bit like she wasn't quite buying that part of the story.

"You always know it's spring when you hear one. The old-timers say you're supposed to drop and roll on the ground three times when you hear the first one each spring or you'll have bad luck all year."

"Is that true?"

"No, it's just superstition."

Jake poked the fire. It kicked up some sparks and the conversation continued. They discussed school and the *American Idol* TV show. Then she asked a question that really surprised him, "How much does it cost to be a member in this huntin' club?"

"Why do you want to know?" he asked very suspiciously. "Did Mom ask you to find out?"

"No, she didn't…really. I'm just curious."

Jake didn't want to lie, so he told her the truth and nothing else was said about it.

Finishing his Coke, he realized it was almost eleven. *It's too late to call Tate's house, even if I could get a cell signal.*

"Let's go to bed. We gotta to be up by 4:45. We have a pretty good walk in the morning." Jake yawned.

"We never told any ghost stories," Katy realized.

"Well, it's late and I'd rather not tonight."

"You're scared...aren't you?"

"No, ma'am, I am not. Now come on, let's go to bed."

"Just one story please.... It doesn't have to be a ghost story. Pleeeease?"

"Okay. Let me think," Jake said poking the fire. "Well, once I was in Dallas on a business trip and we were headed to the airport. There were five lanes of traffic."

"Five—wow!" she replied like she understood.

"Yeah, it's not like West Point at all...anyway...this truck with a bunch of construction workers passes us doing about a hundred miles an hour, and when they pull into our lane, this cooler falls off the truck. It's sliding in our lane and we can't get around it and it's too big to run over. The truck is long gone. So we had to stop and—"

"Who's 'we'?" she interrupted.

"Uh...me and uh, anyway, that's not important," he replied.

"So we stop and I get out to drag the cooler off the highway so it doesn't cause an accident. When I grabbed the cooler it was too heavy to move. Curiosity got the best of me, so I opened it, and guess what was inside?" he said excitedly.

"I dunno," she said growing more interested, her eyes wide with anticipation.

"There was a bag of ice and a Ziploc with a bloody big toe in it."

"Oh, my goodness. I bet they were going to the hospital...did y'all catch the truck?!"

"No. There was no way. They were long gone, and we were in a rush ourselves."

"So what did you do?"

Pausing for dramatic affect, he slowly shook his head and said,

"All we could do was call a tow truck." Jake kept a straight face for a few seconds then broke into a big grin.

She stared at him inquisitively. She smiled as the light clicked on in her mind.

"That was a good one. I believed you for...about one second." Katy was still smiling.

"Come on, let's go to bed."

"Okay."

The camper had warmed up considerably. Katy threw on her pajamas and climbed into her sleeping bag on the top bunk. Jake locked the door, set the alarm clock, checked it again, and looked over their clothes one final time, then turned out the overhead light.

"The turkeys are gonna gobble like crazy in the mornin'," he said, tucking her in. "I have a good feelin' about our hunt."

"Me too, Dad," she said sleepily.

"Good night, Katy. I love you. Thanks for coming," Jake said as he patted her form in the sleeping bag.

"Good night. I love you more."

Jake pulled off his shirt and blue jeans. He would sleep in his boxers in the bunk right underneath Katy.

The whippoorwill was still going strong. Inside the camper was perfectly quiet, except for the buzzing sound of the electric heater. Jake relaxed and thought through the day's events: the hassles of work, the unspoken uncertainty of his marriage, and the joys of being with a gregarious, carefree nine-year-old. Jake smiled and closed his eyes.

"Dad, can I get a horse?" Katy asked.

"Katy, horses are real expensive. And besides you already have four cats, a dog, two hamsters, and a goldfish!"

"If you don't let me have one, I'll tell Mom how much this turkey club costs." She giggled, pleased with herself.

"I see…so I guess you're gonna blackmail me now to get everything you want?" Jake remarked with frustration.

"Maybe." She giggled again.

"Go to sleep, Katy." He shook his head in admiration of the way she set him up. He knew this was only the beginning.

Chapter 4

The county's principal thugs were all gathered at Johnny Lee Glover's double-wide. Johnny Lee was the self-proclaimed ringleader. His résumé included several stints in juvenile detention facilities and various county jails, plus one eighteen-month stretch at Draper Prison in Elmore County just north of Montgomery, Alabama. Prison time had been rough on him. Johnny Lee had had a cellmate nicknamed Meat who had scarred him more than just emotionally. To this day Johnny Lee wouldn't bend over in the shower. He curtsied. None of his running buddies knew about Meat. Johnny Lee had never held a real job for more than a year. He purposely dressed and tried to act like Kid Rock. Johnny Lee was fence post thin and almost always wore a wife-beater. His own momma considered him "wormy-looking."

Johnny Lee's group of outlaws dabbled in a little bit of everything illegal. They consumed and sold drugs; they had attempted to build a meth lab but couldn't quite comprehend the recipe; and they had an old still in which they made really bad corn whiskey. They considered themselves state-of-the-art crime lords. Everybody else thought they were two-bit thugs. Mostly they stole cars, four-wheelers, guns, and about anything they could fence quickly. In the summer they poached alligators in the Black Warrior and Alabama rivers. They knew every back road in the surrounding counties.

The sheriff knew Johnny Lee's group was bad news and kept a watchful eye on them, but they were never caught with the goods, and no one would dare testify against them. The gang was masterful in the art of intimidation. From barn fires to dead cattle, they kept everyone quiet. Local law enforcement had a running joke that they could never get a conviction on the gang because all of the members shared the same DNA.

In early April, it was still too cold for the guys to hang out and skinny-dip down at the sand bar on the Noxubee River. In true red-neck fashion, they loved to sit on their tailgates, drink Old Milwaukee, and listen to Hank Williams, Jr., and David Allen Coe.

Johnny Lee's outlaws included Tommy Tidwell, who weighed in at a shade over 325 pounds. He was always eating something. His favorite meal was fried chicken wings and potato logs—the real greasy kind you get at a gas station. Everybody called him "Tiny." He followed orders methodically. Johnny Lee had met him in the Dallas County jail a couple years back and recruited him to join his team.

Reese Turner was second in command. He and Johnny Lee were first cousins. Since grade school, he had run with Johnny Lee and would walk through fire for him. Both their mothers had done time in Julia Tutwiler Prison in Wetumpka, Alabama, for stealing payroll checks, so the boys had carpooled together on Sundays to visit them. Reese was smarter than Johnny Lee, which wasn't saying much. Reese premeditated his crimes. Johnny Lee was more reactive. Reese's real talent was his ability to think two and three moves ahead. He spent his days surfing the satellite channels watching James Bond movies. He said they gave him ideas.

"Sweat" Lawrence was the "muscle." He had been in the Marines for ten weeks when he was caught holding a colonel's daughter down, forcing her to have sex with him. That was his style. Fortunately for her, some MPs came by and interrupted the party. The military police called it attempted rape, but they couldn't make the charges stick because she had been promiscuous with several of the enlisted men. The colonel had a heart attack listening to Sweat's unnecessarily graphic interrogation. The Corps wasted no time having Private Lawrence dishonorably discharged and sent home before the beloved colonel recovered and killed him.

As soon as Sweat arrived in the area, he fell in with Johnny Lee and never looked back. He sweated profusely, all the time, and never went anywhere without a hand towel. The doctors called it hyperhidrosis. Sweat rarely spoke. When the group needed something done, he was their man. He had yet to disappoint.

What this gang lacked in brains they more than made up for in pure meanness. There was nothing they wouldn't try. They were a pack of opportunistic wolves. Whatever came their way, they worked it for what they could squeeze out of it. They had killed a rival poacher for running their gator lines and then buried his body in an abandoned well. Getting away with that murder gave Johnny Lee and his entire posse a sense of invincibility.

None of these guys had serious girlfriends. Johnny Lee had a few women that hung around for crack cocaine, but as soon as they got their fix, they left. Tiny had been married once for about six months. His wife had left him while he was driving a truck to New Orleans. She had taken everything including his prize coon dog, which he was convinced she had sold on eBay. She sold everything on eBay.

The group's ultimate goal was to steal enough to buy custom motorcycles. Choppers to be more exact. They stopped everything they were doing on Monday nights to watch *Orange County Choppers* on the Discovery Channel. They liked the grumpy old dude. The group envisioned having crimson-and-white bikes in honor of The University of Alabama. To Johnny Lee's increasing frustration, he could never get a return phone call from the guys at Orange County Choppers.

By 10:00 that Friday night the gang had started growing restless.

It had been a slow week. Johnny Lee's main fence in Meridian, Mississippi, was complaining about his lack of productivity. Johnny Lee was contemplating burglarizing a group of cabins on the Tombigbee River. These rarely yielded much, but there was little chance of getting caught. By the time an alarm system alerted the sheriff and he arrived, they were long gone. But Johnny Lee needed a large score to satisfy everyone. His big opportunity was the Green County dog track. He had spent years trying to figure out how to rob it. He knew the security protocols were much more sophisticated than his gang could ever crack. But it was a dream fueled by greed. Johnny Lee especially liked it because it would be a cash haul and he wouldn't have to split it with his fence. He would make enough to get his Orange County Chopper and more. He just had to keep thinking. So he kept drinking Jack Daniel's and well water. He had been drinking steadily since about seven that evening, and he was feeling no pain, growing bolder by the hour.

Reese suggested that they rob the Cypress Inn on the Black Warrior River in Tuscaloosa. This was prom season and spring formals for the sororities, which meant the place was always packed on the weekends. Reese wanted to escape in boats and be picked up downriver. The idea had merit. It sounded to Johnny Lee like a James Bond flick. What would they do with the boat? There would be too many people around…too many potential witnesses. But still he liked the idea.

Johnny Lee clicked the TV off and looked at the group. His gang.

"Well, what do you boys wanna to do tonight? It's after 10," Reese said.

"I dunno…hey, did Bama win tonight?" Johnny Lee asked.

"Nope, we lost 9–7," Tiny replied. "We'll get 'em tomorrow. Our ace is pitchin'."

"Damn. I hate to lose to Auburn at anything." Johnny Lee had never been to the University of Alabama or any other college, but still he considered himself a full-fledged fan. The den of his trailer was filled with prints of great Alabama football moments that he had stolen from an attorney's office in Demopolis and couldn't bring himself to sell.

"Wanna steal some rich kid's car over at the college in Livingston?" Reese asked.

"Nah," replied Johnny Lee, turning on his CD of Hank Jr.

Turning to Tiny, Johnny Lee asked, "Did that guy pay you for the load of moonshine?"

"Yeah, but he was a grand short. He said he'd pay you next week," Tiny reported. "Something about taxes."

"Taxes?" asked Johnny Lee like he had never heard of the word.

"That's what he said," Tiny added.

"Damn, I was gonna buy a flat-screen plasma TV. Remind me to charge him interest, and to tell him about my accountant—he gets out of prison next month."

Everybody laughed. Johnny Lee loved being the center of attention.

"Don't laugh—he's good," Johnny Lee replied to no one in particular.

"You have to have income to pay taxes, Johnny Lee," Reese jabbed.

"My point exactly. Uncle Sam thinks I ain't made a penny in years. I know how to hide it," Johnny Lee said proudly. Johnny Lee always acted like he was a high-roller.

"Hey...I know, let's go break into that camp on County Road Sixteen with the pool table and the stocked bar. We can drink, play pool, and see what they have new to steal," Reese said excitedly.

"Yeah, they don't turkey hunt, so none of them dudes will be there. We ain't broke in there in maybe two years," Tiny added.

"That's not a bad idea...I'll bet they got some of that Maker's

Mark high-dollar whiskey. Let's go, but let's take two trucks." Johnny Lee stood up and stretched as he spoke.

Johnny Lee loved his Ford "Harley Davidson Edition" supercharged pickup truck second only to his double-wide trailer. The truck was jet-black with tinted windows and flames painted down the sides. It would fly. Thanks to a drug buddy getting busted, Johnny Lee had gotten it cheap. But he refused to let Sweat ride in it because of his overwhelming body odor.

Tiny had a 1987 Chevrolet four-wheel-drive that he and Sweat rode in. It smelled like chicken bones and stinky socks. Tiny could never get enough money together to improve his transportation, but it was part of his "starting-over-fresh" plan that was long on wishful thinking and totally devoid of action.

Sweat and Tiny had drunk a case of Old Milwaukee beer since the middle of the afternoon. They called them Walkie-Talkies. Sweat was outside taking a leak off the deck when the plan was formulated. When everybody started sticking pistols and knives in their pockets, he joined right in without a clue of what they were doing. He never even asked.

"Let's steal their pool table," Reese said, excited that his idea was being taken seriously.

"If you can tote it out, I can fence it," Johnny Lee said, pulling on his ostrich-skin boots and stuffing a Ruger Blackhawk .44 magnum inside the right one.

"Mount up boys...the Redneck Posse rides," Johnny Lee Glover said with pride as he rubbed the Doritos out of his dim excuse for a mustache.

Chapter 5

"You're right. This is a perfect place to see the stars. I've never seen so many." Elizabeth slyly grinned. This was the same view she had by her swimming pool. But she wouldn't tell Tanner that.

They had been parked for almost forty-five minutes. If there had been windows in the Jeep, they would have been steamed up. They sat in the back seat looking at the stars. They had been doing some serious necking and a little talking. Elizabeth wanted to do more talking; Tanner wanted more kissing. He loved the way she smelled, the freckles on her nose. She had no idea how beautiful she was. Elizabeth was really enjoying being with Tanner. She loved his Jeep, the music. She loved the wind blowing through her hair. The temperature was a bit cool but perfect for her fleece pullover.

"And it's safe. I locked the gate back and no one would ever come out here this time of year at night. Never," he commented, leaning back and placing his legs across the front seat. Elizabeth then crossed her legs over his and leaned against him and snuggled.

"Are you still excited about going to the University of Virginia?" he asked, smelling her hair.

"No, not really. It's…it's more for my mother than me. She went there and pledged a sorority, so she thinks I should. I'd really be happy to stay home and go to Alabama." She looked up at the stars.

"Mom took me two summers ago and we walked through The Lawn. I really got excited. Mom started signing me up for everything after that. Don't get me wrong, it's a beautiful campus and a great school, but I'll miss everybody, especially you," she said kissing his cheek.

"I think you should do what you want to do."

"I don't want to disappoint her. She's so excited. I think she wants me to do all the things she did and didn't do," Elizabeth explained and sighed.

Well, that's it. Tanner thought. He knew the make-out session was over, and that all they were going to do was talk. He was used to it. He just loved being with her. That was one reason he knew he was in love. It didn't matter what they did…just as long as they were together.

"So we could run off and get married," Tanner said with a sly smile, and he meant it.

"You think?" She grinned as she responded. "You had better get a new car first…and pass English!"

"Is that all?"

"One with a roof."

"I have a roof. It's called a top, and I'll pass English."

"It's plastic, and you can't conjugate a verb."

"Well…that's true…I can't and the top is actually high-grade waterproof canvas and—"

"Kiss me, Tanner. I'm tired of talking," she interrupted before he could finish.

"Yes, ma'am." And he did.

When it was time to leave, he composed himself enough to start the Jeep. He paused, "I sure hope it cranks."

"It better, it would take days to walk out of here; plus, I just noticed my cell phone isn't working," she replied, brushing her long black hair.

"This area's dead, there's no service. It's just too remote," he answered.

Tanner paused another few seconds and watched her brush her hair. *She's got no idea how beautiful she is.* The Jeep cranked and he smiled at her, "I love being with you."

She leaned over and kissed him, "Me too. Crank up the heater. I'm kinda cold," she said, briskly rubbing her hands on her arms.

They started the five-mile ride down the abandoned railroad track that was used for a road. She turned and held his hand and passionately kissed his right ear. Tanner was struggling with shifting and driving one-handed. He was in heaven.

"I'll teach you how to conjugate verbs," she whispered, then laughed out loud.

Chapter 6

By midnight Jake was in the middle of the recurring nightmare he'd been having since he was fifteen years old. It was so real, so vivid. It never changed—he's walking to a deer stand in the predawn darkness. For every step he takes he hears something or someone following him. He walks a bit faster and then stops. Whatever's following him stops and stands still, in step with him. He begins walking and can hear it following him again. It sounds heavy. He shines a flashlight, expecting to see glowing eyes—he can't see a thing. Then suddenly he steps on something out of place. There's a body, someone familiar to him, lying there dead. Brutally murdered. His throat's cut. There's blood everywhere. The exact moment the flashlight turns on, there is a high-pitched cackling scream…demonic…from whatever was following him.

Jake always wakes up at this point, sweating and chilled. He can never go back to sleep. For twenty-two years this nightmare has haunted him. Jake knows a psychiatrist could have a field day with this. He's never told a soul, and to this day he won't go in the woods, day or night, without a flashlight.

Jake was roused from the nightmare by the sound of a vehicle on the gravel road leading into the camp. The camper was toasty from the orange glow of the electric heater. *That's gotta be Tate,* he thought as he sat up and rubbed his eyes. Getting out of bed, he slipped on his boots and checked on Katy. She was sound asleep, snuggling with her Beanie Babies. *I'll ask him to stay in the camp house; his snoring is louder than a freight train,* Jake thought. Wearing nothing but his boxers and boots, Jake cracked open the camper door and immediately heard several male voices and Hank Jr. singing "Whiskey Bent and Hell Bound." Jake couldn't see who it was. The gate was about 150 yards from the camp. He strained to hear what they were saying. Multiple voices. This was odd. His heart was in his throat. He didn't like it at all. Jake could tell that they were arguing. He heard a gravelly voice say, "The gate ain't locked." When he heard another voice say, "Then we won't be breakin' in," Jake knew that he had trouble on his hands.

He quickly stepped to his truck, opened the door, and grabbed his pump shotgun. He fumbled through his turkey vest for his shells. He found the only three he carried on a hunt, fed them into the magazine, and quietly worked the action, loading one in the chamber.

Two pickup trucks slowly approached the camp with their lights off and parked side-by-side with their windows down. Jake had stepped into the shadows next to the camp house. He had no idea what to do next.

"I ain't never seen that camper before," one stated.

Another said, "Let's steal the truck."

"And beat the shit out of the owner," a third one added with way too much enthusiasm.

"Shut the hell up and let me think!" the fourth guy commanded.

All four men got out of their trucks and gathered at the rear of Jake's. Without saying anything, they started approaching Jake's camper like they owned the place. He saw the biggest one pull a pistol and work the action. Jake couldn't believe this was happening. He'd never pointed a gun at anybody. He couldn't imagine shooting someone, but he was in a bad spot and needed to make good decisions. Jake's heart raced so fast he was dizzy.

From the shadows, Jake said loudly, "That's close enough. You boys need to leave right now. I got a gun pointed at you."

They all stopped and looked at the skinniest one in the group. With a wicked laugh and a confident step forward, he asked, "Is it bigger than mine?" pulling a .44 Magnum Ruger Blackhawk from his boot and pointing it in Jake's direction.

This can't be happening, Jake thought. He said, "I'm serious, you need to leave.... NOW! This is private property."

"He ain't got no gun, Johnny Lee!" the fat one yelled out.

"Quit using my name, you stupid shit!" the one with the .44 said in a fit of anger.

"Look; I don't know anybody or remember anything. Y'all just leave right now!" Jake yelled.

"I don't think he's got a gun either. Else why would he hide in the shadows?" one of them said with an air of confidence.

"I'm here turkey huntin', and I've got a shotgun pointed right at y'all, so I suggest you leave." Jake was really getting nervous. He thought about showing himself so they could see his shotgun. *But just how intimidating could I be in plaid boxers?* Jake wondered.

They seemed to be weighing their options. The group didn't look like they were capable of making change much less a decision of this magnitude. Then things started happening in slow motion. Jake could tell that the skinny one, Johnny Lee, wanted trouble. Jake sensed that the others would follow his lead, so he kept the shotgun pointed at Johnny Lee and pushed off the safety.

"They ain't no turkey hunters in this club...I know...he's bluffing. He's out here cheating on his wife with his sport-model girlfriend, I'll bet," one of them said excitedly.

"That true?" Johnny Lee asked calmly although Jake could see his eyes getting wilder. "Where is she?"

The wolves smelled an opportunity and were getting more eager by the second.

Staring straight in Jake's direction, Johnny Lee shouted orders, "Check out the camp house." He motioned to the muscular one, who went through the front door with unbridled enthusiasm. Jake could hear him stomping around, slamming doors and cabinets.

Jake kept his shotgun trained on Johnny Lee.

In a few minutes the big guy was back outside and rejoined the group.

"Ain't nobody inside."

"Check the camper, Reese." Johnny Lee grinned.

"You said my name!" the one named Reese said quickly, not moving yet.

"It don't matter anyhow," Johnny Lee said confidently. "Because I got an idea...a plan."

Jake didn't like the sound of that. His heart was pumping rapidly, and his palms were sweating. He was trying to think of something to say to disarm this situation. An impossibly vivid scenario was unfolding, and to Jake it was like being in some sort of parallel universe, almost like an out-of-body experience. The movement of one of the guys snapped him back to reality. Reese started toward the camper and Jake instantly spoke up.

"No! Stop. Take another step and I'll shoot you!" Jake tried to keep them from hearing the fear in his voice.

Johnny Lee yelled, "Bingo! She's in the camper!" and the whole pack started laughing and cat-calling.

Jake kept quiet. He was thinking. The hair on the back of his neck was standing up. These guys only understood one thing—violence. They weren't rational. He could pump the gun...that would let them know he did in fact have a gun, but he would lose a shell in the dark high grass.

Johnny Lee, sizing up the situation, suddenly looked like he had made his decision.

"I think we'll jack this dude's world upside down. Then we'll take his woman out on a little *date*...and we'll steal his ride," Johnny Lee said calmly to his pack of jackals. Then alluringly he spoke directly to Jake, "Step out of the darkness, my brother, and let me see you. Can you 'squeal like a pig'?"

Everybody but Jake laughed hard.

"What's she look like...black chick?" one asked, laughing even harder.

"It's all good!" another one added, and they all laughed.

"It's just me and this twelve-gauge and I don't want any trouble. Please just leave."

Sweat chuckled and pulled a knife out of his back pocket. He loved forced sex. This was the most excited he had been in years.

Less than ten yards separated the mob from Jake, but they could not see him because of the shadows and the floodlights shining directly in their eyes. He couldn't believe their brazenness.

Should I shoot the leader in the leg? Shoot up in the air? I've only got three shells. I've gotta make 'em count. Looking in Johnny Lee's eyes, Jake saw pure evil. At that moment, Jake knew he would have to kill him. He glanced over his shoulder and thanked God that he couldn't see Katy. He prayed she was still asleep.

Johnny Lee pointed the huge pistol right at Jake's head. Jake swallowed hard, looking straight down its muzzle. Suddenly, Johnny Lee swung the pistol at the camper and fired. *KABOOM!*

Jake jumped with surprise and fear. *Oh my God! Katy!* He looked at the camper then back at Johnny Lee. He was grinning. The rest of the guys were laughing. In slow motion Jake saw Johnny Lee thumb-cock the pistol and aim at the camper again.

Jake screamed, "Nooooooo!" then put the shotgun's front bead on Johnny Lee's chest and pulled the trigger. *BOOM!*

All hell broke loose as fire shot out of Jake's gun barrel, blinding everyone for a second. Johnny Lee was knocked off his feet. Reese shot twice in Jake's direction, then grabbed Johnny Lee by the shoulders, dragging him toward their trucks. The fat one tripped over a barbecue grill. Jake pumped another shell in the chamber and was ready to shoot anyone that moved toward him or the camper. Two more shots rang out, hitting the camp house wall just over Jake's head. They were hiding behind their trucks, frantically talking to their leader. Johnny Lee was screaming in pain. They quickly loaded him in the back of the black pickup. Gravel flew as they backed out and scratched off down the road; then they stopped at the gate. Jake could hear them arguing. One was extremely emotional.

Jake stood in a trance, soaking wet with sweat. Slowly breaking out of the haze, he told himself, *I had to shoot him. They forced me. I had to protect Katy.*

"Katy! Oh, shit!" Jake screamed, running into the camper.

"Oh, God, Katy! Are you all right?! Katy, are you all right?!" he screamed again as turned on a light. Her tiny head was peeking from underneath her sleeping bag. He raced to her and hugged her.

Jake picked her up and ran to his truck. She was about to cry. He put her in the front seat and ran back inside, jumped into a pair of blue jeans and grabbed a shirt. A thought stopped him before he got to the truck. He ran back inside and grabbed Katy's camo gear. Slinging it all into the truck, he could hear the mayhem at the gate.

They were screaming at him, "You killed him! You killed him! You son of a bitch...! We're gonna make you pay...you...you're dead!"

One guy kept yelling over and over, "You're a dead man walking!"

There were only two ways for Jake to get out of the camp. The main one was the gravel road the rednecks were blocking. The other was a seldom-used logging road that snaked through the woods for several miles until it hit an old railroad bed called the Dummy Line that ran for several miles, eventually ending on a county road. Jake had never left the camp by way of the Dummy Line.

Jake caught a glimpse of the gang by the gate as he turned south heading toward the Dummy Line. He was slinging gravel as he slid around the corner.

"Daddy, what's going on? What's happening?" Katy pleaded.

"Some very bad guys were going to hurt us, and I had to shoot one of them. Now we gotta get out of here. Please listen to me and do exactly what I say…okay? Please? I need you to help me. Okay?"

With tears in her eyes, she nodded. Jake grabbed his cell phone. *One bar of service.* He slammed on the brakes, opened his glove compartment and found his address book. His first instinct was to call the sheriff; he didn't know the number or really how to tell anybody where he was, but he tried *HP anyway. The call wouldn't go through. He punched the gas and took off; rounding a couple of curves, he took out several small trees. As it got muddier he slowed and shifted into four-wheel drive. Suddenly he thought of his friend Mick Johnson, who lived only fifteen miles away. Mick had introduced him to the members of this club. He slammed on the brakes again. *Two bars. This might work.* He looked up Mick's number and dialed.

"Come on, come on, go through. Katy, why don't you start getting dressed…there's your stuff.

"It's ringing!" he said excitedly almost out of breath. "And then fasten your seat belt."

Mick Johnson had been in bed since 9:00 that night. He turkey hunted almost every day of the season, and by mid-April he was exhausted. When he heard his phone ringing he immediately turned off his alarm clock and thought how short the night was. His wife jabbed him in the side and told him it was the telephone.

"Hello," he answered groggily on the sixth ring.

Trying not to talk too fast, Jake tried to keep it simple. He didn't have faith that the signal would hold up. "Mick, this is Jake, I need the sheriff at the hunting camp. It's an emergency. There is a bunch of red-necks trying to kill me…Hello, Mick…can you hear me? Mick?"

The call dropped. Jake cussed under his breath. He needed some distance between him and those lunatics. He threw the phone down and drove on, certain they were coming after them. *Damn it! I've got no idea if Mick heard any part of that.*

"Who was that?" Mick's wife asked sleepily.

"I think it was Jake Crosby on a cell phone. It sounded like he said it was an emergency," Mick said, pulling himself up on one elbow.

"Why would he call you?"

"I don't know," he replied, lying back down.

"What kind of emergency?"

"I don't know." He rubbed his eyes.

"Well…what are you gonna do?" she asked as she rolled over.

"I guess I'm gonna go and check on him. I can't sleep now."

"Be careful. Why don't you take Beau?"

"Yeah…I think I will."

He slowly got out of bed and got dressed. Beau, the family's Golden Retriever, met him at the back door, stretching and yawning, tail wagging.

Chapter 7

"Shut up! Shut up! Just shut the hell up! Everybody just calm down!" Reese yelled as he jumped in the bed of the Ford pickup to check on Johnny Lee.

Johnny Lee was gurgling blood and his breathing was extremely labored. It took him several minutes just to say a few words. He was dying and he knew it. Blood ran out of his mouth with his final words: "Get him…get that son of a bitch."

Johnny Lee Glover, one of the most vicious, notorious thugs of west Alabama, died at age thirty-six in the arms of his first cousin.

"Johnny Lee! Johnny…no! Johnny Lee, please! Don't die!" Reese pleaded. He couldn't imagine living without him. Johnny Lee had always been the center of his life.

Tiny didn't say a word. He was horrified. Sweat stood at attention, awaiting instructions.

Reese stood up and faced the camp and screamed at the top of his lungs, "You're dead! You're a dead man! You killed him! You killed him! You son of a bitch! Do you hear me? You're a dead man walking!" Then he grabbed anything he could get his hands on, slinging it as far as he could, screaming over and over, "You're a dead man walking!"

The Chevy pickup came sliding out of the camp house area and disappeared down a road, away from the gang and into the heart of the property.

"Man, he's haulin' ass!" Tiny said.

"And he's gettin' away!" Sweat added.

"No, he's not…he is doin' just exactly what I want him to do."

Reese chuckled out loud. "Okay, boys; the two of you go down this road till you hit the Dummy Line—y'all know where it is. He's gonna try and get out that way. You've got a good ten-mile jump on him. The gate combination is 1992, I think. If it ain't, just shoot the damn thing off. There's only two ways out of this bitch, and we will be on both of them. Kill him and anybody he's got with him. I want that sumbitch to suffer. You hear me?!" Reese was spitting as he screamed.

Looking each of them in the eyes, Reese continued, "I'll follow him this way," pointing in the direction Jake had driven. "He can't make it very far; it's too muddy. That stupid sumbitch is trapped and he don't know it! Go! Now!"

Sweat and Tiny jumped into their truck. Tiny stomped on the gas with all his might, his mud grips shooting a rooster tail of dirt and rocks thirty feet. Sweat checked his pistol. It only took a few minutes to reach the old abandoned railroad track. Tiny nearly lost control of the truck when he turned the sharp corner. In spite of sliding wildly, Sweat never looked up. Miraculously, Tiny regained control and stood on the gas again. After miles of rough road they saw headlights piercing the darkness at the gate. Sweat started cussing. Then they both let out a rebel yell at the top of their lungs.

Reese was trying to figure out what to do with Johnny Lee's body. He decided to leave him in the back of the truck until they killed that scumbag. Reese covered Johnny Lee's head and shoulders with a jacket. He then got into the truck, cranked it up, and slowly drove back to the camp house.

Floodlights illuminated the yard. The camper lights were on. Its door standing wide open. Reese approached cautiously, pistol drawn, peeking in the windows until he was satisfied that no one was inside. He stepped in and looked around. Camo clothes were everywhere. A heater glowed in the corner. On the top bunk he saw a lime-green sleeping bag with a pink pillow and lying on the floor beneath was a stuffed toy of some kind. *That's odd,* he thought as he stepped on it with a twist. He noticed several kids' mystery novels. It started making sense. The scumbag's got a kid with him...probably a girl. *Oh, this is gonna be good – really, really good,* he thought.

As Reese was leaving the camper he noticed a hunting magazine lying on the couch. He picked it up and looked at the small white mailing label in the corner. "Bingo!" he said out loud, a demonic grin forming as he meandered back to the truck. He cranked it up and raced the engine while he thought. The loud dual exhausts gave him energy. He was going to kill the man, just like Johnny Lee wanted...and more.

"I'll get him, Johnny Lee...I swear I will," he pledged aloud.

He picked up Johnny Lee's cell phone and flipped it open. It was a Southern Link radiophone. He switched it to radio, scrolled through the names until he found the one he wanted, and pressed Send. *Beep-beep.*

Twenty seconds later Reese heard "*Beep-beep,*" and a voice responded.

"Yo, Johnny Lee, what's up?" Music was in the background.

Beep-beep. "Moon Pie, this is Reese. I need a favor."

Beep-beep. "Yo dog, you got it."

Beep-beep. "How quick can you be in West Point?" Reese got out of the truck to pace.

Beep-beep. "Twenty. Twenty-five minutes."

Beep-beep. "Okay. Listen. This piece of shit dude just shot and killed Johnny Lee."

Beep-beep. "Son of a...are you serious...shit...man, are you okay? Why? What the hell's goin' on?"

Beep-beep. "We were gonna rob him and he freaked out...it's a long

"Hello? Is anyone here?!" he yelled as he slowly stepped inside.

Mick walked past the pool table. Everything looked like he expected it would. Nothing was seriously out of place. Actually, the place was a mess, but since it was a hunting lodge, no one ever cleaned it up. It always looked like this. He went back outside. *This is weird,* he thought, as he petted Beau gently on the top of the head.

After climbing into his truck, he backed up, looking around one more time. Something was gnawing at him, but he couldn't place it. He said, "Aw, to hell with it. I'm too freakin' exhausted for this crap." He headed home to get some sleep.

When he arrived, his wife was sitting in the kitchen with a glass of milk and some warm raisin bread from the Mennonite bakery in Livingston, sheepishly grinning with guilty pleasure.

"I couldn't go back to sleep," she said. "What's going on?"

"I don't know. The lights were all on, but no one was there. It was kinda strange. I'm a little worried that something's wrong...but...but I just don't know what," he replied.

"Mick, what's that all over your pants' legs?" she asked, pointing at his legs. The bottoms of his blue jeans were covered in something dark and wet.

Mick reached down, touching it. He rubbed his fingers together. "It's blood!" he said with a scared look on his ashen face.

"Oh, my God! Mick!"

"I'll call the sheriff!" he said, reaching for the phone, worried at what this might mean.

CHAPTER 9

"Sumter County Sheriff's office," a husky, cigarette-ravaged voice answered the telephone.

"This is Mick Johnson. I need to speak to Sheriff Landrum."

"Mick, he's not in...It's one-thirty in the morning. But if it's important I'll get him to call you. Are you at your house?" she asked, blowing smoke up into the air.

"Yes, ma'am, it's urgent."

"I'll have him call you right back. Do you need a deputy right now?" she replied and snuffed out her cigarette.

"If you can't get Ollie, then I'll need a deputy for sure."

"Sure thing, Mick. Give me a minute. I think I can get him for you."

Mrs. Martha O'Brien had worked for the sheriff's office for twenty-three years. Since her husband had died four years earlier, she preferred to work the night shift. She couldn't sleep anyway. Her favorite activity in the world was waking up the sheriff. She loved to aggravate him. She never hesitated to call at any hour concerning anything. It drove the High Sheriff crazy. But Martha O'Brien was irreplaceable. She knew where everything was, where everybody lived, and what forms needed to be filled out. The sheriff and his staff constantly asked her for guidance. She relished it. Her celebrity had grown when she slapped a prisoner for making a crude comment about her. The governor had cheerfully vindicated her actions. With true Southern politeness, most everyone called her Miz Martha.

Ollie Landrum was Sumter County's first black sheriff. He was a county fixture now that he'd been in office nine years. Ollie had been a football hero at the University of Alabama—he'd blown out his knee beyond repair during a home game, ending his pro hopes. He'd been a deputy just a few years when the sheriff retired. The Alabama fans in the county showed Ollie how much they appreciated his football prowess in a landslide election to sheriff. He married his college sweetheart, a lady who had dedicated her life to helping educate the poor about Sudden Infant Death Syndrome. West Alabama leads the nation in SIDS, and she was consumed by her task. There were plenty of poor folks in west Alabama. She tried to educate them by day, and Ollie arrested many of them by night. Ollie and his wife hadn't slowed down long enough to even consider having children.

Sumter is a typical rural Alabama county, where legitimate commerce revolves around forestry, agriculture, and hunting. The biggest city, Livingston, with its three red lights, is home to a small, quaint college.

The Sheriff had fallen asleep on the couch watching *Law & Order, SVU.* He loved that show. New York City had the action, the serious crime. On the show, there were no boring driver's license checks like he was forced to do weekly.

Even asleep, when the phone rang, Ollie knew it was Martha. *This better be good,* he thought, pulling himself off the couch. He glanced at the clock, cleared his throat and said, "Hello."

"Chief, Mick Johnson needs you to call him at his house. He says it's urgent." She said, skipping the pleasantries. She lit a menthol cigarette.

Rubbing his eyes, he asked, "Did he say what it's about?"

"No, Chief, he just said it's urgent," she responded, ever the professional.

"Okay, I'll call him, and Miz Martha, please call me 'Ollie' or 'Sheriff'; don't call me 'Chief,'" he begged for the umpteenth time, knowing it wouldn't do any good.

"Yes, sir." She gave him the phone number.

Ollie had been to Birmingham that day to play golf in a charity tournament at the Greystone Country Club. His football legacy made him an in-state celebrity. He was exhausted from the day's events and the not-so-small amount of alcohol he had consumed on the sly. Golf simply wore him out. It must be the sun. He slowly walked into the kitchen intending to microwave a cup of coffee. But he sat down on a bar stool and picked up the cordless phone.

"Mick. Ollie. What can I help you with?" he asked in his most official voice.

"Ollie, I got the strangest phone call from a friend of mine about an hour ago. I couldn't understand all of it, but he said it was an emergency."

"What's his problem?" Ollie asked, with a yawn.

"Well, he's from Mississippi; his name's Jake Crosby. I got him into the Bogue Chitto hunting club. I assumed that's where he was calling from. We got disconnected, so I rode out there. And...well...it's weird...all the lights were on in his camper and the door was open, but he wasn't anywhere around."

"Is that the place that backs up to the big area of wilderness along the Noxubee River on County Road Sixteen?"

"Yeah, that's it, but listen...when I got home my pants were covered in blood...fresh blood."

"Blood?" Ollie became fully alert. "Could it have been turkey blood?"

"Well...I hadn't thought about that...I suppose, but there was a bunch of it."

"Have you tried his cell again?"

"Yeah, I tried, but that area's got awful reception. I couldn't get him."

"I'll be at your house in twenty minutes, and you can follow me. I'm gonna call R.C. and get him on out there. He stays out in that part of the county," Ollie explained, studying the kitchen clock.

"I'll be ready."

Ollie hung up the phone and pondered the possibilities. He needed details. This situation was much more interesting than his typical daily duties. He would call his most trusted deputy, R.C. Smithson. R.C. was a little eccentric, but Ollie could depend on him. He dialed the number. It was ringing when he put the receiver to his ear.

"Yes, Chief." R.C. answered on the second ring.

"Quit calling me Chief, and how did you know it was me...you're too much of a tightwad to have Caller ID."

"You're the only person who ever calls me at this hour."

"Listen. Something serious may have gone down at the clubhouse at the Bo Cheeter something or other hunting club."

"Bogue Chitto. It's Choctaw for big—"

"Shut up, R.C., and listen," Ollie interrupted and paused. R.C.'s trivia drove him crazy.

"A friend of Mick Johnson's from Mississippi called him and said something about some kind of emergency. Mick thinks he was at that camp and he lost communication with him. I'm about to roll and pick up Mick. I'll be there in thirty to forty-five minutes. Go secure the area. See what you can find out. Be careful. We already know there is a bunch of blood near the camp house. Don't violate my crime scene if there is one, you hear?"

"Okey-dokey."

"Quit saying 'okey-dokey'...and get goin'. Call me on the radio if you see anything." Ollie sighed deeply.

"Yes, sir, boss," he said then hung up. He used the remote to turn off the TV. He had been watching a movie on his pirated HBO package.

R.C. Smithson was not unlikable. All he wanted for a career was to be a deputy. He was single. He played video games at all hours of the night and read fly-fishing magazines, though he'd never held a fly rod. Two years ago he'd met a dancer at Danny's Strip Club in Birmingham; he now considered her his girlfriend. They had never been out on an actual date. Their "dates" were always at Danny's, except once when she met him at the Waffle House and they ate Belgian waffles as she told him about her crack-addict husband. She dreamed of being a Playmate. R.C. dreamed of going with her to photo shoots. Twice a month he went to see her dance and give her a couple hundred bucks, one dollar at a time. He talked about her like they had been married for years. Her name was Chastity. R.C. loved her huge fake boobs.

He was rolling down the road four minutes after hanging up with Ollie. He knew exactly where to go. *I was born for this,* he thought, flipping on the car's radio.

Chapter 10

R.C. slowed the police sedan to a crawl as he pulled through the camp's open gate. He turned off the Rush Limbaugh rebroadcast and forced his senses to full alert. He could see the lights of the camp through the trees and immediately stopped to radio Martha O'Brien that he had arrived.

"Bo what?" she asked.

"Bogue Chitto. It's Choctaw for large creek and the Chickasaw Indians used it in their language as well," he expounded, proud of his plethora of knowledge.

"Whatever. R.C., you be careful now," she added.

"Ten-four."

R.C. eased his cruiser into the camp. He parked on the gravel, got out, and walked toward the camp house. He shined his five D-cell flashlight in all the shadows, finding nothing that roused any suspicions. Because the camper lights were on and the door was open, he decided to check it out first.

After peeking in the side windows, with his right hand on the butt of his holstered weapon, he twirled the flashlight over, then with the end of it knocked on the side of the camper, "Deputy Sheriff…anybody home?"

Nothing but silence. Without touching anything, he carefully looked inside the open door. "Deputy Sheriff. Anybody home?" he repeated, then stepped just inside the doorway. The warmth from the heater was inviting. He stood over it a few seconds while casting his eyes around the interior of the camper. Everything looked perfectly normal. Two people had been sleeping inside. One was obviously a child, probably a little girl.

Outside everything also looked in order. R.C. walked back and forth through the yard searching for anything out of the ordinary. Careful of his steps, he methodically grid-searched the area in front of the camper and camp house. Then he saw it. Pools of dark blood that trailed back to the parking area, then ended. There was plenty of it. *What in the hell,* he wondered. *I need to string some tape.* The hair on the back of his neck and arms stood up. With his pistol drawn, R.C. approached the camp house front porch. "Deputy Sheriff…is anybody here?"

More silence. This was unnerving. He wasn't accustomed to so much tension. "Deputy Sheriff. Anyone home!?" R.C. stepped onto the porch. "Sheriff's department!" he yelled, hoping nobody answered. The moment R.C. peered inside the camp house, he was drawn to the Playmate calendars, partly obscured by innocuous swimsuit calendars. He had hit the Pinup Mother Lode. He studied each one, comparing them to Chastity. Time stood still…until his radio crackled suddenly with Ollie's voice.

"I'm here, Chief," he replied while studying, in great detail, Miss November 1999. "There's definitely fresh blood in the yard…and lots of it, but no one's here," he added, shifting his attention to Miss October 1999.

"I'll have Miz Martha call the hospital to see if anyone has come into the emergency room."

"Ten-four. I'll see you in a few minutes."

R.C. radioed Martha. While he waited for her response, he perused the calendars. *Chastity is as hot as any of these girls. Maybe hotter.*

"R.C.?" his radio crackled loudly.

"Yes, ma'am," he said, grabbing the shoulder mike.

"The ER's had two folks in earlier this evenin'. One was a stabbin' from down by the river. It was over a fishin' hole. One guy kept gettin' too close to where the other was catchin' some crappie. Stabbed him in the leg. He's okay. Told the doctor it was an accident. They'd been drinkin'. Apparently the fish are bitin'."

"Well, a good crappie hole is pretty valuable," R.C. responded, nodding his head.

"And the second was a burn victim. Grease got too hot while she was frying chicken livers. Caught the cabinets on fire. Her hands got burned swatting the fire out."

"Ouch!" he added.

"Does that help at all?"

"Yes and no…but thanks, Miz Martha," he replied while admiring another calendar.

R.C. heard vehicles, so he stepped outside. The sheriff arrived first in his Ford Expedition with Mick Johnson behind. They parked behind R.C.'s cruiser and got out.

"Find anything new?"

"No, Chief. I can show you the blood, though."

Ollie glared at him for the "Chief" reference.

"R.C., hang on. Mick, let's start at the beginning…and don't leave out any detail, no matter how small," Ollie said, leaning against R.C.'s patrol car.

Mick told his story. Ollie and R.C. glanced at each other from time to time, trying to mentally put it all together.

"Show me what you found, R.C."

R.C. showed Ollie the pool of blood and how it trailed off, careful not to contaminate the area. The sheriff walked around, looked in the camper, and then walked toward the camp house. He was working several theories in his mind. He really needed daylight. *The grass is so tall it would hide any evidence – if there is any,* Ollie thought. He considered calling Jake Crosby's family to see if they had heard anything from him. He hated to sound any false alarms. *He's just as likely to be at a bar somewhere, drunk.* He knew a lot of guys used hunting as an excuse just to get out of the house. He'd ask Mick later if that was a possibility.

The three men walked into the camp house. Ollie and Mick sat down on bar stools. R.C. otherwise occupied himself.

"R.C., R.C.! Pay attention. Quit looking at those calendars!" Ollie yelled across the room.

"Chastity's as hot as any of these girls," R.C. said with pride.

"What do you think about this situation?" Ollie asked.

"There's not much to go on…the blood bothers me…but it could be any number of things. No one's checked into the ER that fits this scenario. I don't know, boss."

"Mick, do you think a jealous husband could have been chasing him?" Ollie asked, trying to think of the wildest scenario.

"I seriously doubt it. Nothin' less than Charlize Theron would get Jake's attention…Charlize Theron in a camo swimsuit maybe…he's happily married, or certainly appears to be," Mick replied.

"Charlize Theron has not been in the area; I would know," R.C. said, smiling.

"Jake is a pretty levelheaded guy. He doesn't get into trouble. I just wish I could have heard him better," Mick added, growing anxious.

"And I'm pretty sure he's got a kid with him," R.C. added nervously.

Ollie sat quietly, weighing his options. He didn't have the manpower necessary to launch a full-scale manhunt, even if it was necessary – which at this point it wasn't – and he hated to call in any other departments on a false alarm at this hour. He had done that before and sworn he wouldn't ever do it again. Ollie put his face in his hands. He needed to make a decision. He needed some sleep.

Chapter 11

Morgan was looking forward to having the house to herself. She had the perfect evening planned. She rented two DVDs at Movie Gallery. Then she went by the liquor store to purchase a bottle of Barefoot California Merlot. Morgan tried not to be self-conscious in the store. She prayed her Sunday School teacher wouldn't see her. West Point was such a small town, and Jake always bought the wine.

Not wanting to cook, she called Domino's for a pizza packed with mushrooms and anchovies. Jake *hated* mushrooms and anchovies. After eating the medium-sized pizza, she piled on the couch to watch Jack Nicholson and Diane Keaton in *Something's Gotta Give.* The title of that movie described Morgan's life. Something *had* to give. She had material things, but she wasn't happy. She needed more; she wanted more. *I'm entitled to more,* she thought. She had decided to leave Jake—she just had some details to work out. Their marriage had grown to be so boring and predictable.

"Of all the trust-fund-babies I dated, I end up marrying a broke guy who listens to NPR and loves the Weather Channel," she said aloud with no small amount of disdain.

After the movie, Morgan decided to sit in her Jacuzzi, drink wine, and read a self-help book. She was enjoying the lightheadedness and lack of responsibilities. Around midnight, with a slight buzz from the wine, she went to bed.

West Point was such a safe little town; everybody was lulled into a false sense of security. Morgan never even thought of turning on the alarm system. And since Scout was always raising Cain at the deer standing under the feeder Jake had behind the house, she was desensitized to Scout's barking. She didn't pay attention to it tonight, either.

Ethan "Moon Pie" Daniels, a longtime friend of Johnny Lee and Reese's, lived in Tupelo, Mississippi. Moon Pie was making a drug run to Starkville—"Stark Vegas" as he called it—when he got Reese's call.

Moon Pie owed Johnny Lee a big favor. Two years earlier Moon Pie's live-in girlfriend Sheree had been cheating on him with a guy she'd met on the Internet who lived in Jackson. Moon Pie encouraged Johnny Lee to rough him up—send him a message. Moon Pie made sure he was seen at the Tupelo Fire Ants football game—a solid alibi. Sheree knew he had done it. The police suspected it, but could never connect him to the crime. And the computer geek in Jackson couldn't send any more emails because he lost all the fingers on his right hand. Johnny Lee had done Moon Pie right. *That's what friends do,* he thought.

Moon Pie couldn't believe Johnny Lee was dead. He would do his part to reap revenge. The house was easy enough to find. The lots in the area were large, wooded, and very private. *Piece of cake,* he thought. Surveying the scene, he noticed a new Jeep Grand Cherokee that was probably used to haul kids to school. The driveway was big enough for several vehicles, and since only one car was there, he knew the woman was probably alone though she might have a kid or two in there. He hoped not. He wished he had more planning time. He could see a fancy fishing boat and it was certain to have rods and reels worth stealing. Moon Pie loved to fish, but he hated to pay for good tackle. He'd check the boat on the way out.

As Moon Pie slowly approached the house, a large dog barked half-heartedly. Moon Pie had anticipated a dog. Dropping to a knee, he acted as friendly as he could, but the dog didn't buy it. He reached into his jacket pocket and pulled out a hot dog he'd just bought at the Quik Mart, broke it in half, and tossed half to the dog. She stopped barking, smelled the bait, and then ate it. He waved the rest of it and tossed it only a few feet in front of him. She slowly approached, still very suspicious. The dog was accustomed to men in camouflage coming up to the house at all hours. Usually she got fussed at for barking. But this guy had food. Torn between protecting the house and eating a delicious hot dog, the wiener won. She escorted him up the front porch steps.

Peeking in through glass in the front door, Moon Pie could see an illuminated alarm keypad. All the lights were green. He smiled. *This is too easy.* Then, something wet and cold touched his hand. Moon Pie jumped. Quickly looking down, he saw the black dog sitting, wagging its tail.

CHAPTER 12

Jake drove like a bat fleeing hell down the old road, hitting small trees the entire way. He had already knocked the mirrors off one side of his truck. He was in the beginning stages of panic. He kept telling himself to calm down and think. As he approached the top of a ridge, he slowed down to try his cell phone.

"I can't believe I can't get a signal," Jake said with disgust as he threw the phone down and looked in his rearview. He couldn't see any lights following them. Visibility in the deep woods was less than a hundred yards.

Jake turned off the truck, then stood outside to listen. He couldn't hear anything. Maybe they weren't coming? Maybe he and Katy had gotten away? He had no idea how far he could hear, but it should be quite some distance. Katy was busy pulling on her pants as Jake climbed back in. She looked nervous, but he was keeping her busy.

"Put on the heavy gray socks," he said.

"These?" she said and he could hear the fear in her voice.

"Yes, baby." Jake nodded his head also.

Jake cranked the truck and checked his gauges. Half a tank of gas. *Plenty,* he thought. They needed to make it to the Dummy Line and get the hell out of there. He guessed he had about twenty miles to reach a county road. His cell phone probably wouldn't work again until he got back to Highway 17. He wondered about the big mud hole he knew lay ahead as he dropped into gear and drove forward.

Jake couldn't get the image of the shooting out of his mind. He couldn't believe he had shot that guy. He had no choice, but this was unbelievable. *What a nightmare!* Deep down he knew he had made the right decision. But still he questioned whether it could it have been avoided. Should he have stepped out of the shadows and shown his gun? He'd never know. *Who were those guys? What did they want?* Why did Katy have to come on this trip, of all the trips he had been on. *Katy, my dear sweet Katy.* He shuddered to think what might have happened to her. Morgan was going to be pissed.

"Dad, where are my boots?" Katy asked.

Jake realized he had left them in the camper. "Damn," he said under his breath. He had placed them in the camper so they would be warm in the morning. In all the confusion of leaving, he'd remembered her clothes but forgotten the boots.

"That's okay…I left them in the camper. You won't need them. We're going straight to the sheriff's office," he said, trying to sound confident.

Suddenly a long, deeply rutted mud hole loomed in front of them. His headlights would only illuminate part of it. Years of heavy log trucks had really rutted this part of the road. The planted pine trees lined the edge of the road like a wall, preventing him from going around.

Jake looked at the hundred-yard stretch of mud. He had no idea how deep it was. He had a winch, so he figured he would try and make it as far as he could then winch his truck the rest of the way. It was his only logical option. He didn't know if they were chasing him, but he knew he couldn't go back the way he came.

"Fasten your seat belt, Katy, and hang on," he warned as he lined up the truck on the mud hole.

Shifting into four-low, Jake decided to try the right side. He punched the gas and did his best to keep the truck headed straight.

The mud grips were biting chunks of red mud, slinging it everywhere. He turned on the windshield wipers. Katy covered her eyes with her hands. The truck's momentum slowed, but they continued to make progress. The ruts pulled them to the left; then suddenly, with thirty yards to go, the frame hung, slamming them to a stop. Jake tried reversing. No use. He cut his tires left, then right—nothing.

"Katy, I've got to get out and pull the winch cable to one of those trees," he said, pointing down the road. "You stay right here. Everything's okay. Why don't you put in your Hillary Duff tape?"

"I'm okay…can I help?" she asked and meant it.

"Sure, let me go see what I need," Jake replied. He had no intention of letting Katy get out of the truck.

Jake opened his door and stepped into the cold, muddy water. The mud was so deep it nearly pulled off his boots every time he took a step. He ignored the cold. He felt around inside the gull-wing toolbox until he found his flashlight. Then he found the winch control. After slogging to the front of the truck, he laid the controller on the hood. He turned the winch to Free Spool then started pulling out the cable as fast as he could trudge through the mud. Finally, wrapping the cable around a tree just past the mud hole, he plodded back to the truck. He inserted the control into the winch, ran the cable over the hood, and threw it in the driver's side window. Climbing in, he gave the engine some gas, put the transmission in neutral, and then flipped the switch on the winch control. He watched the voltmeter spike and the cable move.

"Yeah, baby. Yeah! Come on! You can do it!" Jake said aloud, nervously tapping the steering wheel with his hand.

When Jake realized he was wet from the knees down, he was cold. He turned on the heater and tried to put it out of his mind. *Maybe I've got some dry clothes in the toolbox,* he thought, watching the cable become taut and begin dragging the truck down the road. Jake loved his winch, especially tonight.

Slowly the truck was being dragged down the road. Jake fought the urge to put it in gear to help out. He feared getting the cable hung up under the truck. He knew this was the safest way to winch out. He kept the truck's RPMs up to prevent draining the battery. *Come on! Hurry! Please hurry!* As the truck eased out of the final bit of mud, Jake hopped out and looked back. He could see lights coming through the woods. His heart jumped into his throat. He ran to unhook the winch line from the tree, cutting his right hand on the cable. Without waiting for the winch to rewind the remaining twenty feet of cable, he quickly wrapped it around the brush guard on the front of the truck and jumped back in.

The headlights were closing in. None of the thugs' trucks that he had seen would fare any better in this mud hole than his. *Getting through it should keep them busy for a while,* thought Jake, as he stomped the gas pedal.

Chapter 13

"Tanner, would you pleeeeease put the top up? I can see my breath it's so cold!" Elizabeth exclaimed.

They were bouncing along the old road listening to John Cougar Mellencamp singing "Jack and Diane." Elizabeth loved old songs. Tanner knew it. They were enjoying each other's company and feeling very alive—the way you do when you're a teenager in love.

"Sure…anything else?" he asked, braking to a stop. She knew he would do anything she wanted.

"Nope, that'll do it…need some help?" she smiled, pulling her fleece jacket a little tighter and putting her hands in the pockets.

"Nope, I can have it up in a sec. Find us another good song," he said, jumping out.

It took Tanner only a few minutes to put up the top and fasten everything into place, including the doors.

Elizabeth loved his Jeep in the summer or on any warm day; but in times like these, she wished he had a car or a truck. Anything with a solid roof would make her happy.

Tanner climbed in and smiled at her. "How's that?"

"Thank you." She leaned over and kissed his cheek.

Tanner ground the Jeep's gears as he tried to find first. Suddenly the Jeep lurched forward as he let the clutch out a little too fast. He loved it when she kissed him. It drove him crazy.

Elizabeth changed the radio stations and found George Strait crooning "Marina Del Rey." Tanner couldn't help but sing along.

Elizabeth laughed playfully, and when the song was over she said with a serious expression, "A little pitchy in places but overall you gave a good effort." She never missed an *American Idol* episode.

Tanner smiled as he slowed the Jeep down at the big yellow gate. The gate had a combination lock on it to allow any of the adjacent landowners access. The combination was 1992—the last year Alabama had won a national football championship. Tanner wondered how many gates in the state had that simple combination. He had just swung the gate open when he saw headlights approaching rapidly. Rapidly was an understatement. The vehicle was flying. Tanner looked at Elizabeth. Her head was down as she searched the radio for another song.

Tanner swallowed hard, climbed into the Jeep and told Elizabeth to look up.

Chapter 14

The recent rain made tracking simple. Reese was careful to stay on the high ground since Johnny Lee's truck was built for speed, not off-roading. He was confident that Sweat and Tiny would block the Dummy Line. *I'm gonna make that sumbitch pay – dearly. Sweat will run him straight to me or I'll push him to Sweat. Either way he's dead.*

Reese flipped open the phone and pressed Send.

Beep-beep. "Yo, dog," came a whispered response.

Beep-beep. "Did you find it?"

Beep-beep. "I'm in the backyard right now; that's why I'm whispering."

Beep-beep. "You think he's got a woman there?"

Beep-beep. "Oh, yeah."

Beep-beep. "Good. Take her…or them…to Johnny Lee's trailer."

Beep-beep. "You got it."

Beep-beep. "Let me know."

Reese continued down the road watching the tire tracks. *This guy's all over the place. He's outta control.* Reese remembered the scoped Browning 30-06 behind the seat. *All I gotta do is just see this guy once. I can kill him from three hundred yards or….* Reese really wanted to see fear in his eyes and watch him suffer. "I'll kill the kid first, then let the sumbitch know that I've got his wife…maybe make him watch Moon Pie and the guys take turns with her," Reese said aloud.

Yanking him back into the present, Reese saw taillights through the woods. He slowed. As he approached the mud hole, he knew this was as far as he could go in Johnny Lee's truck. Reese watched the killer's truck disappear down the road, around a bend. He was gone before Reese could get the rifle pointed out the window. That was fine with Reese. He savored a good stalk hunt.

Putting the truck in park, Reese grabbed the radiophone, a flashlight, and the rifle. He calmly checked for his pistol, stepped out, and shut the truck door. Reese knew this property from years of poaching. He would simply cut off his prey's escape route.

Chapter 15

"See if you can find me a headache powder in that nasty vehicle of yours," Ollie directed R.C.

Ollie was having a hard time making up his mind. He was facing a major decision, similar to one a few years back. He really wished this was not happening. Especially not tonight. He was exhausted, and his head was killing him from drinking in the sun all day at the golf tournament. And his foursome had played awful in the scramble. By the eighth hole he'd had to borrow golf balls. Ollie only played twice a year, and it showed. He loved the game but preferred to watch the pros on television from the comfort of his couch.

A couple of years ago, one of Sumter County's favorite sons had left home in the middle of the night to join the Professional Bull Riders' circuit. He was only fifteen. He didn't tell anyone of his plans. His family reported him missing the next day and put up such a fuss that Ollie called in the Alabama Bureau of Investigation, who called in the Federal Bureau of Investigation. The agencies were convinced they had a kidnapping on their hands. Fox News sent a satellite truck. Ollie gave live television updates three times a day. Then, out of the blue, several days into the ordeal, his parents received a call from the Wadley Regional Medical Center Emergency Room in Texarkana, Texas, explaining that their son was being treated for a broken collarbone sustained at a local rodeo.

Ollie was humiliated. He hadn't forgotten that feeling. Folks kidded him that the young cowboy had ridden out of town on a horse while

Ollie was busy looking for suspicious cars. The incident became known as the Sumter County Kidnapping and was a constant embarrassment to Ollie. Technically, he hadn't done anything wrong. It could have happened to any sheriff, in any county. But Ollie performed in front of the cameras with the dramatic flair and fervor of a television evangelist. His peers always reminded him that if his law enforcement career ever dried up he had a bright future selling kitchen knives on TV infomercials. In reality, Ollie was a great sheriff. He could think on his feet. Once, while on vacation, he had subdued a criminal with nothing more than an emergency defibrillator. Every time the thief made a move to escape, Ollie shocked him. The criminal finally begged for forgiveness and just lay there whimpering until the local cops arrived.

"Sure, Chief. I think I have a BC Powder," R.C. replied as he studied the girly calendars the way an art student studies Monet in the National Gallery. "I'll go get it for you."

R.C. exacerbated Ollie's headache, but he was a smart cop when he got the scent of something. The fact that R.C. had not yet gotten keyed up about this situation served to assuage Ollie's concerns.

"Mick, I'm thinking that we wait until morning—at a decent hour—to check on this Jake character. To be honest, I just ain't got enough to go on," he said with a deep sigh, hoping Mick would understand. Ollie believed Mick about Jake. But he'd seen too many men drink too much and do crazy things when they were away from their wives. This was especially true for the guys who stayed cooped up in offices all the time. They were the worst.

Mick didn't know what to think. He didn't have any experience with anything like this, and found himself deferring to Ollie. *Ollie's the professional. He oughta know how to handle these things,* Mick thought, trying to piece together Jake's jumbled words from the barely audible call, but he couldn't. This, combined with his fatigue, left him at a loss.

"Here you go, Chief," R.C. said handing him a BC packet and placing his hands on his hips.

Ollie didn't even glare at R.C. this time. He was simply too tired.

"You think these guys would mind if we had a Coke?" R.C. asked Mick as he looked in the refrigerator.

"I doubt it," Mick responded, adjusting the cap on his head.

"Chief, I could ride the perimeter roads to see if anything looks suspicious. I don't have anything else to do," R.C. said as he handed Ollie a drink to wash down the powder. "It's way too wet to try the interior roads in my patrol car."

Ollie looked at his watch. It was almost 2 A.M. *What in the world am I doing up at this hour? I'm dying and R.C.'s as ready to go as a puppy with two peckers.* Ollie appreciated his enthusiasm. He watched R.C. take a purple pill out of his pocket and wash it down with a swig of Coke.

"I had some pickled quail eggs for supper and they're killing me. Serious heartburn," R.C. said in response to Ollie's inquisitive glance.

Ollie thought hard. "No. I think we'll wait till daylight. We can't see anything in the dark. String some tape around what blood you can see. In fact, string it across the driveway. We'll look around this whole place later, when it's daylight."

"Mick, why don't you go get some sleep? I'll let you know if we find anything. First thing—about eight o'clock—I'll call the West Point police and have them ride out to this guy's house. With any luck we'll find out the 'emergency' was that he'd run out of money in a poker game and needed a loan. Yep, I bet we find out he was getting killed in a serious game of Texas Hold'em."

"All right...please let me know," Mick said, trusting the sheriff. There were a few honky-tonks in the county, so Mick decided he would swing by the one that was on his way home to see if Jake's truck was there. *I'm gonna be pissed if it is,* Mick thought.

Mick got up slowly and started out of the lodge. He stood in the door to listen and think. He could hear a whippoorwill off in the distance and nothing else. Turning around, Mick said, "I'm sure you're right, Ollie…I just wish I could have heard him clearly."

"I understand. Let us handle it…I promise I'll keep you informed," Ollie answered.

"See ya, Mick," R.C. chimed in.

As soon as they heard Mick's truck crank, Ollie stood, stretched, and said, "I'm goin' home. I need some sleep, and you should do the same. I'll make some calls in the morning. Why don't you hang close to your house in case I need you?"

"No problem. I was gonna go see if I could catch some crappie in the mornin', but I can go later."

"Are they bitin'?" Ollie asked, swatting at some type of bug.

"Apparently; some idiot got stabbed over a fishin' hole late this afternoon. An *accident*," R.C. said, making quotation marks with his hands as he said the word.

"I don't even want to hear about it," Ollie said as he rubbed his forehead and walked out.

Chapter 16

Tiny and Sweat braced for a shootout as they slowed down. They didn't recognize the Jeep. Whoever it was had just opened the gate and was about to drive through.

Tiny stopped about fifty yards away, straight in front of the Jeep, with his high beams shining right at it. Before he knew it, Sweat glided out of the truck like a commando and slithered down into the ditch. Tiny took a deep breath. His adrenaline was pumping at record levels.

Tiny grabbed his pistol as he got out, then started walking toward the Jeep. *I didn't want all this trouble. I just wanted to steal some shit to sell.*

Johnny Lee was always pushing the envelope. And Tiny was a follower, following Johnny Lee right into this huge mess.

Elizabeth nervously asked Tanner, "Who's that?"

"I don't have a clue," Tanner responded, never taking his eyes off the truck. He swallowed hard and climbed out, hoping to find coon hunters. He walked through the open gate and stood in the glare of the headlights.

"Stay in the Jeep," Elizabeth pleaded.

"Hey! We need to get through!" Tanner yelled but got no reply.

"Tanner, be careful!" Elizabeth called worriedly.

Tiny's jumbo silhouette moved through the beams of his headlights, then stood motionless about twenty yards away from Tanner. Tiny could see somewhat, but he couldn't hear well—the truck's glass-packed mufflers were rumbling in his ears. Tanner could see Tiny's pistol. Then he heard a limb crack in the woods and glanced off into the inky darkness, but he couldn't make out a thing. His attention immediately went back to the big guy and the gun.

"We need to get through!" Tanner yelled nervously.

"Nobody's getting through unless we say so."

"Look, I'm Tanner Tillman, and I have been back on my folks' place. I need to come out."

Tanner thought he saw car lights reflected in the treetops, but, when he turned around to look to see if another vehicle was coming up behind them, he saw nothing. His mind was racing. He heard another stick break to his left. The woods were pitch-black and the glare of the headlights blinding.

I gotta get Elizabeth out of here – quick. I'll drive down in the ditch, around the truck and that big redneck with the gun.

As Tanner started to climb in, he heard another noise, and before he could turn, someone grabbed him from behind and slammed him to the ground, knocking the breath out of him, and ground his face into the gravel. Elizabeth was screaming. Tanner was being kicked in the sides. He struggled but couldn't get up. He tried to turn to see who had attacked him.

Tiny ran as fast as he could toward the Jeep. Sweat beat Tanner senseless and then turned his attention to the screaming girl. Sweat wasn't expecting this little piece of good fortune. She was beautiful. His focus had been on the guy standing by the Jeep, and he had never known she was there until she screamed. Sweat reached across the seat to grab her, but she jumped back just out of his reach, screaming louder. Tanner managed to pull himself up and wrap his arms around Sweat's waist. Tanner was way out of his league. Sweat outweighed him by more than a hundred pounds and had honed his fighting skills with years of bar brawls and knife fights. Tanner had been in one fight, and that was in the seventh grade.

Sweat spun around and dragged Tanner to the front of the Jeep where he elbowed him hard in the face, breaking his nose. Pain flashed like a white light through Tanner's brain. Sweat then threw him into the grill of the Jeep. Tanner could barely see or breathe. As he struggled to his knees, Tiny hit him in the back of the head with the butt of his pistol, knocking him flat on the ground.

"Stay down or you're gonna get killed," Tiny advised sympathetically. Tiny didn't like this at all. He wasn't going to kill the kid, but he knew Sweat would without hesitation.

"Elizabeth, get out of here! Run! Run, Elizabeth!" Tanner screamed as he lifted himself to his elbows.

Sweat grabbed Tanner by the hair, dragging him to his knees, then forced his mouth open on the front bumper of the Jeep. Tanner could not move and he was gasping for breath. He could taste the cold metal bumper. Sweat then viciously kicked the back of Tanner's head, knocking out all of his front teeth.

Tiny dry-heaved and turned away.

Elizabeth couldn't see how badly Tanner was getting beaten. All she could do was scream.

Sweat quickly went around to the passenger side of the Jeep to pull Elizabeth out. She frantically looked for something she could use as a weapon. She could hear her mother reminding her that she should always carry Mace in her purse. All she found in the Jeep was a car battery. Scared to death, she jumped to the driver's seat and tried to find reverse, grinding the gears. When she let the clutch out, it was in fourth. The Jeep jerked and the engine died. She leapt out and started running down the Dummy Line. Her mind was racing. She ran blindly. She had no idea where she was going. She just ran as fast as she could.

Tanner struggled to his feet out from under the front of the Jeep and then tried to tackle Sweat. Sweat grabbed him, punched him in the stomach, and then raised him up by the hair and punched him in the throat. Sweat then put Tanner in a headlock that cut off his air. Tanner thrashed around. Sweat tightened his hold. Tanner was screaming but made no sound. His lungs were burning and felt like they were going to explode. Sweat held him until he quit moving. Then he threw Tanner's body into the muddy ditch and turned his attention to the girl.

Tiny was breathing heavily, about to vomit. "What about the girl?" Tiny gasped.

"She's mine. Man, this is my lucky day!" Sweat said glaring down the moonlit road. He could barely make out her outline two hundred yards away, running wildly. *I'll catch her. Where's she gonna go?* he thought.

"What about Johnny Lee? Reese told us—" Tiny asked.

"—Johnny Lee's dead. You help Reese, I'm gonna catch that bitch and have me some fun," he said, interrupting, and turned away.

Tiny knew Sweat was serious and would not be denied. He watched Sweat start walking slowly and deliberately after the girl. They were supposed to help catch Johnny Lee's killer. *I gotta get focused,* Tiny thought. He looked at the blood on the Jeep's bumper and then slid down into the ditch to check on the kid. *I sure hope he ain't dead. Talk about bein' in the wrong place at the wrong time.* After confirming that the kid was alive and not face down in the mud, Tiny went back to his truck for a beer in a desperate attempt to not think about tonight's brutality, which seemed to have just gotten started.

Elizabeth ran for her life, tears pouring down her face. Tanner was in trouble and she couldn't help. She didn't help. *He was fighting for me and all I could do was scream.* Twice she stopped and looked back. The second time, with her hands on her knees and the vapor from her breath glowing against the distant headlights, she saw someone following her.

"Oh, God! Oh, God, help me!" She screamed, running as hard and fast as she could.

Chapter 17

"How you doin', sweetheart?" Jake asked Katy, trying not to let her see his fear. She didn't answer. She was crying quietly to herself.

"Katy, we're gonna get out of here and go straight to the police...someplace safe...I promise...just hang on, girlfriend."

Driving like a maniac, he was trying to put as much distance as possible between them and those lunatic rednecks. If he could just get to the county road he'd feel better. As they rounded a bend, a deer jumped from in front of them, but Jake never took his foot of the gas. He grabbed his cell phone. *No Service.*

"Shit!" he said aloud.

"I'm sorry, Katy," he apologized.

"It's okay. Just go, Dad. Go! I just wanna go home!" she exclaimed tearfully.

"I do too, sweetheart. I promise we are," he said, giving her a quick look.

When they approached the Dummy Line, Jake had two alternatives but really only one choice. A right would take them ten miles to the county road where there was one gate and he knew the lock combination. Turning left would take them several miles until the road dead-ended into several more miles of the Noxubee River swamp. That's the reason the railroad had never completed the line—the swamp proved too vast and expensive to cross. A right it was.

Jake stomped the accelerator. Although the Dummy Line was full of potholes, it was a fairly good gravel road. As they crested the last hill before the gate, he saw headlights. Jake immediately slammed on the brakes. He could see a half-mile ahead. Somebody was coming onto the property.

"F-u-u-…" he said out loud and looked at Katy before he finished the word, "dge!" Jake was unraveling.

"What is it?" Katy said as she sat up to see down the road.

"It's not good."

"Is that the bad guys?"

"I'm afraid so, but it's okay…I've got another plan," Jake lied.

It made sense. The bad guys obviously knew this area. He immediately cut off his lights. Sitting in the dark, he tried to think of solutions. There weren't many. *We can't go out this way. The road's not wide enough to pass another vehicle. Maybe hide the truck, and we'll hide in the woods until daylight. No, not with Katy in tow. Think. Think. Think.*

Jake slammed the truck in reverse and spun around. He sped back the way they had come, going past the turn that led back to the camp. As he roared by, he couldn't see any lights coming down that old logging road. *The thugs must be dealing with the mud hole.*

Jake knew that hiding the truck was going to be a waste of time. The roads were so muddy, tracking it would be no trouble. Jake swallowed hard. *Be calm, use your head, Jake,* he told himself. *That's the only way Katy's gonna survive.*

Chapter 18

Mick Johnson drove slowly away from the camp, trying to piece together the evening's events. He had met Jake eight years earlier at a National Wild Turkey Federation banquet in Birmingham. They had hit it off right away and turkey-hunted together every year since. Jake, ten years younger, was fun, but his job recently had grown incredibly stressful. Mick could see him changing. Jake had commented to him last year that he was thinking of a career change. Mick realized how much he liked Jake and how long it had been since they just simply talked. He made a mental note to have him over for some beers and steaks. Nothing was making sense. One minute he was sure Jake was in trouble, and the next he thought Jake might be off drinking and playing cards.

Mick pulled off Highway 17 to search for Jake's home phone number. He punched it in and hit Send, but hit the End button before it rang. *It's 2:15 in the morning. This isn't necessary.* He stared at the clock, then decided to drive by the Bama Jama Club, a local honky-tonk known to have the occasional recreational poker game in the back. Mick wished the sheriff had been more assertive. But what could he really do? Mick knew Jake wouldn't be there, yet he prayed he was. The highway was empty as he pulled back onto it, heading towards the bar.

Ollie Landrum searched the radio stations for something familiar and soothing. He hated rap—couldn't understand what they were saying. He hated country music—too twangy. He loved Otis Redding. He loved the blues—now that's music. Not finding anything, he switched off the radio, disgusted. All he wanted to do was sleep for about ten hours. He radioed Martha to let her know he was headed home. *I really hope there's nothing to all this,* he thought.

Ollie knew that hunting was vital to the county's economy as a whole, but he couldn't see the real attraction of it. Hunters had to get up too early. Once he had gone rabbit hunting with his jailer and some guys from the area. That one trip had been enough. It was more of a chance to listen to the football games than anything, and Ollie could do that at home, comfortably. He watched all the games on Saturdays, particularly the Southeastern Conference. They were reminders of his glory days. An NFL career had been in sight until an Oklahoma tight end chop blocked him, totally destroying his right knee and his dreams.

So, on his one hunting trip, instead of preparing for Sunday's kick-off, he was hauling around a dozen yapping beagles that smelled to high heaven and occasionally shooting at a rabbit. Mostly, however, they all just talked—telling lies—and ate food he would never eat at home, while listening to the dogs run. Maybe the real motivation for these guys was just to get out of the house and have a moment away from the grind. Now that was a reason he could get his mind around.

Ollie hoped he could relax the rest of the day. His wife was going to the IMAX Theater in Birmingham with a group of kids from church to watch a National Geographic movie. He could hear the imitation leather couch calling his name. And then tomorrow was Talladega, the big NASCAR race that attracted hundreds of thousands of nut cases from all walks of life. The redneck fans were the ones who worried Ollie. He was thankful that the track wasn't in his county. Ollie and the boys always got together to watch the race on TV and drink beer. He had actually gone to Talladega once. There were way too many drunks, and fights, and crazy white guys trying to relive their past. So he and his buddies watched the races at his house and barbecued ribs. They cheered like the drivers could hear them.

After everyone had left the camp, R.C. hung around for a few minutes to finish the calendar girl tour. He turned out the lights but otherwise left the place just as he had found it, minus two Cokes and one really graphic calendar he found hidden in the cabinet above the refrigerator. Climbing back into his cruiser, he radioed Martha to tell her that he was headed home. He then found a talk show on an AM superstation. R.C. wasn't really listening to the yammering about the U.S. military presence in Iraq; he was thinking of calling Chastity. He wanted to tell her that he had just studied dozens of calendar girls and that she definitely had the right stuff to be a Bunny. But she never could talk while she was working. At least that's what the bouncer said every time he called. *I'll just tell her in person tomorrow night.*

R.C. was getting bored and, rather than go straight home, he decided to drive down a few of the old gravel roads. *I wish it wasn't so late and that Hooters wasn't an hour away. Man, I could eat about twenty nuclear hot wings right now,* he thought. All the heaving cleavage, tight butt cheeks, and tiny tank tops was more than he could resist; consequently, he was putting on ten pounds a year thanks to a steady diet of chicken wings and beer.

He slipped his finger and thumb into his Copenhagen to get a big dip, while rooting around under the seat for an empty plastic spit bottle. When he found one, he nestled it between his legs, then eased his foot down on the accelerator.

Chapter 19

So, kids in the house with Momma. This shouldn't be too hard, Moon Pie thought as he petted the friendly dog. He saw a trampoline and swing set in the backyard as he searched for the telephone line. He wanted to cut it to prevent a 911 call, just in case. He wasn't sure he could tell the difference in the TV cable and the telephone line until he saw the BellSouth logo.

Moon Pie had never snatched anyone before. He preferred the word "snatching" to "kidnapping." Kidnapping sounded so federal. But he was more than willing to try it. Moon Pie was thorough, which greatly aided his criminal career. He took the hands-on education he had received growing up on a soybean farm to become the most successful marijuana grower in northeast Mississippi. He was the first to apply modern fertilization techniques and to control the pH levels of his soil. He installed grow lights with a drip irrigation system in two giant chicken houses, boosting yields to twice those of his competitors. Moon Pie struggled with managing the expenses, however, and consequently always found himself a little short. No matter how much money he made, Sheree, his girlfriend of six years, always seemed to spend a little more. She was extremely high-maintenance.

After locating the master bedroom, he worked up a plan. The unknown was how many children were in the house. He eased up the porch stairs and studied the locks. *One deadbolt. I'll just kick it in,* he thought as he set down his bag of tricks. Then it occurred to him that he should simply knock the glass out with a hammer, reach in, and turn the lock. He put a spider web of camo duct tape on the glass to prevent it from shattering, then carefully broke the glass. It always surprised him how little noise it made.

She was awakened by a sound she couldn't place. She wasn't even certain that she had really heard anything. She lay very still listening, warm and comfortable. She thought she heard a board creak, but the old house was full of sounds. Then the heater turned on, drowning out any odd noises. She relaxed.

Moon Pie stepped inside and walked quickly and quietly down the hallway to the master bedroom. Bursting through the door, he took her by surprise. Just as she started to scream, Moon Pie's hand slammed over her mouth. He held her down on the bed and pointed his .40 Glock right between her eyes, the night-light from the bathroom illuminating the pistol. He climbed on top of her and straddled her. Then he lowered his face to within inches of hers, smelling her as he moved the pistol to the side of her head, being certain she could feel the cold steel.

"Don't say a word," he whispered forcefully. "Is there anyone else in the house?" he asked, knowing he couldn't believe her.

Her eyes were wide with terror. Moon Pie was feeding off her fear. She shook her head, "NO!"

"Your husband killed someone that's important to me, and now *you* have to pay!" he said in an intense whisper. "That's how it works."

He saw confusion and fear in her eyes. She violently shook her head and tried to speak but he wouldn't let her. He took duct tape with one hand, stretched it, and tore it with his teeth. He laid a strip over her mouth as he moved his hand away. She struggled to loosen his grip. He forced her arms behind her and began taping her wrists. She fought hard. He ran another strip all the way around her head covering her mouth. She was trying desperately to talk. He then taped her ankles. She was completely immobilized. When he was sure her nostrils were clear, he stood, catching his breath.

She was wearing panties and a tank top. Moon Pie admired her athletic body. Still breathing heavily, he slowly looked around and decided to check out the rest of the house. He searched every room and didn't find another person. *The kids must be spending the night somewhere.* He went back downstairs to the master bedroom.

"Let's go for a ride," he said, picking her up and throwing her over his shoulder like a sack of feed. He walked to the front door, glass crunching under his feet. He shut the front door and walked straight down the driveway to his vehicle. She wasn't very heavy—a buck thirty, maybe. He'd adjusted the interior lights so they didn't come on and betray his presence. He could tell she was about to freak out. She was terrified. He was in charge. He could feel the power, and it aroused him.

The rear seat of the Tahoe was down, so when he threw her in the back, there was plenty of room. Moon Pie climbed on top of her, grinding himself into her. Her squirming only excited him more.

"We're gonna have us a little party," he whispered in her ear, then licked the tears streaming down her cheek, "but not here. I've got somethin' special planned for yo fine self." He lifted her shirt and licked her stomach. He got off her, closed the door, and then hopped into the driver's seat. Pulling off his surgical gloves, he cranked up and drove off. He lit a Marlboro, taking a good long drag. Blowing the smoke out, he picked up the radiophone and hit Send.

Beep-beep. "Yo dog."

Beep-beep. "Talk to me."

Beep-beep. "Got her and she's a gem. One fine piece of ass!"

Beep-beep. "Can you take her to Johnny Lee's trailer?"

Beep-beep. "Sure. I'll be there in about two hours. I gotta drive slow so I don't get pulled over."

Beep-beep. "The key's on the ledge over the door. Call me when you get there."

Beep-beep. "You got the guy yet?"

Beep-beep. "No, but we're close."

Moon Pie hung up and dialed his girlfriend as he rubbed himself. The line was busy. She was on the 'Net. That pissed him off. *She's in a chat room in the middle of the night with a bunch of freaks,* he thought. She'd only surf the 'Net when he was gone. It drove him crazy. *That's it! I'm gettin' rid of her.*

Chapter 20

No matter how many Walkie-Talkies he drank sitting in the truck, Tiny couldn't stop thinking how he'd gotten into this mess. Awhile back, his first cousin had promised him a job at the Indian Casino. He could earn an honest living. Sure, he'd be a maintenance man, but it would be a new start and he could live with his cousin until he got settled. His cousin had a double-wide in a huge trailer park called Sunshine Village in Montgomery. Tiny liked the name. *Why ain't I gone already?* he thought.

Johnny Lee was the reason. He instilled a sense of worth in Tiny when the societal norms dictated the contrary. Johnny Lee convinced him that any day they were going to hit it big. Even criminals dream.

Tiny never thought twice about stealing stuff or selling illegal whiskey, but killing folks wasn't his style. And he knew Sweat was going to rape that girl. That was bothering him more than killing Johnny Lee's shooter. Tiny also knew that he was going to do what Reese asked of him, but he'd made up his mind that he wasn't going to let Sweat hurt the girl. He crushed the beer can and threw it into the pile on the floorboard of the truck.

"After tonight, I'm movin' to Montgomery and startin' over," he said aloud as he turned the truck around in the road and backed it up next to the Jeep, parking so close no one could have gotten out of his passenger's side door. Tiny climbed out without taking anything and walked to the back of the truck. Like so many good ol' boys, he had a four-wheeler in the back. But unlike most, he used his to haul moonshine. He unloaded it and left it idling. With the way the two vehicles were parked, the gateposts, and the big trees next to the road, it was impossible for any vehicle to pass. He had Johnny Lee's killer trapped. Reese would be pleased.

"What the hell am I doin'?!" he yelled looking around. He closed his eyes hard. As Tiny climbed on the Polaris 500, he shifted into forward and gave it some gas. He switched the lights on low beam and started looking for footprints.

Chapter 21

Limbs were hitting Reese in the face, but he didn't care. He walked with purpose—he was on a mission. All his life, his cousin Johnny Lee had been his best friend. Together they weren't afraid of anything. Individually, they always tried to out do each other. Johnny Lee, one year older, was always looking out for Reese. In fact, Reese always thought that Johnny Lee had failed the sixth grade on purpose so they could be in the same class. They played football together until Johnny Lee punched the defensive back coach in the eye for yelling at him. The coaches told Johnny Lee to leave the team. That was the eleventh grade and the beginning of his spiral downward. Two weeks after punching out the coach, Johnny Lee attacked his English teacher. So, rather than be suspended, Johnny Lee walked out of Booker T. Washington High School...but not before he shat in the principal's desk drawer.

Reese somehow managed to stay in school another year. In the following football season, on a cool October Friday night, he chased a running back out of bounds and ran helmet-first into the defensive back coach, knocking him out cold. Reese pointed into the stands after the vicious hit. Rumor was that Reese hadn't actually passed the eleventh grade, but none of the teachers wanted another year of him, so they pushed him through. He was a smart kid; he just wasn't the least bit interested in school, so he quit. He recognized that getting a GED would be the best deal for his career aspirations.

Johnny Lee had earned his GED and his commercial driver's license the year he dropped out of high school and started hauling chickens to the slaughterhouse. At night, he collected for a bookie and did whatever he could to make money.

Reese eventually went to work at a tire store and became quite efficient at stealing valuables out of customers' cars. It became clear who the thief was, so the manager fired him. Before Reese left, however, he stole a key and made a copy. Later that week, in the middle of the night, he let himself into the shop and stole a set of rims and $367 in cash. That was the turning point in his career. He made $220 more that night than he had working the entire previous week, and he didn't have to pay taxes or get greasy. Reese explained all this to Johnny Lee, and they decided right then and there that their fortune was to be made as criminals.

Johnny Lee and Reese experimented with several different schemes but always came back to stealing. Their little enterprise made progress and at times had an impressive cash flow. This allowed them to branch out. The two were always together unless one of them was incarcerated, which was never for long. Johnny Lee and Reese appeared to be Teflon coated. With no mentor, they had to figure out the crime business the hard way. They were productive even in jail. They would listen to the other cons talk about their crimes. They paid close attention.

Reese figured he'd catch up with Johnny Lee's killer on the Dummy Line, or Tiny and Sweat would. Either way, if he kept walking he would eventually get to exact his revenge. Then he would clean up this mess. But right now, he just wanted some one-on-one time with Johnny Lee's killer. The rifle felt right at home on his back. Occasionally, he thought he heard a truck's engine rev, and that just fueled his fire. The night was cool, and he was dressed for it, except for the pointed-toed cowboy boots he always wore. The boots were all show, and he could feel the water leaking through. He had a long walk, but he didn't care. He thought about Johnny Lee. His cold body lying in the back of a truck. He got a tear in his eye.

Reese pulled the radiophone out and scrolled to Tiny's name.

Beep-beep. No response.

Beep-beep. Again no response.

Reese, pissed off, folded his phone, jammed it in his jacket pocket and walked on.

Chapter 22

R.C. headed west from the camp and turned onto the first gravel road. It had been a couple of years since he had driven this part of the county at night, but he was pretty familiar with it. The hunting was great—just too many pine trees for him. The AM station he was listening to began to fade, so he hit Play on the cassette player. Barry Manilow roared to life singing "I Write The Songs," and it just soothed R.C.'s soul. He secretly *loved* Barry Manilow. Once, another deputy had gotten into the car and seen the tapes. R.C. was forced to think fast. He told him it was evidence. The deputy shook his head saying, "We shore got some weird folks 'round here." R.C. reluctantly nodded in agreement.

Tonight R.C. was relaxing and riding the roads at the taxpayers' expense. Spitting into the green bottle, he tried to act official, slowing down occasionally to shine his spotlight into dim roads and paths that went off into the trees. He wasn't really looking for anything. He did not radio Martha to tell her what he was doing, that he hadn't headed home—a serious breech of protocol. But he did it all the time. He passed several roads before coming to the abandoned railroad line. He slowed but didn't turn. *I'll catch it on the way back,* he thought.

May was approaching fast, and R.C. was daydreaming about his upcoming annual redfish trip to Gulf Shores. He'd saved a week of vacation for the trip. *I might even ask Chastity to go this year. It might do her good to get some sun and fresh seafood, and to be away from her worthless, piece-of-shit, crackhead husband.* R.C. had a lot to get ready. Somebody had stolen all his gear from his family's fish camp down on the river. They'd even stolen his $3.97 minnow bucket. He had scoured the county for his gear, but so far he hadn't come up with anything. A group of black guys that were always fishing near the camp finally bought him a new minnow bucket just so he would quit asking about theirs. He never noticed that they didn't have a tag on their old beat-up car.

R.C. kept driving west until he reached the end of the county road—the Mississippi state line. You couldn't tell any difference in the road but the state line was right there, so he turned around and headed back. Barry broke into "Mandy," and R.C. was singing at the top of his lungs when he approached the Dummy Line again. The old road had shooting houses at the top of each ridge. During deer season you wouldn't dream of driving down it in the daylight. There would be a hunter with a high-powered rifle in every one of them. R.C. slowly turned the cruiser down the road and continued singing. "Oh, Mandy…" Occasionally, he turned on the blue lights. He liked the way they reflected off the trees.

Suddenly the radio crackled. It scared him so badly that he spilled his spit bottle. He turned off Barry and picked up the microphone, braking to a stop.

"Base to Unit Three. Come in, R.C.," Martha's husky old voice said.

"Unit Three here," R.C. replied.

"Where are you, R.C.?" she asked, skipping the formal jargon.

"I'm headed back to the house. I was just checkin' a few things out." He hoped that would satisfy her.

"Are you sure?"

"Where else would I be?"

"With you there's no tellin'. Go home. The county can't afford to pay you overtime."

"Yes, ma'am"

"And quit dippin' in the car. The other guys are complainin' 'bout the mess."

He wasn't going to answer that one. R.C. hung up the microphone and started looking for a spot to turn around. *That old battle-ax thinks she runs the place. She smokes like a chimney and has the gall to complain about my dippin'.*

R.C. had two unfailing habits. He dipped whenever he was awake, and he constantly applied Rogaine, hoping to prevent further balding. He believed that if he ever stopped, the rest of his hair would fall out. Consequently, the seats and cup holders in the car were nasty, and the headrest was greasy and stained.

There wasn't a safe place to turn around, so he kept driving, searching. After another mile or so he turned Barry back on, but Martha had successfully killed the mood. R.C. reached up and punched off the tape player with an aggravated jab. *Women, even old women, drive me insane.*

Just when he found a turnaround spot, he noticed reflective lights at the far end of his headlight beams. Orange parking lights. His curiosity piqued, he slowly eased down the road. As he got closer he could see what appeared to be a giant vehicle but then realized it was two vehicles parked side by side. *Either coon hunters or lovers,* he thought. But with the way they were parked, it might be kids passing liquor or drugs back and forth. He sat in his car a hundred yards away wondering what to do. He decided not to radio in and unleash on himself the wrath of Mrs. Martha O'Brien for being alone.

Slowly he crept forward, looking for any kind of movement. Not seeing any activity made him nervous. This was strange. *Where could they be? I need to get out and look around.* Climbing out of the cruiser, he unsnapped his holster and put his right hand on the butt of his pistol. He walked to the side of the truck first and shined his flashlight inside the open window. The smell made him grunt, but he couldn't see anything out of the ordinary. The back of the truck was filled with trash. An aluminum four-wheeler ramp was leaning against the open tailgate. He walked around the back of the truck and tried to squeeze between it and the Jeep. He recognized the Jeep. It was Tanner Tillman's. Thinking they might be hunting, he stood still, listening for dogs running. All he heard was nothing.

Man, I like Tanner's Jeep. I always wanted one. I like the rims, the way it's been restored, R.C. thought as he relaxed, thinking more about buying a Jeep than determining what was going on. He opened the passenger side door and shined his light inside. *I don't like these flimsy doors. But look at the workmanship of this paint job.*

R.C. screamed like a little girl when a bloody hand grabbed his ankle and held on for dear life. He dropped his flashlight. He was trying to get his pistol out of its holster when he squeezed the trigger. The shot missed his foot by less than an inch. R.C. was freaking out.

"Son...of...a...bitch!" he screamed as loud as he could and tried to run but couldn't. Another hand grabbed R.C.'s other leg, causing him to fall on top of whoever or whatever had him. Scrambling to sit up, kicking, he jerked his legs away from what held him. It was not a monster. It was someone badly injured. He wiggled his toes to make sure he hadn't shot himself. He could smell gunpowder and his ears were ringing.

"Tanner? Tanner, is that you?" R.C. asked, hyperventilating and not believing his eyes. "Tanner, what in the hell happened?" he asked as he swung around and bent closer to the bloody face.

Tanner just lay there, struggling to breathe. R.C. couldn't tell exactly what was wrong.

"Hang on, Tanner. I'm gonna get you outta here!" He studied him from head to toe, trying to ascertain his injuries. R.C.'s instincts overrode his training, and he bent down, grabbed Tanner under the shoulders and loaded him into the back of his cruiser. *I gotta get the hell out of here. I gotta get Tanner to the hospital.*

"Unit Three to Base!" he screamed into the microphone.

"Go ahead, Three."

"Miz Martha, I found an eighteen-year-old white male covered in blood and barely conscious. I have him in my car. I'm on the west end of the ol' Dummy Line in the north part of the county. I'll be on Seventeen headed south in eight to ten minutes. Dispatch an ambulance to head north and meet me ASAP!"

"R.C., what happened? Are you okay?"

"I'm fine. I don't know what happened. I rode up on the scene and found him. He can't talk!" R.C. exclaimed.

Martha dispatched an ambulance immediately and got right back to R.C. She could hear the anxiety in his voice. R.C. was shook up.

"R.C., I'll call the sheriff and get you some help out there...where in the world are you?"

"Hang on."

"R.C.... R.C., comeback!"

"Miz Martha, he's trying to talk. Hold on!"

R.C. slowed down and kept looking over the back seat, but he couldn't understand anything Tanner was trying to say. The more R.C. looked at him, the more he realized that Tanner's injuries were extensive.

"Who is it, R.C.?"

He swallowed first and paused a second before speaking, "Miz Martha, it's Tanner Tillman."

He knew that would upset her. Martha O'Brien was rabid about local high school football. Her husband had been the coach for twenty years. She still attended every home game. She talked about Tanner like he was her grandson. She loved the way he ran the wishbone offense.

"You better call his folks," he said with sympathy.

Martha stared at the desk microphone for a second. "R.C."—she began to tear up—"the ambulance is on the way. Take…take good care of him. You hear me?"

"Yes, ma'am. Tell 'em to hurry!"

Chapter 23

Jake hit the brakes hard just ahead of a washed out culvert. By moving the truck forward and back, changing the angle each time, he panned his headlights in search of a way around. There wasn't one. *Damn it!* Jake thought, as he pounded the dashboard. He quickly clicked off his headlights and looked down the road behind him—nothing but darkness—no sign, yet, of anyone following. Remembering that he had a map of the area, Jake fumbled through his hunting vest until he found the aerial photo that showed timber, roads, clearcuts, and food plots. He hadn't been on this side of the property before. This was only his fourth trip to the club, and so far all of his hunts had been in the south section, near the gate. He had killed two turkeys already and was hearing more. He'd had no reason to try new territory.

They would have to get away from the truck. They were trapped. He and Katy would leave it, walk a good distance, and hide. A shooting house would be perfect. It would be a safe vantage point. He knew there was a good chance of finding a shooting house on any food plot large enough to be seen on the map. Studying the wrinkled piece of paper, Jake decided to walk south on a dotted line called Rattlesnake Road. At the end of that road he could see what looked like a large field. On the map it was called Little Buck Field. *Surely it had a shooting house. If not, there's another field about a half-mile through the woods.*

Jake parked the truck on the north side of the Dummy Line behind some big buckeye bushes that were in full bloom. *We'll slip back across the road and head south, hopefully creating some confusion,* Jake thought. He looked at Katy and searched for words to comfort a scared little girl.

"Katy, everything is going to be fine. Trust me," he said confidently. "All we have to do is wait on daylight. We're gonna find a shooting house and climb up in it to hide."

He could see that she was clutching one of her Beanie Babies. *I'm glad she's got it. She seems so small and innocent.* He vowed to do whatever it took to protect her, both physically and mentally. He was getting pissed.

"Hey, I'll bet Ashley Kate and Mary's adventures don't even come close to this," trying to loosen her up and check her awareness.

"It's Mary Kate and Ashley, Dad," she said with a knowing sly look.

"Oh. Oh, yeah," he replied. *Thank goodness she's still together. She's tougher than I expected.*

"Okay, are you dressed?"

"Except for my boots."

"It's all right. I'll carry you," he replied as he grabbed his old Mossy Oak hunting vest and slipped it on. He checked the vest pockets. He had a compass, a map, and a pocketknife. He checked the pockets for anything else that might be useful. *At least I've got a flashlight.* He leaned his shotgun against the side of the truck.

Katy was in full Mossy Oak camo, heavy gray socks, and no boots. He was wearing wet, muddy blue jeans, an old button-down shirt, work boots, and his hunting vest. He searched the truck and toolbox in vain for dry pants or a jacket.

Slinging the shotgun over his shoulder, he grabbed his cell phone off the seat and put it in his pocket and said urgently, "Grab your gloves and your hat. It's pretty cold. If you're ready, let's go." He added, pointing at the mouse Beanie Baby, "...and don't forget Cheddar."

"How'd you know his name?" She smiled in wonderment.

"I'm your dad; it's my job to know that kinda thing."

Jake grabbed Katy, who grabbed Cheddar. He put her on his left hip, holding her with one arm. He leaned away from her for balance as he started walking through the woods holding the flashlight, which he kept turned off, in his right hand. Jake's adrenaline level masked her weight.

They had traveled a hundred yards or so when Katy whispered loudly in his ear, "Dad, you're shaking!" She sounded as concerned about him as he was about her.

"Am I? I'm just cold and wet." He tried to sound calm. He knew the longer this lasted, the greater the chance they wouldn't make it.

"I'll keep you warm," she replied and hugged him as hard as she could.

"Lord, please help us," he prayed in a whispered voice. He readjusted his fifty-pound passenger and started off again in search of Little Buck Field.

Chapter 24

Elizabeth was running for her life…and she knew it. She had run non-stop for twenty minutes when she slipped and fell face-first into the mud. Her knees and hands were skinned, her clothes were soaking wet with mud, and her legs were aching. Although she jogged three or four times a week, panic began to overwhelm and exhaust her. Not knowing what to do or where to go, she had stayed on the road because the moon lit the way. Her lungs were burning, and her right side ached. Standing back up, she looked east and thought she saw red lights heading away from her. She stared. The lights vanished. *Were those really car lights?* A chill ran up her spine. Elizabeth got up and started running in the direction of the lights she prayed that she saw.

"Please, God, help me," she said aloud, "and please, God, help Tanner, please let him be…let him be all right."

Every now and then she passed one of the shooting houses lining the road. They were very ominous and resembled miniature prison guard towers. She had been hunting with her dad once and had sat in one very similar to these. But tonight the moon shadows made them creepy. She was worn out and couldn't go much further. Not wanting to hide in the woods, she decided the next shooting house would be her refuge. There it was, fifteen feet or so off the ground, wooden, about four feet square and almost tall enough to stand up in. It was old but appeared to be in better shape than some of the others she passed.

She stood at the base thinking. She was too tired to run any further. This made sense. Before she started climbing the ladder, she shook it to see if it would hold her. Quickly she climbed up and cracked the door. As soon as the door opened, there was a loud shriek and a blur of something big flying by her head. She screamed, "Oh, God!" as she slipped from the ladder. She hit the ground with a thud. Her right ankle immediately began throbbing. With exasperation, she made a fist and pounded the earth a couple of times.

An owl or a hawk, that's what it was, she thought as she climbed back up and eased the door open again, ducking as she stuck in her head. All was silent. She quickly crawled in and shut the door. She ran her hands up and down the edge of the door until she found the latch and hooked it. She stared out the eight-inch-wide opening but couldn't see anyone coming. She then eased down to the floor and pulled her legs underneath her. She loosened the laces of her right shoe and started to shake uncontrollably. She sobbed silently.

Chapter 25

R.C. was hauling ass. His blues were flashing, but he'd turned off the siren in a vain attempt to hear what Tanner was saying. His mind was racing even faster than he was driving.

"R.C., what's your twenty?" Martha asked calmly.

"I'm on Seventeen headed south. Just passed the Kendalls' farm. Where's the ambulance?"

"They just crossed the interstate headed your way. You should see their lights in about five minutes."

"Yes'm," he replied trying to keep both hands on the steering wheel as much as possible.

"Ollie's on his way here—expect him to radio you any minute."

"Let me get Tanner transferred to the EMTs, and then I'll tell Ollie what I know."

"Ten-four. I dispatched Larson to take the Tillmans to the hospital."

"I'm guessin' they'll airlift him to Tuscaloosa or UAB."

"Dear Lord…is he that bad, R.C.?"

"Yes, ma'am."

"R.C.…Ollie wants you to come here as soon as possible."

"Ten-four."

Ollie had gotten the call just after crawling in bed and turning off the lights. His wife never woke up. Jackie was used to this sort of thing. Ollie told Martha he would be right there and to make some fresh coffee. Driving to the office, he listened to the police radio, resisting the urge to question R.C. He could tell he had his hands full. If

R.C. got too distracted, somebody could get killed. Ollie switched on the blues in his tan Expedition and punched the gas. *What a night,* he thought.

"I see them up ahead. I'm pullin' over!"

"Ten-four, R.C. Hold on." Twenty seconds passed, "They've got a visual on you, too."

"I'll radio as soon as they have him!"

"Ten-four, Unit Three."

The ambulance did a quick U-turn and stopped next to R.C.'s cruiser. Within seconds, the EMTs jumped out, opened the back doors, and slid out the gurney. It automatically opened and they rolled it next to the rear quarter panel of the car. R.C. opened the back door but didn't know what to do next. He was anxious to help but was at a loss. The two EMTs were very professional. They had seen it all.

"I don't know what all's wrong with him. I think he's been beat up. I knew I could get him out here faster than y'all could get there," R.C. said hopefully.

"You did good, R.C.," said the female EMT, reaching for Tanner's wrist. The male EMT shined a light in Tanner's eyes, checking for dilation. The EMTs looked at each other and nodded in agreement.

"Let's roll!" the woman said and then grabbed Tanner under his arms. "R.C., hold his head."

R.C. helped the EMTs make certain the gurney straps were tight. Then he looked at his hands and casually wiped the blood on his pants and asked, "Do you think he needs airlifting?"

"I don't know. Once they clean him up and x-ray him, then they can tell," replied the male EMT with a grunt as they lifted the gurney into the unit. The female EMT jumped in the back, and the guy slammed the doors.

"That's Tanner Tillman…you know, from the football team?"

"No way?" he said, surprised. "Well, he's in good hands now!"

R.C. looked in through the side window and saw the EMT placing an oxygen mask on Tanner's blood-covered face. As the ambulance raced off, R.C. stood watching, listening.

"Three to Base," R.C. finally called in.

"Go ahead, R.C.," Martha replied.

"Is the sheriff there yet?"

"He's walking in the door."

R.C. dropped the car in gear and headed straight for the sheriff's office. He had driven about a mile when the radio crackled.

"Base to Unit Three."

"Unit Three."

"What happened out there, R.C.?"

"Chief, I don't know. I was ridin' roads near that camp and turned on the Dummy Line and about three miles down there were two vehicles but no people. I got out to check on things and found Tanner at the edge of the road."

"What do you think happened to him…what's your gut saying?"

"I think he got the crap beat out of him in a fight."

"Not some kind of an accident?"

"No. This was on purpose."

"Was anyone else there? What was the other vehicle?"

"I didn't see anyone. The other truck looked familiar, but I can't place it. I left so fast I didn't look at the plates—sorry," he added quickly.

"What is your ETA?"

"Five minutes."

"Hurry up," the sheriff said, then stood.

Ollie poured himself a cup of coffee. Cream, three sugars. Martha was on the phone with the hospital. Ollie walked to his desk and sat down to look at a county map. His eyes drifted to the massive wilderness bordering the camp. *Could these incidents be related,* he wondered? He planned to quiz R.C. and then go to the hospital to see the kid for himself.

R.C. ran in and plopped down in the chair in front of the sheriff's desk. He was obviously proud of himself.

"Hey, Chief," R.C. said, expecting accolades.

"R.C., do you think these two, well, incidents are or could be related?"

"Tanner probably got into a fight over some girl or the football game," R.C. continued, "but, if that's what it was, the fight got way ugly. He had the crap beat out of him."

"High school fights don't get that brutal," Ollie said, sipping his coffee. R.C. shrugged, then nodded tentatively in agreement.

They both looked up when they heard someone running down the hall. Martha rushed into the room with a panicked look on her face.

"Ollie, Tanner Tillman's mother just told me that Tanner had a date tonight with Elizabeth Beasley…she's asking where the Beasley girl is."'

Ollie and Martha wheeled to R.C. His eyes got wide and he jumped up.

"Holy shit! That's what he was trying to say…Elizabeth! She's out there! I'm on my way!" R.C. yelled, racing down the hall.

Ollie grabbed his cowboy hat as he ran toward the door. "Who else is on duty tonight?" he asked holding the door open.

"Larson and Shug," Martha quickly responded.

"Have them meet me wherever R.C. is saying this happened. I'm on my way. Radio R.C. to slow down long enough for me to catch up. Tell them both no sirens, just lights."

"Yes sir, Chief!" Martha replied. As soon as the door closed, she lit another cigarette.

Chapter 26

Standing silently along the creek's edge, Reese listened for his prey. His shortcut through the woods had worked. He was about half a mile from the Dummy Line. He could hear a vehicle speeding east. *That had to be Johnny Lee's killer and his kid. He musta seen Tiny and Sweat and they flushed him back my way. If I coulda been here a few minutes earlier, I'd-a killed him as he drove by – just like shootin' a rabbit.* The killer had nowhere to run. There were only two ways out and they were blocked. *This guy's screwed and payback's comin'.* Reese smiled at the thought.

Reese flipped open the phone, found Tiny's number, and hit Send.

Beep-beep. No response.

Beep-beep. Again no response.

"Dammit!" he said aloud. *Tiny never remembers to carry his phone. Hell, that lardass couldn't even remember to turn it on. He drives me crazy. I gotta do all the thinkin'. I hate incompetence.* Off to his right, a pack of coyotes started howling.

Poaching and drinking while driving were Reese's favorite pastimes, and most of the time he combined them. It had been several years since Reese had been poaching on this property. The timber was a bit bigger now, but he knew where he was and where he was going.

I'll kill the kid first – that'll really punish him – and then I'll steal his truck, Reese thought. After everybody was back at Johnny Lee's trailer, he could send Tiny to hide the truck until they could either paint it or fence it in Meridian. They'd have to get their story together and say Sweat shot Johnny Lee by accident as they were loading up to go turkey hunting. Nobody ever got convicted—or even charged—in a hunting accident. That made sense. Plus, they had the trump card—the killer's old lady. That guaranteed cooperation. After they inflicted all sorts of pain and suffering on him and the woman, they'd simply shoot both of them between the eyes.

Reese knew to temper his revenge with caution. They needed to get out of here before daylight. He glanced at his fake Rolex and smiled; it was not quite 2:21 A.M. Time was on his side.

Chapter 27

The shooting house was filthy. It was full of leaves, spider webs, and what appeared to be some sort of nest in the far corner. Elizabeth felt around, hoping to find something useful. All she discovered was a hunting magazine, two empty Mountain Dew cans, an empty rifle cartridge, and one unopened can of what she thought was pork and beans. A swivel chair was in the opposite corner. She tried it but was more comfortable on the floor, with her foot elevated.

Slowly and silently she looked out the small opening again. Nothing, but she could hear a four-wheeler not too far off. She settled back down and wondered about Tanner. *He fought for me and I ran. I had to,* she told herself. It was killing her. She prayed that he was okay. She wanted to go home.

Suddenly she had an idea. She eased up on her knees to take another look down the road. The coast was clear. She took off her fleece jacket, then took off her shirt and tied one of the long sleeves into a knot at the wrist. She slid the can of beans into the arm. She twisted the shirt until it was tight and then put back on her fleece jacket, zipping it up tight. *I'm gonna fight like hell...like Tanner did,* she thought, as she brushed her hair behind her ears and let out a deep breath.

She settled in to wait. After several minutes she could hear someone walking on the road. On her knees, she peeked but couldn't see him yet. Her heart was racing as she clenched her weapon. A little more than a hundred yards away, she began to see his outline coming towards her. Every few feet, he shined a small flashlight on the ground. She watched until he was almost to her when she realized that he was following her footprints. She wanted to scream. *How could I be so stupid*? She thought. She was cornered.

She watched him walk by without so much as looking up, and then suddenly he stopped. He flashed his light around on the ground, turned around and backtracked a few steps. Then he quickly flashed the light up at the deer stand. She ducked down, hitting one of the empty cans.

In the moment of silence after the can rattled, she could hear the four-wheeler coming closer. *Who's that? Is someone gonna help me?*

"Hey, little girl...you got a real man comin' up to see you...not some schoolboy!" he said, licking his lips.

Elizabeth huddled in the corner of the shooting house and prayed.

"You'll never be the same after me. You'll throw rocks at all them college boys after you've had a little of this!" he said, laughing as he approached the shooting house. His sadistic laughter and lewd comments made her hyperventilate.

Suddenly she felt the structure shake. She couldn't see who was shaking the shooting house but saw the fat guy with the pistol drive up on a four-wheeler. She let out a bloodcurdling scream. The shooting house rocked more and more as the goon climbed closer. Then the door shook, but it didn't open immediately.

"Sweat, is that girl up there?" the fat guy called as he slowed to a stop.

"Yeah, man; but you're gonna hafta let me bring her down there for you. This ladder ain't gonna hold yo big ass!" Sweat said with a laugh.

Elizabeth curled into a ball, praying the latch would hold.

"Leave her alone, man. I can't let you hurt her!" Tiny hollered up at Sweat.

"Shut the hell up!" Sweat said as he worked his hand between the door and the frame.

"I'm serious, man. I ain't gonna let you hurt her," Tiny replied climbing off the four-wheeler.

"You and whose army's gonna stop me?" Sweat answered as he splintered the plywood door with his hands. He threw the pieces to the ground, and like Jack Nicholson's character in *The Shining*, stuck his head inside, smiled and said, "Heeeeerrrrreeeee's Johnny!"

WHACK! The sound of the can smacking Sweat's nose could be heard a hundred yards away.

Sweat rocked back, dazed, then slipped off the ladder. When he hit the ground he bit off the tip of his tongue.

Elizabeth rushed down what was left of the ladder. She climbed as low as she could and jumped. Landing on her good foot, she rolled as she had learned in cheerleading camp.

Sweat reached out and caught her as she stood up. He slapped her as hard as he could, knocking her down. Then he kicked her in the ribs. The salty taste of his blood was making him crazy.

Tiny jumped on Sweat's back. Sweat stumbled, but he still had Elizabeth solidly by the jacket. Sweat was dazed and confused and covered in his own blood.

"Let her go!" Tiny screamed trying to hold on to Sweat.

"Get off of me, you fat bastard. I'll kill you too! You sombitch!" Sweat yelled as he struggled to stand.

Elizabeth was screaming, trying to pull herself free. Tiny was choking Sweat with his weight and grip around his neck. Sweat was not letting go of either one of them. They finally fell in a pile. Tiny landed squarely on Sweat. Elizabeth screamed in terror. They all lay in the road for several seconds. Elizabeth was trapped but was scrambling to regain position. As Sweat got to his knees, Elizabeth suddenly stood up. He still had a grip on the bottom of her fleece but not her right arm.

WHACK! She hit him again in the side of the head, breaking a cheekbone and stunning him. As she slipped from his grip, her jacket ripped and came off. With her ankle throbbing, she ran the best she could. Her strides became a one-legged hop, but nevertheless she was getting away. And she still had her weapon. Elizabeth continued down the Dummy Line, never looking back.

Sweat watched her run while fighting with Tiny. Now that he didn't have to hold the girl, he rolled Tiny on his back and punched him several times as hard as he could. Tiny simply curled into a giant fetal position and tried to absorb the beating.

Sweat finally got to his feet. He was wet all over. By the four-wheeler's headlights, he could see that it was blood. His hands hurt, part of his tongue was gone, and his face was on fire. Every heartbeat sent flashes of pain through his face. He looked at his hands, down the road toward the girl, then down at Tiny. Then he kicked the crap out of Tiny one more time.

"You stupid asshole!" he growled. He spat a gob of blood on Tiny, wiped his face with his shirt-sleeve, and then staggered after the girl.

Chapter 28

After only twenty-five yards, Sweat stopped. He bent over and placed his hands on his knees. He had swallowed a large amount of blood and was about to puke. *She's a fighter. I like that.* He had been able to catch that skinny boy by surprise. That was his trademark. He wasn't expecting her to attack him, catch him off balance. *What the hell did she hit me with? It felt like a brick. Bitch broke my nose.*

Standing quietly in the moonlight, Sweat could see her limping down the road. *She's hurt.* He smiled at the thought, blood trickling down his chin. He spat hard. She'd be easy to catch now.

Sweat turned and stared at Tiny moaning and unable to get up. "What the hell's your problem, man? I don't want to hurt you. We're partners, dude. But you was way out of line. Ain't nobody gonna keep me away from a taste of that sweet stuff."

Glancing back at Elizabeth, he lusted after her athletic build and long legs. She had dark hair like that of a Cajun girl he had loved once. Seeing her in that black bra and jeans just made it worse. He couldn't believe his good fortune. *To hell with Reese and Johnny…I now got my own business to tend to.*

Sweat knew his injuries weren't life-threatening. They hurt like hell, but he wouldn't let them distract him. Four years ago while working as a flunky for a fishing guide near Lake Charles, he had been high and accidentally put the gas nozzle in a rod holder. Fifty gallons later, the transom was full of gas. He cranked up and was idling back to the boat ramp when he lit a cigarette. That's all he remembered. He had sustained serious burns on his legs and feet, but if he hadn't been blown into the water, it would have killed him. Since then, the pores of his skin had not functioned properly, so he smelled bad all the time. Shortly after the explosion, his dark-haired girlfriend had dropped him and taken up with an offshore mechanic. As soon as Sweat recovered, he tracked her down and then beat her nearly to death. He had left Louisiana with a taste for abusing women. It was a release he craved. *And this little half-naked teenage sorority bitch is just what I need,* Sweat thought.

Tiny acted seriously injured so Sweat would leave him alone. He could hear Sweat walking off in the gravel and mud. Sweat had landed several good shots to his ribs, and it burned when he tried to breath. He got to his knees and thought, *I can't let him hurt that girl.* He finally stood and, with no small amount of effort and pain, straightened up. He slowly shuffled to the four-wheeler and painfully swung a leg over the side. He sat there for a few minutes, thinking, watching Sweat walk after the girl. *Where's Reese and where's the dude who shot Johnny Lee?* He cranked the four-wheeler, shifted into low gear and eased his thumb on the gas.

Chapter 29

Ollie finally caught up with R.C. as they crossed over Interstate 20. He fell in line and was drafting the same way the NASCAR drivers did on Sundays.

"Miz Martha?" He spoke calmly into his microphone.

"I'm here, Chief," she replied. She was on a caffeine high and a nicotine buzz.

"Call the Beasley girl's parents and make sure she isn't home asleep, please. And don't scare 'em. I don't know how to do it, but I'm sure you'll think of something."

"Yes, sir," she replied.

"R.C.? You copy?" Ollie asked.

"Yes, sir."

"Larson and Shug are on the way. Let's approach silently."

"Sure thing, Chief," R.C. replied.

Ollie's adrenaline was pumping. This was action, although he hated that it involved kids. This was why he had become a cop. He had idealistic notions of actually helping people who couldn't help themselves.

Ollie had been driving in silence for almost twelve miles when his radio crackled.

"Ollie, I got the Beasleys. As you can imagine, they're pretty shook up. I told them what we just found out and that you were all over it—not to worry. They're on their way here."

"Okay…all right…get a Livingston police unit to escort them."

"Ten-four. I've done it." Martha typically stayed one or two steps ahead of everybody. It bothered some people. Ollie appreciated her efficiency, which had saved his butt on more than one occasion.

"Thanks, Miz Martha. As soon as I know anything, I'll let you know."

"Ten-four, Chief."

Elizabeth's mom had met Zach Beasley at a Campus Crusade for Christ retreat in Panama City. Within fourteen months they were married and setting up house. After five years of marriage they had not been able to get pregnant. Olivia started trying fertility drugs. After two years, Elizabeth came along, and they lavished their attention and affection on her. Olivia was never able to become pregnant again; consequently, Elizabeth was everything to them. Their whole lives revolved around this beautiful young girl. From the time she was born she had always had the best of everything—the best clothes, the best kindergarten, the best bikes, ballet, piano, and more. Elizabeth responded to all the positive stimuli by being a great daughter. Her parents were very proud.

The Beasleys are good folks, thought Ollie. Zach Beasley was a pillar of the community. He attended church every Sunday morning, belonged to the Rotary club, served on the school board, and could always be counted on for a donation whenever needed. The county needed more men like him. He didn't really know Olivia Beasley that well.

When Olivia heard the phone ring she instinctively knew it was about Elizabeth. Elizabeth always came in and woke them up to tell them she was home after a date. She hadn't tonight. After listening to Martha, she explained the situation to Zach. They both ran upstairs to look for Elizabeth. She wasn't there. Olivia searched her mind for the last conversation she'd had with Elizabeth about her and Tanner going to Tuscaloosa and then coming back home. She called Elizabeth's cell phone several times, getting only: "The subscriber you are trying to reach has either turned off their telephone or has left the coverage area. Please try your call again." They dressed quickly and then drove to the sheriff's office.

Flying up Highway 17 at ninety miles an hour, the two sheriff's department cars approached the turnoff. Ollie grabbed his mike, "R.C., take me straight to where you found the kid."

"Ten-four."

"Miz Martha, where's Larson?" Ollie asked, totally ignoring radio protocol.

"He and Shug are about ten minutes behind y'all!" she replied, buzzing like an air traffic controller.

"Ten-four."

A few minutes later Ollie and R.C. turned on the Dummy Line and sped toward the crime scene. All Ollie knew was that it was twenty miles long and no one lived on it. He concentrated his attention on areas where the voters were, and the best places to eat.

Both vehicles slid to a stop with the lights flashing. Ollie got out and stood staring at the truck and Jeep parked ridiculously close together.

"What's the deal, R.C.?"

"The Jeep belongs to the Tillman kid. I don't know about the truck."

"Run the tag," Ollie said.

"Yes, sir, boss," he replied, expertly placing a fresh dip in his lip.

Ollie noticed blood on the ground in front of the Jeep. He shined his light on everything looking for some clue as to what had happened.

"It ain't got a tag."

"What?" Ollie straightened up and looked at R.C. "Well, look through the inside and see if you can find anything."

Ollie walked around both vehicles. "Where was the kid?" he asked.

"Right here, kinda down in those weeds a bit," R.C. said, pointing while walking around to the Jeep. The truck smelled so bad he was looking for any excuse to delay his search.

"Here's your flashlight...you must have left in a hurry." Ollie grunted as he bent down and reached under the Jeep to retrieve it. Ollie took his time looking at everything.

"Look here, R.C. A nine-millimeter shell," Ollie said as he kneeled down and stared at the small empty brass cartridge lying in the gravel. Ollie finally had a clue.

"Uh...well, uh...I'm afraid that's mine, Chief," R.C. replied as he reached for his flashlight.

"What? You fired a round? You never said you fired a shot!"

R.C. told him the story. The sheriff simply stared at him for a few seconds. Ollie took a deep breath and let it out. Nothing was making sense tonight. He continued his search, shaking his head and mumbling under his breath. R.C. was used to it.

"Quit spitting everywhere; you're contaminating the crime scene," Ollie growled. "When are you going to quit that nasty habit?"

"I can't. I'm too good at it," R.C. said honestly, while shining his light in the Jeep.

"Chief, look at this!" he said excitedly.

R.C. held up a small, expensive-looking purse. Ollie looked at the purse and then back at R.C.

They unzipped the bag, reached in, and pulled out the matching wallet. Ollie took a deep breath and opened it. There was Elizabeth Beasley's driver's license. He clicked off his flashlight then let out a deep frustrated sigh and looked up at the stars.

"This ain't good, boss," R.C. replied.

"No shit, Sherlock."

Chapter 30

"Okay, chunk, you gotta give me a break," Jake said in a half-whisper, setting Katy gently down on the ground.

Jake's left arm was starting to go numb. They had only covered about half a mile, but it was around trees and over logs. He could tell he had spent way too much time behind a desk and none in the gym. He jogged a few days a week; at least he tried to, and some weeks he actually did. Most weeks he was too busy; jogging was the last thing on his list. And he ate way too many Krispy Kremes. Jake never counted carbs or calories, and every step he took carrying Katy reminded him of it.

"Oh, Dad, it's wet!" Katy whined, standing on one leg in her sock feet.

Jake reached in his hunting vest and dug around until he found a black garbage bag that he carried but never used. He unfolded it and placed it on the ground. Katy stepped on it. He couldn't remember why he had originally put it in his vest or kept it—it was always in the way.

"My legs are soaked," he replied, as he watched her sit down Indian-style on the bag.

"Yeah, but you're used to it," she shot right back.

"I've got some gloves you can put on your feet. Don't laugh. At least they're dry."

Katy looked at him like he was crazy and then said, "Sure, I'll try 'em."

Jake dug around in his vest and found a pair of thin cotton gloves with extended wrists. They slipped right over her feet and actually fit rather well though the fingers dangled awkwardly. Katy giggled. She was glad to have dry warm feet again.

"We gotta keep those dry; it's all I have."

"Yes, sir," she replied, wiggling her toes.

Jake punched the side of his Timex. It glowed like a firefly. *Over three hours until daylight. Damn. If I ever get out of this mess, I'm takin' up golf,* he thought. Nobody robbed a clubhouse and chased golfers all over the course at night. Maybe he'd get serious about fishing. Jake shook his head. *I've gotta concentrate. I've got to get us out of this.*

"Okay, Katy, I think we have about another half-mile till we reach the field. Can you ride on my back?"

"Sure. I did at Disney World."

"Let's go," Jake whispered. He bent down while she crawled up his back. Two years earlier, he had carried her for miles so she could see everything, and he figured he could sure do it again to save her life.

Suddenly every hair on Jake's neck stood up straight as he heard a loud hysterical scream off to the west. Chills coursed down his spine. A woman was screaming for her life. And she kept on and on. Katy instantly squeezed tighter around his neck. It was scaring Jake as well. It reminded him of his recurring nightmare.

"What's that?" Katy asked in a loud whisper.

Jake listened, and then he responded, "I don't know. I'm not sure. I mean, I'm pretty sure it's a girl screaming."

"Why's she screaming? Who is it, Dad?" Katy asked excitedly.

The screaming stopped. Jake stared off in its direction, "I don't know, honey. I have no idea."

They could hear her screaming again, this time more muffled, but it still had terror in it. Whoever it was, she was scared to death. Jake squatted down, picked up his shotgun, and started walking as fast as he could carry Katy in the direction of the screams. He had to help.

"Katy, hang on and be very quiet," he whispered over his shoulder. One hand held her arms around his neck and the other held the shotgun. He decided he was better off without a flashlight even though vines and limbs were cutting his face every other step. Fortunately, Katy was small enough to mostly hide behind his head and shoulders.

Jake had covered quite a bit of the initial distance when the screaming stopped. He needed to rest and get his bearings. He had taken off in such a rush that he had forgotten the trash bag, so he had to find a log for Katy to sit on. He put one finger to his lips and whispered, "Sssshhhhh." He stood up and listened intently. Jake thought it wasn't too far…maybe half a mile, but in the stillness things sounded closer or maybe farther—he wasn't certain.

Nothing but silence. Jake didn't like this at all. *Whatever made that girl scream that way had to be evil. I saw evil once tonight and I never want to see it again.* Jake sat down on the log next to Katy.

"Is she okay?" Katy asked in a whisper.

"I don't know, but we're going to help her if we can. I just don't hear anything any more."

Jake knew the direction, but without hearing a sound to gauge the distance, he feared walking up on whatever it was. He needed the element of surprise. He also had Katy, and he wasn't going to leave her alone. Jake decided to slowly move ahead. He bent down, and Katy again climbed up on his back. He eased off in the direction of the screams. He couldn't get that sound out of his mind.

Reese also heard the woman. He tried several times to raise Tiny on the radiophone. Finally, he had heard enough and headed toward the screams. When the screaming finally stopped, Reese quit walking, stood very quietly, and listened—utilizing all his predatory skills.

Two unique criminally-related sounds in one hour—a gunshot on the far west side of the place and the panicked screams of a girl nearby. All this had to be connected. Reese was loving it. Jake hated it.

Chapter 31

Sheriff Ollie Landrum stood in front of Tanner Tillman's Jeep thinking. He had his cowboy hat in his hand and was scratching his balding head. Deputy R.C. Smithson awaited orders that he hoped wouldn't involve searching inside the nasty-smelling pickup truck. The sheriff was visibly stressed.

"R.C., please check the truck out for anything indicating who owns it. That truck is the key to all this."

"Yes, sir," said R.C. and with a resigned sigh opened the driver's side door. A cloud of funk filled the air and four empty beer cans fell out. "He stinks and he drinks cheap beer."

"Do what?" Ollie asked.

"He drinks cheap beer…see? And a lot of it," R.C. replied as he held up a can of Old Milwaukee, then threw it in the bed of the truck.

"Yeah, well…keep looking, Columbo," Ollie said, walking back to his Expedition.

Picking up the microphone, he radioed into the office, "Miz Martha?"

"Yes, Chief."

"Can the Tillman kid talk or maybe write and tell us what happened?" Ollie asked, hoping it could be that simple.

"Chief, the hospital said he was in so much pain that they knocked him out as soon as he was stabilized. He was beat up pretty bad. He lost several teeth, and his windpipe is partially crushed…and he has some broken ribs."

"Son of a…." Ollie began to reply, then exhaled deeply.

"Chief—and the girl, Elizabeth, she's an honor student, cheerleader. You name it. She's a great girl. She isn't the type to get into any trouble."

"Hang on, Miz Martha." Seeing Elizabeth's purse again gave Ollie an idea. He opened the purse and looked inside. There it was...a cell phone. He hit power and it came to life.

"It wouldn't work out here, boss. There is a huge hole in cell service in this area. You might get through if you were lucky...but it would be for only a few seconds," R.C. commented.

Returning to his search of the truck, R.C. held his nose, "Hey, this might do it. It's a receipt from a butcher near Camden. They're a dang good deer processor. You like deer sausage, Chief?"

"No, R.C., I haven't had any lately. What name's on the ticket?" Ollie asked aggravated.

"Uh...Tommy Tidwell, and it's got a phone number, actually I think it's his cell phone number. I know of him...most folks call him Tiny. He's trouble if he's with the wrong crowd."

"You think if we call he'll answer?" asked R.C.

"Not at this hour and not if he has Caller ID. Give me that, though."

"Sheriff?" Martha called.

"Yes'm?" Ollie's patience was running thin.

"The Beasleys will want to know what you're gonna do," she said, trying to be prepared.

"You know procedures," he said, then added, "call me the second they arrive. Also, I want you to call a number for me. Don't use the office phone...use someone's cell phone. In fact, go to the evidence room; there's a phone that belongs to that kid we locked up earlier. Use it to call 555-1456. If they answer just hang up and call me immediately...either way."

"Ten-four, Chief."

Ollie and R.C. looked up at the same time and in the direction of the sound of a vehicle heading fast toward them. They then looked at each other.

"Larson," Ollie said. "I hope. I don't need any more surprises."

About that time they saw the bright blue lights reflecting in the treetops. Larson slowed to a stop and got out. Larson Hodges had been a deputy for five years. He constantly hoped for something big like this to happen. He watched *COPS* all the time. He read and reread every issue of *Police Marksman* magazine. Two years ago he had talked Ollie into buying a canine officer. Larson went to Columbus, Ohio, and picked out the dog and trained to handle him. They were constant companions. The German Shepherd had been named Luger and was called Lug. Before he got home, Larson changed it to Shug in honor of one of Auburn University's greatest football coaches, Ralph "Shug" Jordan. Not everybody in west Alabama cheered for the Crimson Tide.

Of course, Ollie suspected the K-9 Academy had not named the dog Shug, but since it seemed to respond to it, he didn't say anything about the name. The commands were in German. Initially, both Larson and the dog stayed in a constant state of confusion. After a few weeks, Shug began to understand Southern-flavored German.

"Mornin', Sheriff. What can I do?"

At that moment, the cell phone on the dash of the pickup rang. R.C. reached in, grabbed it, and then tossed it to Ollie. He opened it and saw the Caller ID. Martha was calling from the phone Ollie had asked her to use. It only had one bar of service, so rather than try to have a conversation he simply let it ring until it quit. He dropped the phone in his pocket.

His radio cracked, "Chief, no answer and no voice mail."

"Ten-four. Thank you."

"Larson, you have Shug?' Ollie asked. Larson nodded.

"Let him smell around these vehicles. R.C. found the Tillman kid all beat up right here, and we have reason to believe that the Beasley girl was with him."

"Yes, sir!" Larson replied.

"Achtung, Shug!" The overweight brown-and-black police dog jumped from the cruiser and sat at attention. Larson walked Shug to the front of the Jeep and said, "Finden!" Shug appeared to go to work. First he found what they thought was Tanner's blood, and once that area was searched, Larson encouraged him to work elsewhere but after only a few minutes it became clear to all that Shug had found the only thing that really interested him when he laid down in the middle of the road and began licking himself vigorously.

Crestfallen at Shug's failure, Larson dragged him back to his car. Ollie turned away in disgust, shaking his head. R.C. stifled a chuckle.

In an attempt to take some of the heat off Larson, R.C. said, "Hey, Chief. Let's move this Jeep. I'll put it in neutral and we can push it out of the way. We *gotta* go down this road where the four-wheeler went," R.C. pointed down the Dummy Line.

"Where does this road go anyway?" Ollie asked.

"It dead-ends into the Noxubee River Swamp...the road is twenty miles of potholes and mud with a shootin' house about every five hundred yards. Not much else."

"Yeah...you're right. R.C., let's do it," Ollie replied.

As they all got ready to push Tanner's Jeep out of the way. R.C. noted, "Hey, the keys are in it!"

"Well, crank it up and move it," Ollie told him.

Chapter 32

"Oh, God, no…I can't take any more," muttered Elizabeth. She was limping along as fast as possible, her ankle becoming more tender and painful with every step. She slowed, almost stopping, and looked back. She could hear the four-wheeler, and somewhere in between she could see a form lumbering towards her. She looked around. The monsters were chasing her. It appeared that miles of muddy road lay ahead and that there were miles of dense woods on either side. She headed into the woods, hoping it would cover her tracks.

It was difficult for her to walk, much less run. Limbs, vines, trees, and stumps were difficult to negotiate in the dark. After twenty yards she was wondering if she had made the right decision. She looked down to see if she was leaving footprints. She couldn't tell. She assumed she wasn't. As she pushed forward, she realized that the fat guy had helped her. *What did he say? I can't let you hurt her.* She kept replaying that scene over in her mind. She knew they had been fighting as she ran off. Elizabeth soon came to a small flowing creek. It was knee-deep, and the cold water felt good on her bad ankle. When she stepped out on the far side, she left her bad ankle dangling in the cold water for a few seconds and thought of her parents and Tanner's folks, *They'll all be worried and nobody knows where we are.* "Oh, God, Tanner. Please, Lord, please let him be okay," she prayed quietly.

She had been making so much noise going through the brush that she didn't hear how close the four-wheeler had approached. While she was standing listening, she heard a stick pop and then another and realized the goon was on her trail in the woods and he was close. She began to run. She tried to be as quiet as possible. She was running blind. She grimaced in pain from her ankle and the briars that dug in and ripped her flesh.

A few moments later, she heard a splash as he went through the creek. "NO! NO!" she said, realizing he was gaining on her. Looking back, she could see he had a flashlight. She could make out a small opening up ahead and ran for it as hard as she could, dragging brush with her. She was numb. She was trying to run faster than her body could keep up. *Run! Run! Run!* She could hear limbs cracking and his footsteps as he raced through the woods toward her. Her leg caught in something, stopping her dead in her tracks. She screamed as loud as she could. *The opening's right there!* Struggling to free herself, she lost her grip and dropped her improvised weapon. She didn't have time to pick it up as she freed herself and lunged into the small opening.

"Help me! HELP!" she screamed as she struggled through the dense brush.

Sweat closed in. When he was within twenty yards, he sprinted as fast as he could and tackled her. He landed on top. She took the brunt of the blow, landing hard. The ground scraped her bare stomach and chest. She struggled to catch her breath. He lay on her breathing hard. Elizabeth was screaming for her life. He didn't care. He had her. Sweat had his reward.

Sweat's weight prevented Elizabeth from moving. He bent over and wiped his bloody face on her back and laughed. Holding her down, he sat up so he could breathe better.

"Please, PLEASE. Don't hurt me, PLEASE, awwww, PLEASE!!" she begged.

He pushed her face down in the dirt while he thought about what he was going to do first. *I'm gonna be slow, and thorough, and enjoy all of it...right down to her last gasp of air.* He placed his flashlight in his mouth while he took his knife out of his pocket and eased the sharp blade under her bra strap. He made sure she could feel the steel. He was slow, methodical.

Elizabeth could feel the knife pressing against her skin. She screamed even louder. The fear of being butchered and raped was paralyzing. She was about to pass out from fear and dread.

The black strap fell away from the cut of the razor sharp knife, exposing her naked back. Sweat stabbed the knife in the ground just out of her reach and then leaned back to admire her body. This was it. His favorite fantasy was about to play out.

Elizabeth continued to scream for help. Jake heard her and was scrambling toward her as fast as he could. Reese also heard and was headed that way too. Tiny's eyes welled up when he heard it, and then he shed tears of frustration and shame standing next to the four-wheeler.

Sweat's right hand held both Elizabeth's arms fully extended over her head as he rolled her over. He wanted to see her face and breasts. He was careful, he wasn't going to let her hit him again. Blood from his nose dripped on her stomach. He positioned his weight over her hips and legs so she couldn't move. Her shoulders and chest were scratched and covered in dirt and blood. With his left hand he began scraping it away. Elizabeth was sobbing uncontrollably and begging him not to do it. Sweat couldn't hear anything. He wasn't aware of anything other than this opportunity.

Jake and Katy were less than two hundred yards away when the screaming started the second time. He was trying desperately to get close enough to see what was going on. He had never heard screams like that before. Jake crossed a four-wheeler trail with a ground-level shooting house on the side. He thought about Katy and what he was hearing and what was surely about to occur.

"Katy, listen to me. I need you to stay right here for just a few minutes while I go help that girl; please, I gotta go right now. Here's the flashlight. I swear, I'll be right back," he said with his most serious voice. He opened the door to the shooting house and shined the light around. "Just sit right here, sweetheart. I have to go."

"No, Dad, don't leave me," she said with tears in her eyes. Her whole body was shaking.

"Please, Katy; trust me, honey. Please. I don't have time to explain," he begged.

Katy didn't say anything, but he knew she understood. She didn't want any part of what was making that girl scream. Katy did as she was told.

"Katy, please don't leave this shooting house, baby. I mean it now. Stay right here."

"Be…be careful Dad," she said softly as she watched him disappear into the woods towards the screams. She was shaking so badly she couldn't hold onto the flashlight and dropped it.

Jake stopped twenty feet from the shooting house, turned around for just a second, thinking about leaving Katy. Every fiber in his body told him not to. But he had to help. He turned back around and ran as fast as he could.

Reese crossed the Dummy Line. He had about another four hundred yards to go. He could clearly hear the screams and knew his crew was involved. He pulled out his radiophone while he ran and hit Send. Maybe they had caught the dude and he had a woman with him, too. He grinned.

Beep-beep. "Tiny." He spoke excitedly.

There was a long pause and just as he was about to put the phone back in his pocket, *beep-beep*. But there was no voice afterwards.

Reese stopped and took a deep breath. He leaned his rifle against the tree.

Beep-beep. "Yo, Tiny what's going on...who's the girl?" He asked.

Sheriff Ollie Landrum was dumbfounded. He about jumped out of his skin when the phone beeped. He didn't know what to say. Here was a chance to get additional information that he desperately needed. Caller ID had given him another suspect, Johnny Lee Glover.

Ollie hit Send again, but he didn't verbally reply.

Beep-beep.

Reese sensed that something wasn't right. He stood still, trying to think.

Jake crawled to within forty yards of the shocking scene. He recognized the big muscular dude with the flashlight in his mouth. He had been with the gang at the camp; now he was holding down a nearly naked young girl. *Shit! She's covered in blood.* She was begging him to leave her alone. Jake also could see a knife stuck in the ground. To make a killing shot with turkey loads, Jake knew he needed to be a little closer. This guy was taking his time but there was no doubt he intended to rape this girl.

Sweat never noticed that Jake had slipped up to within twenty yards and was on his knees about to shoot. Jake could clearly see Sweat holding down the girl with one hand and trying to loosen his pants with the other. She was bucking like a mule but couldn't resist much longer. Jake couldn't let him rape her. Twice in the same night Jake did something he had never done in his life. He placed the front bead of the shotgun on the guy's chest and took a deep breath.

KABOOM!

Sweat collapsed forward, lifeless, on top of Elizabeth. She was stunned but instantly started trying to free herself from under the heavy weight of the dead man. Screaming louder and louder, she pulled herself loose. Jake was shocked, motionless. He hadn't shot. Jake then saw the fat guy from the camp house standing in the edge of the woods, a pistol hanging at his side. *What in the world?* Elizabeth got up screaming, running in Jake's direction. Half-naked and running blindly, she was screaming at the top of her lungs. She didn't know Jake was there. Jake took one more look at the fat guy. He briefly thought about killing him, but didn't. *This is crazy.* The fat guy appeared to be in a trance. He was staring at his dead buddy whom he had just killed. He didn't seem to care about the girl at all.

Jake got up silently and took off running after the girl.

Chapter 33

R.C. and Larson were talking when they heard a distant gunshot. R.C. pointed and explained that the shot had come from the west; Larson pointed south. Ollie was staring intently at the radiophone and didn't have a clue; he never offered a guess.

"It's hard to course a direction on a single unexpected gunshot," R.C. explained, "'specially in these thick-planted pines."

R.C. and Larson argued for a minute about the direction and whether it was related to any of the night's events. In the country, gunshots are heard at all hours. A single shot this late at night usually meant some stray just got dead getting into someone's trash. Ollie returned his attention to the phone.

"Damn it…that phone call caught me off guard," Ollie said.

"Well, at least you know it's Johnny Lee Glover. That's a starting point, Chief," R.C. said.

"Johnny Lee always has Reese Turner with him. Those guys are joined at the hip. That Turner dude makes my skin crawl," Larson added.

"Should we call him back?" Larson asked, holding Shug's leash.

"That's not a bad idea. But what should we say?" Ollie responded.

A minute passed in silence.

"Let's think about this. Obviously they're not together, but somehow Johnny knows something about the girl," Ollie said. "Where does this Tiny character live?"

"I don't know," R.C. replied.

"Find out."

"Yes, sir, boss."

"Larson, do you know where the—what the hell's the name of that hunting club?" Ollie asked looking at R.C.

"Bogue Chitto. It's Indian for—" R.C. started, but never finished.

"Larson, do you know where that camp is? It's maybe fifteen miles back down this road," Ollie interrupted, rolling his eyes at R.C.

"Yes, sir, sure do."

"Go there. See if that mutt can find anything besides his balls. We found some blood earlier tonight in front of the camp house. It may be turkey blood. I need to know if there's anything else in the high grass. All this may be connected. Radio me when you get finished. I'll probably have something else for you to do. In fact, I may want you to go to this Tiny character's place and check it out."

"Yes, sir," Larson said as he ran to his car.

"R.C., all this must be connected but I sure hope it isn't. I need you to stay here and keep your eyes and ears open. Don't try and be a hero. I'm gonna ride down this road while I radio the Beasleys."

"You got it, Chief. Be careful."

"Stay close to your radio."

Ollie pulled his Expedition even with the big Chevy truck, easing between it and the gateposts.

"Unit One to Base."

"Go ahead, One," Martha promptly responded.

"Are the Beasleys there yet?"

"I expect them any minute. Mr. Tillman just pulled into the parking lot." That surprised Ollie. He would have expected him to be at the hospital.

"Call me when they all arrive. Miz Martha, get me Sheriff Marlow. No, no, I'll get back to you on that."

"Ten-four, Sheriff."

Ollie didn't want to deploy another county's deputies until he had more facts. He laid the microphone across his leg and stared down the road. *Where in the world were Elizabeth and Tiny and Johnny Lee and the four-wheeler? They could be anywhere. It's miles and miles of woods. The shot could have been anything.* Just as he started easing down the Dummy Line, the radio crackled.

"Sheriff, they're here."

"Okay, put them by the radio so they can hear me."

Ollie stared out the window for a second trying to decide how much to tell them. He decided to concentrate on the events around Tanner and Elizabeth. He nodded his head as he decided not to tell them about the mysterious phone call. It might not even be related. He grabbed the microphone.

"Mr. and Mrs. Beasley, let me tell you what we know. One of my deputies just happened to find Tanner Tillman on the old road they call the Dummy Line. As y'all know, he was beat up pretty bad. We did find your daughter's purse in the Jeep, but we haven't found her yet. We don't have any serious leads right now. We just don't have anything. I need to know who was with them, if anybody, where they were going, and establish a timeline. There could be other kids missing. This could be some type of an accident…we just don't know. We don't need to jump to any conclusions."

"We'll get you the answers, Ollie," Steve Tillman responded.

"We also need to know if there are any conflicts in Tanner's life right now…any enemies?" Ollie said. "But let me add…finding Elizabeth is our top priority right now, so we need to know everything."

Elizabeth's mother started crying again. She was hanging on every word said. Elizabeth's father, Zach, had a lump in his throat and could hardly speak. Olivia remembered speaking to Elizabeth as she and

Tanner left the baseball game at about nine o'clock. She was pretty sure they had been by themselves, but they might have met some friends after the game. She didn't know. Elizabeth usually got back home by eleven. Sometimes Tanner stayed for a while and they watched television. Tonight the Beasleys were exhausted from the tax deadline and the drinks celebrating the end of tax season. So they had gone straight to bed after arriving home past midnight.

Tillman truthfully said he wasn't aware of any problems in Tanner's life. He added that he owned 160 acres that was accessible off the Dummy Line. Maybe they had gone there for some reason.

Ollie agreed that it would be worth a look since all this was just unfolding. He assured them that he was doing all he could and would keep them informed.

"How is your son, Mr. Tillman?" Ollie asked, genuinely concerned.

"It's serious, Sheriff, but they don't think its life-threatening. The doctor said he should be okay with some time...he was just in so much pain when he got there. I haven't spoken with him. He's heavily sedated. His condition is listed as stable. I'd be glad to come and show you where the property is if you need me to. There's nothing I can do at the hospital, and I just had to come here to try and understand...maybe make sense out of...and I want to help find Elizabeth." Tanner had recently asked his father how he would know when he met the right girl to marry, and he knew he was referring to Elizabeth.

Ollie could tell that Mr. Tillman was beginning to choke up. "That's not a bad idea, sir. Let me call in some deputies and get one to bring you out here. Mr. and Mrs. Beasley, it might be best for you to go home and sit by the phone. She might try to call or actually come home. Call the sheriff's office if you hear anything."

Olivia Beasley insisted on going to the hospital in case Tanner said something that might help. She needed to be there. Ollie understood all these emotions, and he agreed, but he asked that Zach return to their house.

"Y'all give Miz Martha all the info—anything you can think of. She knows what to ask and she'll pass it on to me. The whole sheriff's department is focused on this right now."

They all agreed. Tillman hugged Mrs. Beasley. They felt each other's pain. They didn't really know what to say to each other. They didn't have to say anything.

Ollie started back down the Dummy Line.

Chapter 34

The cracking sound of the gunshot piercing the silence of the night made Reese jump. It was obviously very close. The screaming escalated after the shot. He took off running in the direction of the screams as fast as he could manage through the dark brush. Reese knew how to cover serious ground. He desperately wanted to be a part of whatever was going down. As he dodged limbs and jumped logs, he wondered who had answered Tiny's phone. That bothered him. It was a mystery and he hated mysteries.

As Reese approached the scene of all the commotion, he stopped to listen. He thought he heard a girl's muffled screams; he definitely could hear a familiar man's voice. He was sobbing and mumbling. Reese was very confused and extremely careful as he began to slip forward. About a hundred yards ahead, Reese could see a faint flashlight beam. He crept closer, careful not to make a sound. Reese eased the Browning rifle off his shoulder and carried it in front of him with the safety off.

"I told you…I warned you…why didn't you listen to me?"

Hearing Tiny's ramblings added to Reese's confusion. Reese silently worked his way closer. From the edge of the clearing, he could see a body lying in the field. Tiny was standing next to it holding a pistol. A small flashlight was lying next to the body, shining ominously through the grass. Reese couldn't see anyone else.

"Tiny. It's Reese. What's wrong? What the hell's goin' on?"

Tiny, startled, jumped back a few feet and pointed the big stainless steel revolver at Reese.

"Shit, Tiny! It's me, Reese!" he exclaimed, "Put that damn hand-cannon down!"

Tiny dropped the pistol to his side and fell forward on his knees. The gun fell out of his hands into the grass.

Reese approached cautiously. He was horrified to realize it was Sweat who was dead. Apparently, Johnny Lee's killer had also shot Sweat. Reese didn't liked Sweat very much, but he hadn't wanted him killed.

"Tiny, what the hell happened?" Reese asked. He bent over to check Sweat. He could see a huge hole in the back of his head. "What the hell happened!?"

Tiny began to sob louder. His head hanging, he mumbled, "I told him not to…I told him I couldn't let him hurt—"

"Hurt who?…the kid?…where's the guy who killed Johnny Lee? What the hell's goin' on?" Reese asked, jumping to conclusions. He stared at Sweat's body. It looked like a cold-blooded execution.

"Tiny, what happened. Did he shoot Sweat? I don't…where is he? Tiny! Tiny! Listen to me. Pull yourself together, man. Tell me what the hell happened!"

Reese quickly looked up at the sound of someone running through the woods. He held up his hand for Tiny to be silent. Then he turned toward Tiny. "Tiny, where's your phone?" Tiny was in another world, gazing at Sweat's body. Reese knew he wasn't going to get any answers.

Reese was beyond pissed-off. He really didn't know what had just happened, but his best friend was dead and now so was a member of their gang. He assumed the same guy was responsible for both. Revenge was all he could think about.

"Tiny, where's Johnny Lee's killer? He didn't get by you, did he?"

"The Dummy Line's blocked. He can't get out," Tiny mumbled finally.

"So he's still in here…that makes sense. I heard him driving east—twenty or thirty minutes ago," Reese thought aloud. "How'd ya get down here?"

"Four-wheeler."

Reese needed stealth to stalk his prey. But the four-wheeler would be helpful to get out later if he didn't find the killer's truck. *What do I do with Tiny? He's worthless now. What do I do with Sweat's body? Shit. I got too much goin' on.*

"Okay, get yourself together. I'm going after the killer. Where's your phone? Your radiophone that Johnny Lee bought you. Where is it?" Reese demanded, exasperated.

"I think…it's at home." Tiny was finally coming around and he began to realize that Reese didn't know that he had killed Sweat. He knew he had done the right thing. He had a sister who had been raped. He had seen the trauma she endured. He revered women. Hearing Sweat joke about abusing women made him sick, but he had to keep Reese from knowing the truth about Sweat.

It made sense to Reese that Tiny's phone was at his house. Some drunken idiot had probably answered his call. But why didn't Tiny have the phone with him? Reese let the question slide for now.

"Who was doin' all that screaming?"

"It was a girl, maybe seventeen or eighteen," Tiny weakly replied.

"Really?" Reese said and thought, *Could it have been the killer's girlfriend? Wife? His daughter? What about the toys, the small sleeping bag. Nothin's makin' any sense.* Reese's head was beginning to ache. He wanted to avenge Johnny Lee's death and now, to a lesser degree, Sweat's.

"What was going on?" he calmly asked, hoping Tiny would open up and talk.

"Sweat was trying to…you know…have his way."

"That's our boy. Sweat went out doin' what he loved, huh? Was there a little kid?" Reese asked coldly, thinking about the books and toys.

"I didn't see one." The less Reese knew right now the better.

"Okay, Tiny…that's okay. Which direction did they go?"

Tiny, with his head still down, simply pointed.

Reese could do this by himself. In fact, it might be better if he did. Tiny couldn't move silently through the woods, and based on his current mental state, he wasn't going to be much help.

"I'm going after 'em. There's no way you can pick up Sweat's body and get him in the back of Johnny Lee's truck by yourself. Go get your four-wheeler and wait for me right here. Keep your eyes open. Okay?" Reese said, bending down to look in Tiny's eyes.

"Hey, Tiny? Look at me," Reese said and added when Tiny raised his eyes to him, "If I'm not back by daylight, get the hell outta here and meet me at the trailer. Got it?" Reese snapped authoritatively.

Tiny nodded. Reese slung his rifle over his shoulder and took off in the direction Tiny had pointed.

Chapter 35

Jake sprinted through the woods to catch the panicked girl. Getting close wasn't easy. He was trying to be as quiet as possible. He didn't want to shout and knew that the moment he touched her she would freak out. She was struggling to keep her balance and fell twice before Jake got to her. She was getting up from her last fall when Jake grabbed her arm. Elizabeth screamed and starting slapping at him trying to get away.

"Calm down, calm down, please! I'm not gonna hurt you. I'm here to help you," he said in a hushed whisper. "I heard you screaming and I came to help." He looked her straight in the eyes, while holding a hand over her mouth. He saw only raw fear.

"Don't scream. Don't scream. I'm here to help you. I'm gonna let go. Okay? Don't scream."

Elizabeth nodded and immediately started trying to cover her breasts with her arms. She began sobbing.

Jake laid down his gun and took off his hunting vest. He then slipped off his button-down shirt and gave it to her. She turned around and quickly put it on. Jake slipped his vest back on and noticed her hands were shaking too much to button the shirt.

"Here, let me help," he said. He gently pushed her hands away so he could button the shirt. Afterwards, her arms immediately folded around herself. Her whole body was shaking uncontrollably.

"I'm Jake Crosby. I'm here turkey hunting, and those same guys raided my camp. I have my daughter hidden over there. We need to go get her and then we'll get outta here. Okay? You're safe now. I promise nothing will happen to you. Follow me and be as quiet as you can." Jake paused, trying to read her expression. "Do you understand? Good. Come on."

Jake picked up his gun and started walking toward Katy. The girl followed silently right behind him. Once they were in sight of the shooting house, Jake was relieved to see a small light moving around inside.

"Katy…Katy, it's me," Jake said in a hushed voice as he approached the shooting house. Katy's small face popped into the window, her eyes smiling in obvious relief. "Unlock the door, Katy."

"Dad, I heard a gunshot!"

"I know, I know; it's okay," Jake reassured her.

The door opened and Katy hugged him immediately before she even noticed Elizabeth.

"This is Katy, my daughter. She's nine but she acts fifteen," Jake said, trying to put everyone at ease. Elizabeth was still shaking and crying. "Say hello, Katy."

"Hey. Are you okay?" Katy said barely above a whisper. Katy was eyeing her worriedly, instantly compassionate. Katy was a mother hen to any person or creature in distress, and she loved to hang around "big girls." Jake didn't think Elizabeth had been raped but knew she had been beaten badly. She was covered in blood, and Jake had seen the source of most of it.

"I'm Elizabeth Beasley…thank you so much for…" was all she could say.

"Those guys that were chasing you tried to kill us. It's all crazy. I'll get us outta here, I promise. Let's put some distance between us and them. You're limping. Are you okay? Are you hurt anywhere else? Wipe your face on your sleeve…it's clean."

"My ankle's sprained," she whispered, adding, "but I can keep up."

"Okay. I'll take it easy. Come on, Katy...get on my back," he ordered.

Jake wondered what she was doing out here. He'd ask questions later. Jake carried Katy and Elizabeth followed along right behind as they headed back to the field they had been going to before the ordeal with Elizabeth. Occasionally Jake heard Elizabeth grunt in pain, and he could feel Katy watching her. They had walked about four hundred yards when Jake needed a break. Carrying Katy in the woods was killing him. He set her on a stump and plopped down beside her. Elizabeth eased down on a log across from them. Katy smiled at her.

Jake finally caught his breath after a minute and asked, "Elizabeth, what in the world are you doin' out here?"

"I was out here with my boyfriend, Tanner, on a date. They blocked the road and started beating him and I took off runnin'." She was wringing her hands.

"Where did all this happen?"

"Tanner was unlocking a big yellow gate, and then they started trying to attack me, and I just ran and left him. I'm so worried about him."

"Wow, you've covered four or five miles. You did the right thing to run," Jake replied.

"They chased me the whole way," she explained.

"Those guys are trouble. I'm sorry all that happened to you. I got the whole thing started when they showed up at our camp. I had to shoot one of 'em. It was getting really ugly."

"And you shot the guy who was attacking me!" She blurted out and saw Katy's eyes grow wide with shock.

"No. I was about to. But there was a big fat guy who walked up and shot him the second before I pulled the trigger. It was really strange."

Elizabeth began to realize what had happened. *But why?* she thought. It was all too much. She started crying again.

Jake dug in his vest and pulled out a cotton camo facemask and gave it to her, "Here, wipe your face with this."

Katy was trying to understand. Jake stood up and stretched. His back was aching. He stepped up on a stump to listen for anything out of the ordinary. Jake punched his watch. It softly glowed 3:02 A.M. He checked his phone again. No Service.

"All right, girls, let's move," he whispered to them.

"Can you make it?" Katy asked softly.

"Sure. I'll do anything to get outta here," Elizabeth replied as she stood up. She winced as a pain shot up her leg.

"Mr. Crosby, what about my boyfriend?" Elizabeth whispered after a few moments.

Jake stopped and turned around. He paused a moment, "I don't know, Elizabeth. Let me get you girls someplace safe first, and then I'll think of something."

Chapter 36

"Get ready, old boy. This could be our big break," Larson said to Shug, who momentarily stopped his ceaseless grooming and looked at him with a cocked head. "If we find something significant at the camp, Sheriff Landrum might expand the K-9 program."

Deputy Larson Hodges and Mrs. Martha O'Brien had a fair working relationship. Although she didn't care for the dog, she admired Larson's attitude and seriousness. She just thought he needed to spend more time talking to humans. Radioing her, Larson gave her a quick update on the status of the investigation and where he was headed. Martha in turn filled him in on Tanner's current condition since she was in constant contact with the hospital.

The Chief Resident, Dr. Sarhan, a Vanderbilt grad from India, had come in to oversee Tanner's case. The town folks could hardly understand Dr. Sarhan, but he was unquestionably the most talented physician they had ever had in the area. He was so well thought of, one restaurant had added curried chicken to its menu. Tanner was in good hands.

The latest hospital report indicated that Tanner had multiple fractured ribs and a broken nose, had lost five teeth, and had a mysterious grazing wound on his right hand. There were too many bruises and cuts to list. Concerned about Tanner's neck, Dr. Sarhan called in a special x-ray team. Tanner was heavily sedated and would be for awhile. Dr. Sarhan was cautiously optimistic about his initial prognosis.

Martha was chain-smoking menthol cigarettes and drinking black coffee. She was itching to find out what might have happened to Tanner. *They must have driven up on a drug deal gone bad,* she guessed. She immediately set out to determine the whereabouts of Ray Ray Walker, who was at the heart of almost every crime in Sumter County. Without instruction, she called Ray Ray's house. His woman du jour answered. When Martha asked to speak to him, the woman said that he was incarcerated in Montgomery and that she was going to kill him when he got out. Martha verified Ray Ray's incarceration with the Montgomery Police Department and promptly forgot even hearing the girlfriend's ranting. Martha O'Brien was back to square one.

Larson pulled into the camp and turned off the ignition. He opened his door and stepped out, taking a moment to stretch and look around. Shug sat in the back seat, licking. Opening the door, Larson called, "Achtung," and the dog jumped out and heeled on the wrong side.

"Finden!" Larson said in his best German accent, and the dog began searching the high grass. Larson reached back in the patrol car and looked for his long search leash.

Shug barked excitedly several times as he ran around. Larson looked up curiously, *What's goin' on? Shug never barks.* Larson clicked on his flashlight and as he walked over to Shug, he stumbled on something, nearly falling.

"Holy moly!" Larson exclaimed as he trained his light at his feet and saw a .44 magnum revolver. It was huge. "This is our big break, Shug. Ollie's gonna be thrilled. We might even get another K-9 officer for this find. Good boy, Shug!"

Hearing himself praised, Shug trotted back to Larson.

"Quit licking it!" he scolded Shug, who paid absolutely no attention to the command.

Larson pulled Shug away and wondered what he could use to pick up the weapon. He finally stuck his pen through the trigger guard and carefully lifted it. He held it up to the car lights. It was a

Ruger Blackhawk, a very powerful handgun. He smelled the end of the barrel like they do on TV.

"It's been fired!" Larson exclaimed, then placed it in a Burger King bag he had on his front seat and hurried to radio the sheriff.

Larson's hands shook as he grabbed the mike. "Unit Five to Unit One!" Larson used his best radio voice. He was dying to tell someone.

"Go ahead."

"Sheriff, you'll never believe what I...what Shug found over here!" he said as fast as he could.

"Hang on. I'll be right there," he said matter-of-factly, hoping Larson understood what he was doing. In case the Beasleys were still at his office, Ollie didn't want Elizabeth's parents hearing an excited deputy describing what might be their daughter. He was thinking the worst.

"You don't want me to tell you?" Larson was disappointed.

"No. I'm on the way." Ollie looked for a place to turn around.

Twenty-five miles away at the sheriff's office, Mrs. Martha O'Brien was on the edge of her seat. Her intuition kept her from saying anything.

Ollie had hit the brakes immediately upon hearing Larson's report. He backed up thirty feet, found a wide spot in the Dummy Line to turn around, then headed to the camp.

Just past the reach of the Expedition's headlights when Ollie stopped, in the center of the road, lay a black fleece jacket that was ripped almost in half. It smelled of perfume. Sheriff Ollie Landrum never saw it.

Chapter 37

Mick slowly pulled into the Bama Jama Night Club parking lot. He recognized a few of the redneck locals' trucks. Those same guys always patronized this fine establishment. They were mainstays in the late-night pool hall scene. Mick didn't see Jake's truck, so he decided to ride through once more, looking for any Mississippi tags. *Maybe he had a new truck. This is stupid. Jake's not here. He doesn't play high-stakes poker and he certainly wouldn't call me for money.* A car flew by at eighty-five miles an hour just as Mick started to pull out onto the road. "Jeez um! That was close!" Mick yelled at the idiot driver.

"This is crazy," he said, then let out a deep breath. "Nothin' makes sense."

Mick carefully looked both ways, pulled onto the road, and headed home. He wanted to sit down, clear his head. Maybe his wife could help sort it out.

What had he heard? The words he remembered were "Mick," "Jake," "club," and "kill." He thought he had heard "emergency." Maybe he had imagined that. The telephone connection had been awful and he hadn't been fully awake. Could it have been a hunting accident? Not that late at night. Mick smiled as he thought that, to Jake and any die-hard turkey hunter, killing a turkey *was* an emergency.

It was beginning to get foggy in the low areas. Mick noticed that the sky was clear and the stars were out as he pulled into his driveway and parked. He lowered the tailgate and allowed Beau to jump down.

"Night, Beauregard, I'll see ya in the mornin'."

Beau wagged his tail as he watched Mick go inside. He then went to the corner of the porch, circled three times, and lay down on his monogrammed camo dog bed.

Mick's wife was waiting up. Their two kids were sound asleep. She was flipping the stations between CNN and the Weather Channel. She got up when she heard the door open.

"Well...what's going on?" she asked.

Mick hung up his coat and answered, "Nothing. Ollie thinks it was nothing and he wants to wait till about eight in the mornin' to call Jake's house and check it all out."

Mick sat in a kitchen chair and ran his hands through his hair.

"I don't know...I don't really know what I heard."

"What about the blood?"

"Ollie thought it could be turkey blood."

"Yeah? I didn't think about that," his wife responded. Clearly she'd been worrying about it.

"You huntin' in the mornin'?" she asked, folding a quilt she had been using.

"Yeah...I better get some sleep. Maybe I can get an hour or so," he said, again running his hands through his hair.

"Are you okay?" She asked, placing the quilt on the end of the couch.

"Yeah, I just can't get it all straight in my head. The camp lights were on...even the heater was on...but no Jake. That doesn't make sense."

"Did Ollie take it serious?"

"I think so...I mean he and R.C. drove all the way out there and looked around. I suppose they know what they're doing."

"They don't know Jake."

Mick looked at her and thought, *She's right. But what could I do? All I can do is go to sleep and hope for answers in the mornin'*. He said,

"I'm too exhausted for all this. I'm goin' back to sleep."

"It's gonna be clear and cool in the morning, and it's going to rain Monday. President Bush is vacationing at Camp David, and the stock market isn't looking very promising," Mick's wife babbled like a TV news reporter.

Mick stopped, looked back at her, smiled, and said, "Come on, let's go to bed, honey."

Chapter 38

Zach Beasley was a wreck. Lately there had been several abductions in the news and the outcome was never positive. He tried to block that out of his mind and think of what he should do. How could he be proactive? Zach liked Ollie but wasn't convinced Ollie was sheriff material. He'd give Ollie an hour, and then he was going to start calling people that he knew could make things happen. He checked to make sure the phone was working and sat down at the kitchen table to make his call list.

Zach decided to first call the chief of police in Livingston. He was a close friend. They belonged to the same Rotary club and both served on the school board. *Yes, sir, that will be my first call in fifty-two more minutes. Then I'll call the district attorney of Tuscaloosa County.* He knew he had a fraternity brother who was in law enforcement somewhere, but he couldn't remember exactly where. If only he could think clearly. Zach took a deep breath, stared at the clock on the wall, and swallowed hard.

The silence in the house was killing him. Zach went upstairs to Elizabeth's room, passing numerous photos of her along the way. He stopped at the picture of the family skiing in Steamboat Springs. His eyes misted thinking of how much fun they had. Replacing the photo, he trudged up the stairs. Walking into Elizabeth's room made him break down and cry—her schoolbooks, her stuffed animals, and the hundreds of photos of her with her friends. He opened her closet door and breathed in deeply. She was his baby girl. His life. His greatest love. He had to find her. He sat down on the bed and sobbed into one of her sweaters.

Wiping his eyes with the neck of his shirt, Zach stood up and went downstairs to start making phone calls. Elizabeth was way too important to him to play any political correctness game. Ollie would just have to get over it. Elizabeth had to be found at any cost.

Olivia Beasley sat in her car in the ER parking lot. She stared at the hospital. Tanner was in bad shape. She looked out at the stars and thought, *God only knows where Elizabeth could be right now.* "Please protect her," she prayed as tears rolled down her cheeks. Elizabeth had been born in this hospital. Now Olivia was here hoping for some information that might help them find her. She took several deep breaths, attempting to calm herself. She made a plan to call a select few family members and friends to start a prayer chain. Her Prayer Warriors.

Before turning off the ignition, Olivia prayed as hard as she had ever prayed for anything. She didn't know what else to do but turn to God. She found great strength in her religious convictions. After dialing Elizabeth's cell phone one more time, she placed hers in her purse and crossed herself after saying another silent prayer. She touched the Lock button on her key chain and heard the "chirp-chirp" sound as she ran inside the hospital.

Tanner's mother sat in the ER/ICU combined waiting room wringing her hands and praying. Tanner was her baby. His older sister taught fourth-graders at a private school in Montgomery. Mrs. Tillman was too upset to dial long distance from the pay phone. A perceptive nurse recognized this and brought her personal cell phone over and handed it to her.

"Honey, just use it all you need," she offered kindly.

Mrs. Tillman thanked her repeatedly. She put on her reading glasses and tried her best to compose herself as she dialed the tiny buttons. Tracy Tillman Bonner answered on the fourth ring. Mrs. Tillman was so upset she could hardly speak.

"Hello," Tracy answered.

"Tra...Trace...Tracy," she stammered.

"Mom? Mom is that you? What's wrong?" she asked, sitting up in bed. "Mom."

"Tanner's hurt, Tracy. He's hurt bad."

Tracy turned on the light on the nightstand, waking her husband.

"Mom, what happened?"

"We don't really know, but he was beaten up and he's in intensive care right now."

"Where are you, Mom?"

"What happened?" her husband asked and cleared his throat.

"Ssshhh!" Tracy replied harshly.

"I'm at the hospital in Livingston."

"We'll be right there. It'll take us three hours, but we're on the way."

"No, you don't have to drive..." she tried to reply but ended up sobbing.

"No way, Mom. We're coming. I'll have my cell phone. Call me when you can and update us, okay? Promise you'll call?"

"I will. Y'all please be careful."

"Mom, I love you. Everything will be okay. Call me now."

"I will. Bye, dear." She felt better. Tracy had that effect. She would take charge. Mrs. Tillman needed her daughter.

"Get up!" Tracy exclaimed to her groggy husband as she ripped the covers back and jumped out of bed, "Tanner's been hurt!"

* * * * * * *

Steve Tillman sat sipping coffee, staring at the bland walls around the sheriff's office. Everything was overwhelming. He was anxious to get back to the hospital. Thankfully, Martha was keeping him updated. He also felt an obligation to help Sheriff Landrum find Elizabeth. He hated sitting, waiting.

"Can you call again, Miz Martha?" He asked in a meek voice.

"Sure," she replied and picked up the phone and dialed a direct ER line. Martha O'Brien had friends in the ER and ICU who always took her calls.

"Anything new?" she asked curtly.

"No. Not at all…the doctor's with him now but he's sedated, still unconscious."

"Call me if anything changes. His father is here waiting to help."

Tillman listened and couldn't take it anymore. He wanted to see his son.

"Miz Martha, I'm going back to the hospital. If Sheriff Landrum needs me, just let me know. I'll do whatever you need, and please call me if you hear anything."

"Steve, I understand. Go…we'll call. Sometimes these things just take a little time to unravel," she said compassionately.

And with that, Steve Tillman walked out the front door, heading to the hospital.

Chapter 39

R.C. reclined in his police cruiser, spitting into a green plastic bottle. He heard Ollie tell Larson he was on the way. He kept watching down the Dummy Line. He rolled down his window as Ollie pulled next to him.

"Did you see anything, Chief?" he asked.

"No. I want to get over to Larson. I could hear the excitement in his voice. Come on, follow me," Ollie said in a hurry and stomped the gas. As quick as he started, he slammed on brakes.

"Hey. If there are keys in that truck, grab 'em," he said.

As soon as he was certain that R.C. understood, he tore off down the road. Ollie hoped that Larson hadn't found a body. He cringed at the thought of Larson broadcasting that he had found a raped, mutilated woman. He flipped on his blue lights and pushed the Expedition as hard as he could.

R.C. climbed out, ran over to the Jeep, and removed the keys. He looked inside the truck. No keys in the ignition. He ran around to the other side, opened the driver's side door, and found them lying on the floorboard. Satisfied with himself, he tossed both the truck and Jeep keys on the cruiser's front seat and took off. Ollie was out of sight, but R.C. wasn't far behind.

Larson was so excited about finding the gun he didn't know what to do. He called for Shug to heel. The dog never looked up.

"Damn it, Shug, come here!" he hollered.

Larson finally walked over, hooked the leash to his collar and dragged the dog back to the police car. He looped the leash through the handle on the back door and leaned against the car. Shug tested the leash. As soon as the leash was tight, Shug sat down and resumed licking.

"Quit lickin' your nuts, Shug." Larson talked to the dog is if it could understand. "You gotta start behavin' more like a police dog. This is our big break."

Larson reached through the passenger window and grabbed the Burger King bag and admired the pistol. *This is significant.* He leaned against the car and listened to the whippoorwill while he waited.

It wasn't long before Larson heard the sounds of fast-approaching vehicles. He was about to pee on himself he was so excited. He tried to prepare the story he would tell that would make Shug look like Rin-Tin-Tin.

Ollie slid to a stop. R.C. turned the corner behind him. By the time Ollie had radioed Martha to let her know where he was, R.C. pulled up and stopped.

Larson got so excited he forgot the details of his concocted story and simply held up the bag, proudly exclaiming, "Look what I—I mean Shug found!"

"He found a bag of hamburgers?" R.C. chirped.

"No. He found a gun, I mean a pistol, and it's been fired!"

"He found a gun in a Burger King bag?" Ollie asked.

"No." Larson was growing aggravated. He simply pointed in the general direction of where "Shug" had found the gun. Larson was pointing at the grass. Ollie thought he was pointing at the camp house.

"Larson, this is a hunting lodge, so please tell me he didn't find the gun in the camp's gun cabinet!"

"No, no, no. We found it in the grass over there!" he said emphatically.

Larson removed the massive pistol and held it up for everyone to see. He stuck his pen through the trigger guard to preserve any fingerprints that Shug hadn't licked off.

"Wow!" Ollie exclaimed. Larson's chest swelled with pride.

"And it's been fired recently!" Larson proudly pointed out.

Ollie bent over to smell the muzzle, then nodded in agreement.

R.C. leaned in and said, "Smells like a Whopper to me."

Larson ignored him.

"Good job, Larson. That dog's finally done somethin'," said Ollie.

"Yeah, yeah, yeah. Good job," R.C. said sarcastically.

"This could be a big break. I need you to focus, R.C.," Ollie stated.

"Sorry," R.C. said as he looked again at the pistol.

"So what do you make of all this, Ollie? Is what happened at that gate related to this gun and the occurrences around here?" R.C. asked waving his arms around the yard of the camp.

"I don't know. I'm havin' a hard time connecting the dots. Normally, I'd say they were coincidences...but now.... We just don't know what happened here."

Ollie carefully took the pistol from Larson and opened the cylinder. He was taking a chance that he might destroy fingerprints, but he had to know. Sure enough, a dent in the primer. Easing the cylinder back shut, he let out a deep breath and said, "That's it. I'm calling in reinforcements. We have to find that girl."

R.C. and Larson nodded in agreement.

"Larson, do you know where Johnny Lee Glover stays?" Ollie saw him slowly nod after thinking about it a second. "Go by his trailer and see if he's there. No accusations. I just wanna know his whereabouts. Go!" Ollie commanded.

"Yes, sir!" He ran and jumped into his car.

"R.C., you know what happened last time I called in the big boys. But I don't see any other choice; do you?"

"No, Chief. I support you a hundred percent…for whatever that's worth."

"I think we'll use this camp as our temporary command post."

They saw Larson slam on the brakes after he had traveled about seventy-five yards down the road. He jumped out, ran around to the passenger's side and unhooked an exhausted, very confused German Shepherd and loaded him in the back seat. Larson acted like nothing happened. He never looked at them.

R.C. and Ollie turned to each other and laughed.

"I'll start making some calls," Ollie said, walking to his vehicle.

"Yes, sir, Chief. I'll call in the serial number on this pistol to see who owns it."

Chapter 40

The more Ethan "Moon Pie" Daniels thought about his girlfriend being on the 'Net, the more pissed he became. He couldn't trust Sheree, but he couldn't live without her either. Whatever she did, whomever she did, he always took her back.

He drove carefully through Aliceville and all the way down Alabama Highway 17. Constant whimpers and sobs were coming from the back but Moon Pie didn't pay any attention. He was as cold as ice when needed, and he never experienced remorse. This combination made him capable of anything.

Moon Pie thought about a new drug he'd just heard about called Ketaset. It was used to tranquilize bears. This fascinated him. Supposedly, it could fully paralyze an adult bear, while allowing it to see and hear everything going on around it. Biologists used it to "haze" bears that had become bold around people. Historically, brazen bears had to be destroyed, but this new drug and hazing techniques were working wonderfully. They basically beat up the drugged bear, terrifying it of humans. Moon Pie wanted some of that drug. He smiled, imagining what he would do to his girlfriend's computer lovers while they were helplessly paralyzed, watching. *I wish I had some right now. I'd try it on that whiny chick in the back. I'm gettin' me some Ketaset as soon as I'm done with this little project.*

Moon Pie had a good idea of what was going to happen to his little gem in the back. He hoped he could have some fun, too. But Reese was calling the shots, and Moon Pie would do or not do whatever he said.

He couldn't believe Johnny Lee had been killed. That really threatened some of his plans. He and Johnny Lee had been planning on running drugs on the Tombigbee River up from Mobile, Alabama, into north Mississippi and Alabama, and on into Tennessee. Their elaborate plan had taken months to devise. Johnny Lee had the balls to make the deliveries. Moon Pie had the customers. Johnny Lee's death was going to change everything, but he also knew that Reese would step into Johnny Lee's shoes and he'd want to try to keep the project alive. Moon Pie stood to make a lot of money and he couldn't do it alone. He was highly motivated to stay in Reese's good graces.

Moon Pie drove straight to Johnny Lee's trailer. He backed up to the front door then got out to have a look around before unloading his cargo. He walked to the edge of the yard and peed on a set of old tires that had been there for years. Moon Pie lit a cigarette and decided to take a look at the woman. She was curled into a tight ball, and he could see the fear in her eyes. He ran his hands up her bare legs, commenting that they needed shaving. *That don't really bother me none.* She tried to scream. He took a deep drag from his cigarette and blew the smoke in her face. Their eyes locked. He waited until she looked away before moving. Stepping back, he shut the doors and went to see if the trailer key was where it was supposed to be.

Moon Pie let himself in. When he turned on the lights, two roaches ran for cover. There were empty pizza boxes and beer cans everywhere. The ashtrays were full. There was barely room to walk around because of the trash. The kitchen was even worse. It appeared to have been months since the dishes had been washed. Down the hallway, he found a small bedroom with enough room to lay the woman on the floor. He left the light on and went to get her. On the way out, he counted a dozen empty Crown Royal bottles and chuckled, "Johnny Lee always had good taste."

"Whew!" he said aloud when he stepped outside. "That place is rank."

Moon Pie carried the woman inside. She was shaking uncontrollably as he set her down on the floor. He considered cutting her shirt off but decided to wait. He squatted down and looked her in the eyes again. He smiled at her and made a kissing motion as he rose to leave. He turned out the lights.

"I'll be back with a few of my friends. We're gonna have us a little party," he said softly, laughed, and shut the door.

The room was pitch-black. Her hands and ankles were bound, her mouth taped shut. The more she cried, the harder it was to breathe. She knew she was going to be gang-raped. She lost it. Urine trickled onto the dirty brown carpet as she wept.

Chapter 41

"How y'all doing?" Jake softly asked Katy and Elizabeth.

They weren't making as much progress as Jake had hoped. Katy was getting heavier with each step, and the going was slow through the hardwood bottoms. Even so, Elizabeth was having difficulty keeping up.

Jake was impressed with her mental fortitude. *She saw her boyfriend being severely beaten, successfully eluded a violent attacker for miles, and at the moment she was about to be raped, her attacker was shot in the head. Certainly a tough night for anyone, much less an eighteen-year-old girl.*

Katy was glad to have Elizabeth along. Although she noticed that Elizabeth was wearing her dad's shirt, she didn't say anything. Elizabeth's presence was comforting to her. She had never seen her dad scared before. Katy was pretty sure that he was and that frightened her.

Jake's right arm was getting numb. He stopped and stood Katy on a dry oak stump. He leaned against a tree to catch his breath. Elizabeth caught up, and Katy scooted over on the stump to make room for her to sit down. Jake pulled out his map and unfolded it. He shined his flashlight on the girls to make a quick assessment. Katy squinted her eyes. She had a bad scratch on her forehead that she hadn't said anything about. Elizabeth had a swollen eye and a bad bruise on her cheekbone. Jake noticed that she was shaking and cold. He didn't have any more clothes to offer her. His plan was to make their way to Little Buck Field where they could get warm and rest in a shooting house. He touched Katy's scratch and brushed off some dried blood.

"Dad, I wanna go home," Katy instantly replied.

Elizabeth simply nodded her head. Jake understood.

"I do, too, girlfriend. Let's rest here for a few minutes; then we'll go straight for a place to hide out."

When there was no response, Jake immediately clicked on the light and said, "Hey, girls...look at me. I'm going to get us outta here, I promise."

They both nodded. Jake rubbed Katy on the top of her head and smiled assuredly at Elizabeth. He studied his map. Checking his compass, he confirmed their location. *We're traveling southeast, so we must be here,* he thought, pointing confidently to a spot on the map.

"Are you cold, Elizabeth?"

"I'm okay," she replied.

"You can have my gloves," Katy offered.

"Thank you...no, you keep 'em." She smiled at Katy.

"Let's get moving. Come on. We'll warm up as we walk," Jake said, squatting down for Katy to climb onto his back.

Chapter 42

Tiny was beginning to think clearly and was feeling better about the situation. Reese hadn't seen what happened. He believed that Johnny Lee's killer had also killed Sweat. *To get out from under this, I'll tell Reese how the guy took me and Sweat by surprise and that they fought hand-to-hand and that I chased the girl and before I could get back, the guy shot Sweat. I'll come up with something to say about the boy and the Jeep and tie it all together.*

Tiny looked hard at Sweat's body and saw all that was bad about his own life and future. He was at a crossroads. This was his chance to change course. He started back toward his four-wheeler, proud that he had stopped the rape and murder of the girl, but hating that he'd had to kill Sweat.

After climbing onto the four-wheeler, he sat a moment, thinking. *I'll load up, then just drive away from all of this mess. Reese won't even know where to look for me. I got $3,800 cash money in my old mayonnaise jar—my startin'-over money. I'm done.* Tiny smiled. He switched on the lights, started the engine, and headed back to his truck and a new beginning.

As the four-wheeler's headlights reflected off his truck, Tiny eased back on the throttle. He shifted into low, lined up the tires on the ramp, and goosed the throttle. The engine revved and slowly crawled up the ramp into the back of his truck. Switching off the ignition, he stood up and looked around. Something was different. *Oh, shit, the Jeep's been moved!* Tiny's heart stopped. It wasn't blocking the road any more. If Johnny Lee's killer had escaped, Reese would be furious.

"Shit!" he said aloud.

He quickly slid the ramps into the back of the truck and shut the tailgate. *Just drive right out of this screwed-up situation.* After climbing into the truck, he slammed the door and reached for his keys. They weren't in the ignition. *Shit!*

He climbed out and raked out all the trash from the floorboards. Still no keys. He checked under the seat, feeling with his hands. *I need a light,* he thought, as he reached up on the dash and grabbed his flashlight. "Now," he mumbled as he clicked on the light.

He found a knife he hadn't seen in over a year, a screwdriver with interchangeable bits that he had been certain Sweat had stolen from him, but no keys. He looked in the side pockets on the door and in the drink holders, but he knew they weren't there. There were only two places they could be…in the ignition or on the floorboard. *Dammit!*

Although a professional criminal, Tiny didn't know how to hotwire anything. He was stuck, and this was supposed to be his getaway—his freedom ride. He wanted to scream. He also wanted to cry. He walked over to the Jeep and opened the door. He reached for the ignition. It was empty. Tiny's heart sank.

Tiny figured that his keys must have fallen out of his pants when he and Sweat fought. He stuck his flashlight in his pocket as he walked to the truck. He dropped the tailgate, pulled out the aluminum ramps again and set them in place. After backing out the four-wheeler, he headed back down the Dummy Line to look for a needle in a haystack.

Chapter 43

Anxious and frustrated, Reese stood silently on top of a stump, listening for anything that could be Johnny Lee's killer. He had never been caught poaching and was rarely even seen. Reese could tell when someone was approaching by the way the sounds of the woods changed. He took great pride in his predatory skills. He knew he had the advantage. But he could not hear anything. No running, no limbs cracking, no voices.

Reese shifted his weight and reached for a cigarette. His lighter fired up the first try. After a long drag, he blew the smoke out up into the night sky. He thought about Sweat and Tiny. *I can't wait to hear this story. Sweat's an idiot, and Tiny ain't too far behind or ahead – as the case may be.*

A barred owl hooted in the bottom off to Reese's right. *Owls are awesome hunters.* Tonight, more than ever, Reese wished he could glide silently through the trees and see in the dark. He finished his cigarette and mashed it out on the pine tree in front of him. *I've gotta cut his tracks,* Reese thought, grabbing his rifle. He then slipped off silently through the thickest woods in the county.

Chapter 44

"Unit One to Base," Ollie said with frustration, leaning back in the bucket seat of his Expedition. He dreaded making this call and the added burdens that surely would follow. There were just too many unanswered questions. Ollie hated unanswered questions.

Several seconds slowly ticked by before Martha responded, "Go ahead, One."

"Have you learned anything from the parents that I need to know?"

"No, not a thing," she replied.

"How's the Tillman kid?"

"No change."

"Call Hale County and get them to have Sheriff Marlow call me on frequency four," Ollie said flatly, weary resignation in his voice.

There was a long pause. Martha understood Ollie's reluctance to involve other jurisdictions. Sheriff Marlow was arguably the most respected sheriff in west Alabama. He had been in office for almost thirty years and had run unopposed in the last three elections. It was widely known that he could make things happen and that he was a close personal friend of the governor. The problem was that Marlow always came to the party with an attitude and a hidden agenda.

"Absolutely, Ollie. Hang on."

Martha O'Brien dialed the Hale County Sheriff's office. A young man whose voice Martha didn't recognize answered on the second ring. The rumor was that Marlow let trusties answer the phones, cut his grass, clean his fish, and do various other personal jobs. She explained who she was and that Sheriff Landrum needed Sheriff Marlow's assistance. She could hear him jotting down names and instructions.

"I'll see what I can do…it's three-fifteen in the morning, you know," he said condescendingly.

"I am well aware of the time. This is urgent or I wouldn't be freakin' callin'! Now, get me Sheriff Marlow," Martha erupted. She mouthed the word "idiots" to herself and let out a deep breath. Martha O'Brien was constantly amazed at others' incompetence. She had zero tolerance for it and them.

"Yes, ma'am," he replied, respectfully this time.

"Sheriff Landrum will be waiting on frequency four," she said, lighting another cigarette.

"Yes, ma'am," he said, then hung up and began cussing.

She hung up the telephone and then pushed the radio microphone button.

"Sheriff?" she asked, "I expect he'll be calling you any minute."

"Thank you, Miz Martha."

"Anything else?"

Ollie thought he heard a trace of sympathy in her voice, "I may need you to call Tuscaloosa. I'm thinking we'll need a helicopter. But wait till I talk to Marlow. Stay in touch with the Tillmans and Beasleys, and radio me if there's something I should know."

"Ollie, listen to me. You find that girl," she pleaded.

"Yes, ma'am. Let me change channels. I don't want to miss Marlow," he replied, then leaned down to adjust his radio. Ollie couldn't decide how Marlow would react.

Ollie looked at his watch, rolled down his window for some fresh air, and settled into his seat. He thought about the pistol and the role it might have played in this crazy scenario. The camp looked sinister in the dark shadows created by the maze of floodlights. R.C. was in his vehicle trying to run down the pistol's serial number. That would take some time, unless it was stolen. Somewhere there was a missing girl. He hoped this wasn't going to turn into a high-profile case that put him under a microscope.

"Hale County Unit One to Sumter County Unit One," a gruff voice crackled over the radio.

"Unit One here," Ollie responded and thought, *Okay, here we go.*

"Ollie, what the hell's goin' on?"

"Sheriff, I've got a situation over here that's really got me worried." He gave him an abbreviated account of Mick's phone call and the camp house. He quickly explained about finding Tanner Tillman and that Elizabeth Beasley was missing. The girl was his priority. Sheriff Marlow said that he knew Zach Beasley—Zach did his taxes. Ollie tried to be concise yet stress the uncertainty of it all.

"Ollie, this is serious. I agree that we should concentrate on the girl. Let me get some deputies over there and we'll start canvassing. It'll take an hour," he replied, staring out his bedroom window.

"Sheriff? I was wonderin' if we should call in a copter to search at daylight?" Ollie asked.

"The closest one's in Tuscaloosa, and I know it's broken down. If the National Guard wasn't in the Middle East, we'd get one of theirs. I tell you what…I might call the governor to see if he'd dispatch his helicopter. Let me get there; then we'll make a plan. Remember last time?"

"Yes, I do."

"I'll have my deputies call your office for directions. I'm on my way, son."

"Thank you," Ollie replied, feeling an immediate sense of relief. Help was coming and Marlow hadn't been arrogant or uncooperative.

R.C. was standing by Ollie's door nodding his head in agreement. "A helicopter could do a fast search of this area."

"True, but the more I think about it, the more I think they've left. Why would they hang around? And where? It's cold, wet, and muddy out there. They had to leave. That may be why the truck's tag was missing. Trying to buy some time," Ollie explained.

"You're probably right. Unless it's teenagers, and then they may not have anyplace to go."

Ollie nodded. He hadn't thought about that. "Any word on that gun registration?"

"They're gonna call back," R.C. explained.

"R.C., I want to find that girl. I'm afraid.... I can't even go there—we just gotta find her and fast."

"I know. I feel the same way...but where do we start?" R.C. threw up his hands in frustration.

"That's the problem. We could tie up all of our manpower in the wrong direction."

Ollie pulled the radiophone out of his pocket and studied it. "This might be our ticket. If we could get them to disclose their location or at least give us a clue."

"You're right...or...it might tip 'em off and make 'em run." R.C. shook his head in confusion.

They looked at each other and then at the phone.

Chapter 45

As the trio approached a small creek, they stumbled upon an Indian mound. Any other time, Jake would have been excited to explain to Katy the significance of this site. Jake loved Native American history and over the years he had found a number of arrowheads while planting food plots. It always amazed him that the last person to touch the artifact had been an Indian.

Jake, needing to rest, found a spot to set Katy down. Elizabeth stumbled up, leaned against a tree, and slowly lowered herself to the ground. He looked at them both. Katy was still terrified, and Elizabeth looked like she could be going into shock; he wasn't sure. Jake sat down between the girls. He checked the safety on the shotgun then laid it at an angle across his lap.

The words of the Conway Twitty song kept going through Jake's head. And that's what he was doing right then—everything to keep Katy safe with him. It was Jake's job; it was what he did. He breathed in deeply.

"Y'all okay?" he asked.

"Sure," Katy said tiredly.

Elizabeth just grunted. Jake could tell that she was just going through the motions.

"Elizabeth, tell me about yourself," he asked, trying to distract her. "Do you go to school?"

"I'm a senior at Sumter Academy. I'll probably go to the University of Virginia this fall," she said in a monotone voice. There was no emotion in her eyes or voice.

"I guess you live around here somewhere?" Jake asked, trying to keep the conversation going.

"In Livingston."

"What does your father do?"

"He's an accountant."

Katy joined in, "Do you play sports?"

"I played softball until the tenth grade, but not anymore," Elizabeth answered.

"I play softball and basketball," Katy said proudly.

Elizabeth managed a small smile. Jake thought, *Maybe she's holding up. Katy seems to be calming down, too.*

Elizabeth looked off in the distance, then back at Katy, "I'm a cheerleader," she said; then, looking squarely at Jake, she added, "and my boy…my boyfriend plays football." Elizabeth burst into tears.

Katy looked at her dad with a sad, bewildered look, and he shook his head at her, signaling that it was all right.

"Elizabeth, I've been thinking about him. After I get y'all safely in a shooting house, I'll go get him," Jake remarked assuredly.

"No! You can't leave us…they can track us…please, don't leave!" she said in a panic and added hopefully, "We'll go with you!"

"Okay, okay, I won't. I won't leave y'all," he promised. Jake placed a hand on Elizabeth's shoulder to comfort her, but he was thinking how he might be able to turn the tables on the rednecks and become the aggressor.

"Listen to me—both of you. We're going to get out of here. But we have to really push ourselves. We're all hurtin', tired, and scared. Katy, you have to do everything I say…immediately, no questions. Elizabeth, I know you're worried about your boyfriend, but right now you have to think about helping yourself first. You can't help him right now. Since he's a football player, I'm sure he's a strong, tough guy. I have a plan. It'll get us out of here. Y'all understand? Helpin' yourself helps us all; that's how it works. Got it?"

They both nodded in agreement. Jake didn't have a plan yet, but he was going to get these girls out of there even if it killed him.

Turning to Katy, he wrapped his arms around her and looked her in the eyes, "You believe me, don't you?"

"Yeah, Dad, I do," she answered and hugged him.

Jake kissed her cheek and held her tight. "I love you."

"I love you, too, Dad."

"Is your boyfriend in love with you?" he asked Elizabeth. She smiled slightly. With enough light, he might have seen her blush.

"Yes, sir, he is," she responded with a smile.

"Well, think about that...that's a good thought," Jake said, standing.

"Let's go," he said as he stretched. "It can't be much farther."

"Dad?" Katy asked.

"Yeah, baby?"

"Mom's gonna kill you when we get home."

Jake smiled and said, "I know." And then he thought, *If someone doesn't beat her to it.*

Chapter 46

Larson drove as fast as he could to Johnny Lee Glover's trailer. All local law enforcement knew his address. The sheriff's department had spent years watching Johnny Lee, who was suspected of drug manufacturing, possession, distribution, and other crimes. He had no apparent means of legitimate financial support.

It had only been about six months since the last time Larson had been to Johnny Lee's place. The sheriff's department had received a call concerning gunfire. Larson had been the first to arrive. There were two naked teenage meth addicts in the back yard shooting a .22 rifle into the trees trying to kill the "tree people." At the sight of Shug both kids cooperated. Larson found it sad how they insisted the trees were full of people who wanted to kill them. As he was loading the junkies into the police cruiser, Johnny Lee stepped out of the trailer and thanked him. He said that he couldn't sleep with all the noise. Larson knew the kids had bought the drugs from Johnny Lee; he just couldn't prove it. The boys were only sixteen years old.

Larson cut off his headlights about two hundred yards from Johnny Lee's double-wide. As he eased closer to the trailer, he saw a black Tahoe or Suburban backed up to the front door. Larson didn't recognize it but was certain it wasn't Johnny Lee's. Then he saw the small orange glow of a lit cigarette on the front deck of the trailer. Larson decided to pull up and ask a few questions. He told the ever-licking Shug, "*Achtung,*" as he flipped on his headlights and braked to a stop. The guy sitting on the front steps was blowing smoke rings.

The black Tahoe had chrome spinner rims. Larson looked around carefully before he got out of his car. He rolled down the back window in case he needed Shug.

"Evenin'…or I guess I should say mornin'," Larson said as he closed his car door.

The guy simply nodded.

"You got a name?" Larson asked.

Moon Pie took a long drag on his cigarette and decided to tell the truth. "Ethan Daniels," he said after he blew smoke into the air and flipped his cigarette butt into the gravel. "I'm down here to do a little fishin'."

"Oh. I see. Where's Johnny Lee?"

"He went to get us some bait," Moon Pie replied, cool as could be.

Larson wasn't buying whatever this guy was selling, but he didn't have much to go on. He played along in hopes of learning something.

"I really need to talk to him," Larson said, trying to look through the tinted windows of the vehicle.

"Until he gets back, I don't know how to get in touch with him."

"What about his cell phone?"

"I don't know if he's even got one."

Moon Pie slipped a cigarette between his lips and offered the pack to Larson.

"No, thanks," Larson replied. "You a chain smoker?"

"I like 'em well enough I guess," Moon Pie replied, then cupped his hands around the cigarette and lit it. He expertly blew a smoke ring.

"As soon as you see him or talk to him, tell him the sheriff's department wants to speak with him immediately. Tell him to call us as soon as you see him. Here's my card. I'm serious."

"Glad to. I always support the Law."

Larson walked to the back of the Tahoe and shined the light on the tag. As he was memorizing the plate number he asked Ethan where he called home.

"I'm from Noxapater, Mississippi, but I live in Tupelo," Ethan replied, knowing better than to lie about that.

"How do you know Johnny Lee?"

"We went to med school together," he replied.

That made Larson laugh. "So you're a comedian. I need to talk to Johnny Lee, or any of his other runnin' buddies, right now," Larson added in a very serious tone.

"When I see him…I'll tell him."

"I mean it now, you tell him to call us." Larson gave Moon Pie a very determined look.

"No problem, officer."

Larson climbed back in his cruiser and rolled up the back window. He decided to tell the sheriff the latest. Staring at Ethan, Larson radioed Ollie.

"Go ahead, Larson."

"Sheriff, I'm at the suspect's residence. He isn't here. There's a guy sittin' on the porch, says his name's Ethan Daniels from Tupelo. He has a Mississippi tag. He says they're goin' fishin'. Claims the suspect has gone to get some bait."

"Jailbait," R.C. whispered under his breath. He was listening to the conversation.

"Why don't you back up and keep an eye on him. Stay close to the radio. I've called in reinforcements. They should be here shortly."

"Ten-four, Sheriff."

Larson backed up and drove away, trying to give the impression that he was leaving. After about a mile he turned around and, without lights, slowly eased the patrol car to within two hundred yards, just out of sight of the trailer, and parked.

Moon Pie heard the deputy return. He wasn't falling for that old trick. He needed to report this to Reese. He climbed into his Tahoe and shut the door.

Beep-beep. "Reese?"

Approximately thirty seconds crawled by before any response.

Beep-beep. "Yeah."

Beep-beep. "Yo, I'm here and Deputy Dawg super-cop come by asking questions 'bout Johnny Lee. He acted like he was leavin', but he's parked just down the road. He can't see the trailer or me. He got my tag number, but I didn't tell him shit."

Beep-beep. "Where's my package?"

Beep-beep. "Stored inside."

Reese's mind raced. He wanted revenge, but having the girl was getting too risky. That wasn't smart. He was trying to think about what was going on with the cops. *There could be a thousand reasons why the cops wanna talk to Johnny Lee. That ain't out of the ordinary. But tonight? At this hour? We gotta ditch the woman!*

Beep-beep. "Hey, sit tight a minute."

Beep-beep. "All right...Look, I wanna help, but I don't need no trouble. No, make that *we* don't need no trouble," Moon Pie replied, growing anxious. He owed Johnny Lee a favor—that's what had gotten him involved in this mess—but Moon Pie was willing to stay in it because of the huge potential profits from running drugs on the rivers, and that venture would be decimated if Reese was in prison.

Beep-beep. "Just hang on."

Beep-beep. "Deputy Dawg's gonna follow me if I leave."

Reese realized Moon Pie was right, and he didn't want the woman in the trailer if anything went down.

Beep-beep. "I said hang on. I'm thinkin'."

Moon Pie shook his head and then said quietly, "Dammit!" and thought, *Now I'm lookin' at federal time for kidnappin'. Reese has got ten minutes. That's it, then I'm gone!*

Chapter 47

Sheriff Ollie Landrum and Deputy R.C. Smithson stood side by side with their backs against the front quarter panel of the sheriff's Expedition. They stared blankly into the cold darkness just beyond the camp's lights. They had not spoken for several minutes.

Ollie was feeling the mounting pressure to act. The clock was ticking. His palms were sweating. *Somethin' gotta happen and pretty damn quick.*

R.C. blurted, "Just call him. Tell him who you are and that you need to see him ASAP."

"Is that the best you can do?" Ollie asked. "I was hoping for something a little more tricky comin' from you."

"We could get a known associate of Johnny Lee's, maybe Ray Ray Walker, to call him...but that would take hours to put together. Let's just push the envelope ourselves...maybe use that old ruse where someone calls anonymously tellin' 'em a search warrant's been issued."

"Well, Ray Ray is doing time, so he's not a candidate. Besides, I don't think he'd go for it anyway. That punk would enjoy seeing us squirm. Let's—"

Before Ollie could finish, the radio crackled to life, and they both spun to listen.

"Base to Unit One."

"Go ahead, Miz Martha," Ollie replied, hoping for some good news.

"Sheriff, I just gave two deputies from Hale County directions to your twenty. They're coming through Livingston right now."

"Redirect one to Larson's location. Have him watch the trailer and report anything unusual. Larson can give him the details. I need Larson and Shug to be flexible for the search."

"Ten-four."

"Sheriff Marlow's about five minutes behind 'em."

"Thank you," Ollie replied.

Ollie pulled out the radiophone that R.C. had found in the pickup and stared at it. He hit the Menu button and found the Recently Received Calls. There was Johnny Lee Glover's number. *All I have to do is hit that button,* he thought.

"Okay. I'm goin' to do it. I'm just gonna call him. Straight up," he told R.C. confidently. "I've got to *do* something."

R.C. nodded, and Ollie hit Send, heard it beep twice, and waited.

Just a few seconds before he heard "*Beep-beep,*" Reese thought he glimpsed a flashlight beam for a split second across a clear-cut. He stopped, leaned his rifle against a tree at the edge of the cut-over, and pulled his phone from his pocket. He looked at the screen. Tiny? *His phone's at his house,* he thought. *This is weird.*

Reese hit Send, and the phone beeped twice. He didn't say a word. Reese listened intently.

Ollie and R.C. had their fish on the line but didn't know what to do next. Ollie took a deep breath and went for it.

Beep-beep. "Mr. Glover, this is Sheriff Landrum. I need to speak to you."

What the hell?! How'd he...? Reese thought, shocked. He stared at the phone, trying to make sense of what he heard. *Shit! Do I respond? Ignore him?* Reese decided to see what he could learn.

Beep-beep. "I'm kinda busy right now, Sheriff. Maybe tomorrow."

Beep-beep. "No. I need to talk to you face to face. Right now. Where are you?"

Reese was scrambling to think this through. *Maybe he went to*

Tiny's house, searched it, and found the phone. Maybe Tiny left it in his truck at the gate and they found it there. If that's the case, he's on the property. But he thinks he is talking to Johnny Lee... so they haven't found his truck yet.

"Shit!" Reese said out loud.

Beep-beep. "Johnny Lee, where are you? This is important."

Beep-beep. "Where are you, Sheriff?"

Beep-beep. "Johnny Lee, we're looking for a missing female. You know anything about it?"

Reese's mind was swirling.... *Is he talkin' about the woman I had Moon Pie kidnap? Maybe it's the "female" I heard screaming with Tiny and Sweat?*

Beep-beep. "Sheriff, I don't know anything about that at all. How 'bout I call you tomorrow sometime?"

"That's not Johnny Lee!" R.C. said. Ollie looked at him like he was crazy.

Beep-beep. "Johnny Lee, no...I need some answers. Now!"

There was no response. Only silence.

Beep-beep. "Johnny Lee?"

Beep-beep. "Johnny Lee!"

Reese had no intention of talking to him anymore. He had to get Moon Pie. Reese hit End, then dialed Moon Pie's number.

Beep-beep. "Moon?"

Beep-beep. "Yo."

Beep-beep. "Get rid of the package and get the hell out of there. But I need you to hang around and wait for me to call you back. I'll need you to pick me up on Highway Seventeen, 'round the Noxubee River bridge at about daylight. Be close but not too close. Go hang out at the truck stop off Twenty...that's maybe ten miles from me."

Beep-beep. "Whadda I do with our girl? They're gonna follow me."

Reese thought for a minute. There were too many unanswered questions. He needed some time. He needed vengeance, but he decided to eliminate a liability first.

Beep-beep. "Blindfold her. Tie her hands, then push her into the woods behind the trailer…she could walk for days back in there. Has she seen ya?"

Beep-beep. "Shit, man, yeah. This is screwed up, dude."

Beep-beep. "I really need you on this one, Moon. Get rid of her and hang tight."

Beep-beep. "I'll be there…you call, I'll be there."

Beep-beep. "Hey, Moon?"

Beep-beep. "Yeah."

Beep-beep. "This shit's serious, man. He killed Johnny Lee *and* Sweat. So whatever happens tonight, I need to know that you'll help even the score...and then some."

Beep-beep. "You got it, dude. Go get him. I'll meet you at the bridge."

Moon Pie slithered out of his Tahoe and crawled to where he could look at the cop's car. The moonlight made it easy to see the lone deputy's outline slouched behind the wheel.

He hurriedly went inside the trailer, straight to his victim. She jumped when he whipped opened the door. He could tell she had been trying to get free of the duct tape.

"Get up, bitch!" he said jerking her up by one arm. The room reeked of urine. Because now she was going to live, he was careful not to let her get a good look at him in the light. He stood her up, then cut the duct tape from her ankles. He checked her wrists. They were still secure. She could barely make a sound with the tape over her mouth. He led her to the back door, unlocked it, stuck out his head, and looked both ways.

Beyond Johnny Lee's trailer lay miles of swamp that eventually ended at the Tombigbee River. Gators, moccasins, and rattlers awaited. If she wandered west, she could reach a catfish farm or the giant landfill. Moon Pie didn't care just so long as she was as far away from him as possible.

"Listen to me and listen good. This is your lucky night...but only if you do one thing. So you better listen good *real* good, you hear? You walk straight ahead and do not come back in this direction...don't turn right and don't turn left. You forget everything that has happened, you hear?" Then he whispered in her ear, "If you talk to anybody...*ever*...remember, I know where you live."

"You hear me?" he asked, cupping her breasts from behind, and then he nibbled on her ear. She nodded, tears streaming down her face.

He pulled off an eight-inch piece of camo duct tape and put it over her eyes. She cringed. But when she opened her eyes she could see parts of her bare feet. She was shaking so violently she could hardly stand up.

"If you want to live, you walk straight ahead and forget any of this ever happened. Understand?"

Again she nodded, overwhelmed with relief at the thought that she might actually live.

"Go!" he slapped her butt like she was a football player and watched her follow his directions to the letter. He then hurried back inside and looked around before bolting out the front door.

Inside his Tahoe, he breathed a sigh of relief, cranked up, and rolled out of the gravel driveway. He didn't like this at all. Johnny Lee would never be this disorganized or take these crazy risks. Moon Pie knew he had to keep his cool for just a little longer. He turned onto the pavement and gave his ride some gas.

Larson saw the lights and sat up straight. He grabbed his microphone and excitedly shouted, "Ollie?" *Come on…hurry up,* he thought.

"Go ahead," Ollie responded.

"Daniels is leavin'…whaddya want me to do, Sheriff?"

"Follow him. Let's see where he goes. Give the Hale County deputy good instructions—have him watch the trailer. You should be able to reach him on the radio now. And Larson…be careful."

"Ten-four." Larson was so excited he couldn't replace the microphone on the small metal clip. After three tries he dropped it on the seat.

Chapter 48

Ollie and R.C. debated the call with Johnny Lee, or whoever it was, for a few minutes. They couldn't agree as to its probative value. They'd pushed the envelope, but it did not appear to have paid off. One thing was certain—they'd tipped off Johnny Lee or his accomplice that they were onto him.

Ollie monitored the radio traffic to make certain Larson's replacement knew where to go and what to do. He should be in place in a few minutes. Ollie learned from Larson that Ethan Daniels was headed toward Livingston.

A few minutes later, Martha reported that the .44 Magnum Ruger had been stolen from a Selma man's truck two years earlier.

Ollie was trying to get everything straight in his mind, so he could thoroughly explain the situation to Sheriff Marlow, who would be arriving in a few minutes. Ollie's headache worsened.

"R.C., go get me another Coke from in there, please," he said, pointing at the camp house with one hand and rubbing his furrowed brow with the other. His cowboy hat lay upside-down on the hood of his Expedition.

"Yes, sir, Chief," R.C. responded, heading toward the camp house.

Ollie grabbed the microphone to touch base with the kids' parents. Instead, he leaned his head back, trying to clear his mind. *I'll wait a few minutes more.* After a while, he realized that the calendars had distracted R.C. again. He was about to honk the horn, then raised the microphone to his face.

"Miz Martha?"

"Yes, Sheriff?" she said, blowing out a lung full of smoke.

"Give me an update…how's everybody?" he asked.

"Well, Tanner is still sedated. I understand Mrs. Beasley is standing there waiting on him to crack an eye open. Mrs. Tillman seems to be doing pretty good, but they say Mr. Tillman is pacing the halls."

"What about Zach Beasley?"

"I haven't heard from him. He's supposed to be at home in case Elizabeth calls or shows up."

"Call them all and tell 'em that I have reinforcements coming, and we expect to have as much help as the state can provide by daylight."

"Hang on, Chief. Somebody's cuttin' in!" she said excitedly.

Ollie watched R.C. approach with a Diet Coke. He shrugged his shoulders and mouthed, "It's all I could find." Everyone knew Ollie hated diet drinks.

"Ollie, go to frequency three and hurry!" Martha exclaimed.

Ollie set down the can and switched the channels. He heard a Hale County deputy in the middle of an excited explanation, "I have the girl in my car now and she seems to be okay but she's unconscious," he said in a very high-pitched, excited voice, "but I think she's all right."

Ollie was stunned. He heard Sheriff Marlow's voice speak, "Great job, Lewis. Take her to the hospital emergency room in Livingston. I'll meet you there."

Ollie couldn't take it anymore. "This is Sheriff Ollie Landrum. Please apprise me of the situation."

"What's that, Ollie?" Marlow asked.

"Tell me what's going on, Marlow!"

"Well, it seems my young deputy Lewis was instructed to stake out a trailer north of town. As he explained it to me, he got a gut feeling and approached the trailer where he saw a girl with her hands tied behind her, blindfolded, wandering around. Lewis is on the way to the hospital with her. Good thing you called us…it only took us about three minutes to resolve this for you!" he boasted.

"And she's all right?" Ollie asked, almost out of breath, ignoring Marlow's last comment.

"Apparently," Marlow said, chuckling like he did this every day.

"Hey, Marlow? Thanks, man, I really appreciate you guys. I'm on my way. I'll meet you at the hospital."

"I'll be there. I want to see my old buddy Zach Beasley."

"I understand…Miz Martha, are you listening?"

"Yes, sir."

"Call everybody and tell them!"

"Yes, sir. Good job, Ollie!" she was clearly proud and about to tear up.

Ollie signed-off, then bear-hugged R.C. They high-fived each other. R.C. howled like a dog and yelled, "Yes, yes, yes!" *This nightmare's over,* Ollie thought, *My worst fears were for nothin'.*

"Let's go!" Ollie exclaimed, grabbing his hat.

They both jumped into their vehicles. As Ollie hit the gas, relief flooded his body.

The sheriff thought about Martha calling him "Ollie." She didn't do that often. He still had the crazy Mick Johnson cell phone call to think about, but he would do that later. There was one more person to call right now. He switched back to the main frequency.

"Larson? Larson? Come in."

"Yes, sir, Sheriff." He sounded very despondent.

"Arrest that guy you're following. Where are you?"

"Larson?"

"Larson!"

"I'm in town, but I lost him."

"What? What happened?" Ollie was furious. Marlow had deputies with uncanny accurate gut feelings, and his deputy couldn't even keep a tail.

"It's crazy. This guy just vaporized. I'm really sorry, Sheriff."

"I can't believe this!" Ollie said out loud to himself. This was a classic Larson screw-up—just another example of his crazy-making behavior.

"Larson, give Miz Martha his name and vehicle type," he said sternly. "She can put out an all-points bulletin."

"Yes, sir, I'll do just that." Larson knew he had screwed up. He felt like he was going to vomit.

Ollie wanted to see the family reunited. He stomped the accelerator. They had found Elizabeth. *What a relief,* he thought. He was frustrated that he and his men had spent hours trying to resolve this crisis, and Marlow's deputy had it handed to him on a silver platter within minutes. *I'll catch hell about it, but at least the girl's alive and in good shape. That's the really important thing.* He took off his hat and laid it on the seat next to him, ran his hand over his head, took a deep breath, and with no small amount of relief said out loud, "Thank you, Lord!"

Chapter 49

How's your ankle?" Jake asked Elizabeth when she caught up.

"It's worse, Mr. Crosby," she whimpered. "I can hardly put any weight on it."

Jake got Katy off his back and then kneeled down to take a look at Elizabeth's ankle. It was the size of a grapefruit and hot to the touch. He knew she must be in excruciating pain. Jake slipped off her shoe, then searched his hunting vest for his pocketknife. He removed her shoelaces and cut out the tongue of the shoe. He then cut the top off, leaving just enough to cover the sides of her foot. He hoped her toes and heel would keep it on her foot.

He quickly stood, grabbed his shotgun, then unloaded it as quietly as possible—hating that he had to do it. He slipped the shells into an easily accessible pocket. Then he unzipped the cushion seat off his hunting vest and dropped it on the ground. He reached into the back of his vest and found his old Primos Turkey Wing, which had a six-foot piece of parachute cord tied to it so he couldn't run off and forget it when things heated up during a hunt.

The girls just watched silently.

"Elizabeth, hold this straight up,"Jake said as he put the gun barrel down onto the cushion. Using both hands, he squeezed the cushion around the barrel and used the parachute cord to tie it tightly around the barrel, looping the cord through the ventilated rib to prevent the cushion from pulling off in the mud.

"Okay. Now you have a crutch," he said proudly. "Put your

armpit right on the butt of the gun like this. The end of the barrel shouldn't sink too far in the mud since the cushion's so wide. See?" Elizabeth had to lean over slightly, but other than that it really made a pretty good crutch. *If I need it, I can shoot though the cushion,* Jake thought

"Cool, Dad," Katy said proudly.

"Thanks, Mr. Crosby. I've used crutches before. But what about if we need…you know?" she said, testing her crutch.

"You'll have to give it to me, fast. Listen to me; it's very, very important that you keep the cushion on the end of the barrel. If it comes off and you jab the barrel in the mud, I can't fire it. Understand?"

"Yes, sir."

"This is really important. You have to watch it all the time."

"Yes, sir."

Jake bent over, and Katy jumped on his back. They were off. After a few yards, Jake turned to watch Elizabeth as she hopped along at a much better pace. Jake prayed that the cushion would stay on.

The trio had traveled about another quarter of a mile when Jake thought he heard something. Years of shooting had taken its toll on his hearing, especially in his right ear. He turned to face the sound.

"Shhhhh," he whispered to the girls.

There it was again—a unique high-pitched beeping. Jake recognized it as a radiophone. *Was that the sheriff or the police or those freakin' lunatics. SHIT!* he thought. Fear shot through him again. He strained to hear; suddenly there it was again—maybe two hundred yards across the clear-cut. Whoever it was, they were tracking him and the girls…and they were close.

"Come on, girls. We have to be extra quiet from now on." He was right up against their faces as he whispered urgently. He wouldn't tell them what he had heard. He'd insulate them from as much as possible.

Katy held onto him with all of her strength. Jake kept a constant eye on the cushion. He had to push Elizabeth so they could cover ground faster, but she was really gutting it out. The crutch made travel much easier once she got into a rhythm. Jake considered every step to make tracking them as difficult as possible.

Chapter 50

Deputy Lewis Washington had been on Sheriff Marlow's staff for only six months. He was certain this event would jump-start his young career. He kept looking back over the seat, checking on the woman, doing his best to hold the car in middle of the road as he raced toward Livingston. The blue lights and siren fed his adrenaline rush. He nearly sideswiped a mailbox while talking on the radio. He tried to calm down—to analyze what had just happened. He'd have to explain it to his superiors...maybe even to the press. He was going to be a hero.

Lewis had not totally understood his assignment. Instead of stopping two hundred yards short of the trailer and observing, he had accidentally driven up to the trailer. When he slowly pulled into its driveway to turn around, his headlights illuminated the entire area. Lewis thought, *Looks like white trash lives here,* observing the Rebel flag hanging from a pole in the yard with old tires stacked around it. *A brother wouldn't be flyin' that flag.*

As he backed away, movement caught his eyes. He flashed his searchlight. Standing under a giant oak tree was a half-naked woman with duct tape over her eyes and mouth. Her hands were bound behind her. He slammed the cruiser into forward and drove right to her. Pulling his weapon as he jumped out of the car, he frantically searched the shadows for anyone else. The woman ran from the sound of the approaching car. Lewis caught up with her, grabbed her, and held on as she jerked and twisted. He quickly explained several times who he was. She then collapsed in his arms.

Lewis wanted to get out of there as fast as he could. He was spooked and expecting all hell to break loose at any moment. He quickly laid the unconscious woman on his back seat. Jumping into the driver's seat, he locked the doors and slammed it in reverse. Once on the pavement, the rear tires boiled smoke as he punched the gas and headed toward Livingston.

His first thought was to radio Sheriff Marlow. He did and could tell that Marlow was very pleased with the news. That feeling made Lewis drive even faster—he was headed to praise and glory.

By the time Lewis crossed the I-20 overpass, he had the story and his future career worked out in his mind. *I'll wait for Sheriff Marlow to retire and then I'll be elected Sheriff—the county will belong to me. After one term, I'll move on to the FBI. This is indeed a great night for Deputy Lewis Washington, law enforcement officer extraordinaire.*

Chapter 51

Ollie leaned back and relaxed as he headed to the hospital. He was relieved, the stress draining from his body. This could have been the ugliest of all possible scenarios. A missing, then murdered, teenage girl, besides being a devastating local tragedy, would have made national news instantly, inviting constant media attention. Ollie shuddered at the thought. CNN and Fox News were absolutely relentless. When they had first descended upon Ollie's investigation a few years ago, he'd enjoyed it. He'd loved seeing himself on television, the daily press conferences feeding his growing ego. After the truth was uncovered, Ollie had realized that he had allowed the hype to adversely affect his judgment. He'd vowed never to let that happen again and rededicated himself to the job—with the help of a good therapist. Apparently, the end of his football glory days had left an "attention void." He *needed* to feel and be important.

Yesterday's golf tournament had given Ollie a much-needed fix. A radio talk show host who had been a kid when Ollie played football had been in his foursome. Ollie couldn't help but like the guy. He had been on his radio call-in show a dozen times. This guy could recite all of Ollie's stats and knew the big plays step by step. And a businessman had paid $1,000 just for the privilege of being in Ollie's foursome. Ollie loved it.

With his blue lights flashing, Ollie crossed Interstate 20, a few miles from the hospital. He thought about all that still needed to be done. Martha could help with the details. As long as the Beasley girl was okay, everything else would fall into place.

Sheriff Marlow called the Tuscaloosa television stations to tip them off about the breaking story. They couldn't be there when Lewis arrived with the girl, but it would make a great news story anyway. Marlow planned to retire in a few years. He didn't need the publicity for career advancement but never missed a chance for it either. Marlow had never met a camera he didn't like.

Marlow arrived at the ER and started preparing for his photo opportunity. The first thing he did was to go into the men's bathroom to put a little dab of Brylcreem in his gray hair. He smoothed the starched shirt covering his pot belly. He was proud of Lewis. He would have to think of some way to reward him—maybe a dinner at some swanky Tuscaloosa restaurant. This whole affair was worth getting up in the middle of the night. *I bet Zach Beasley never charges me again for doing my taxes.* He checked his teeth in the mirror, then walked out to put on a show.

Martha O'Brien called Zach Beasley to give him the good news. He was elated and headed straight for the hospital. Olivia broke down crying and promised to pass the word to the Tillmans. Martha called her nurse friend at the hospital ER to get the details of the girl's initial exam.

Afterward, Martha got up and walked out the front door for some fresh air and a cigarette—a cup of coffee in hand. What a night! Tanner would be fine, eventually, and the Beasley girl was found. *Thank you, God,* she thought happily. She finished her coffee, took one last drag, then went back inside.

R.C. was following closely behind Ollie. Things were looking up for him. They still had to catch the bad guys, but they had a great lead. He was confident that they would be tracked down. He was proud of his instinctual decision to ride down the Dummy Line. This was proof of a sixth sense for investigative police work. R.C. had always liked and understood Ollie. They appreciated each other. Since R.C. had no ambition to be sheriff, Ollie trusted him completely. R.C., the devoted deputy, clearly understood the nature of their relationship. He smiled as he fast-forwarded the tape to "Copacabana," then cleared his throat, preparing to sing along with Barry.

Deputy Larson, on the other hand, was sinking into a deep depression. He had gone from peak exhilaration when he found the gun to complete frustration when he lost the guy he was following. He had given Martha the details of his vehicle including his tag number. It was just a matter of time before they would find him again, but that didn't help his mood. Adding insult to injury, the Hale County deputy had found the woman just minutes after Larson left the stakeout—just his rotten luck. Even over the airwaves, he could feel the weight of Sheriff Landrum's disappointment. Larson glanced over his shoulder at Shug lying in the back seat, licking away.

Steve Tillman was elated to hear about Elizabeth. He prayed silently that she had not been raped. She was so young, vibrant, and full of life. Tanner had told him last month that she tested in the top ten percent of high school seniors nationwide. He hoped that she had been able to somehow protect herself. As he stood near the ER nurses' station, he heard the head nurse instruct someone to take a wheelchair and a gurney to the entrance.

"I'm on my way!" the female nurse's assistant replied excitedly as she hustled to the door.

Tillman followed her while Olivia punched Zach's cell phone number into hers and waited.

Chapter 52

The four-wheeler strained under the load that was Tiny. He finally got up enough speed for it to shift into a higher gear. Halfway down the Dummy Line, Tiny remembered a spare key that he'd wired to the truck's frame a couple of years earlier.

"Yes!" he yelled, slamming on the brakes as he turned the wheel, sliding into a one-eighty. He goosed the throttle. He felt energized. *If the key's still there, I can get the hell out of this life…right now.* He drove as fast as possible.

When he reached the truck, he jumped off the four-wheeler without turning it off. He bent over at the back of the truck, feeling underneath the truck body. His hand found clumps of dried mud but no key. "Dammit," he muttered as he strained and grunted. Finally, he lay flat on his back and fished the flashlight from his pocket. Turning it on, he searched the underside of the back bumper. Solid mud. He hadn't washed the truck in months. *There!* Under a thick layer of red mud was the wire. Tiny grabbed it and pulled. Nothing. He pulled with all his strength, and the key popped out.

Tiny scrambled up. He jumped into the truck and cranked it, letting it idle while he quickly loaded his four-wheeler. With no thought of Reese or Sweat's body, Tiny dropped the shift lever into Drive and stomped on the gas. His oversized mud grips threw gravel as he scratched-off, heading home to pack and grab his starting-over cash. The last thing he planned to do in Sumter County was to toss his pistol into the Tombigbee River as he crossed it. *I finally got some options.*

Chapter 53

"Dad, I'm thirsty," Katy whispered into Jake's ear.

Jake and the girls were making much better time now. Jake guessed he had about another five or six hundred yards to Little Buck Field. He was having difficulty keeping his cool, but he knew their lives depended on it. And he couldn't let the girls know he was scared to death.

"I am too, baby…just try not to think about it," realizing just how thirsty he was.

"Don't you have a bottle of water in your vest?"

"No, ma'am. Just don't think about it, okay?" he whispered back.

"I'll try," she said, not really understanding.

Jake stopped and, without taking Katy off his back, waited for Elizabeth to catch up. "How's your foot? Is the crutch helping?" he asked in a low whisper.

"Yes, sir, it is." Elizabeth grimaced.

Jake could see his breath when he exhaled.

"Are you still cold?" Jake asked Elizabeth, knowing Katy was warmer than anyone because of her camo outfit.

"I'm freezin', but I can make it."

Jake took a fleece neck warmer from his vest and pulled it over her head, then back up over her chin.

"That'll help."

"Thanks."

"We'll be outta here before you know it," he whispered, then looked behind them for lights.

"Come on, we gotta keep movin'," Jake said, shifting Katy's weight on his back as he trudged further through the swamp.

Chapter 54

As Hale County Deputy Sheriff Lewis Washington turned his cruiser into the hospital parking lot, he noticed the crowd gathered in anticipation of his arrival. He quickly checked his rear-view mirror to make sure his hair looked good. He glanced into the back seat. The girl was still passed out. Lewis didn't know why she had fainted. He'd let someone else determine that. His job was done. He turned off the siren but left his blue lights flashing as he pulled under the hospital's ER awning.

Ollie had almost caught up with Lewis. He was about sixty seconds behind him. Ollie knew there'd be a horde of people waiting. He kept reminding himself that this was about Elizabeth Beasley. Whatever else happened or whoever got credit for the rescue was immaterial compared to her well-being. The focus had to be on her. He just hoped that Marlow wouldn't pull his usual stunts, getting his kicks at Ollie's expense during the news conference.

"I'm here, Miz Martha," he informed her, then put the microphone on its hanger.

"Ten-four, Sheriff."

Ollie parked his Expedition to the side of Lewis's car. As he got out, he watched the scene develop. Nurses and orderlies gathered around Lewis's car trying to get Elizabeth out of the back seat. The news media were jockeying for position to get video. In front of the car, Lewis was describing the events to Sheriff Marlow. He was using his hands to describe how dramatic and dangerous the past twenty minutes had been. Ollie walked by as the chaos reached a fever pitch.

The crowd gasped when they saw that the woman was still bound and had duct tape over her eyes and mouth.

Marlow immediately got in Lewis's surprised face. "You idiot! Why in the hell didn't you take the tape off of her?" he asked furiously. "That looks real bad."

"I was in such a rush...I didn't even think about it, Sheriff," Lewis tried to explain.

Ollie was halfway across the covered area when a man screamed. He saw Zach and Olivia Beasley hugging each other like something was wrong. *What the hell's going on now! They oughta be excited,* Ollie thought as he rushed to their side.

"What's the matter, Zach?!" he asked, watching the orderlies lay the woman on a gurney.

"That's not Elizabeth!" Zach Beasley screamed.

"What!" Ollie exclaimed.

"That's not her!" Zach Beasley replied. "That's not Elizabeth!"

"Where's my baby?!" Olivia Beasley screamed at Ollie. Zach put his arm around her, trying to calm her.

Ollie stood in shock. The gurney with the mystery woman was being wheeled past them. She was obviously traumatized. *Who the hell is she?* Ollie thought.

Ollie's eyes caught those of Steve Tillman, who had just watched the gurney roll by him. His eyes said it all—that this horrible night was worse than anyone could have imagined. Ollie was totally confused. He needed to determine who this woman was and where she had come from. He needed to restart the Beasley investigation. He stood in the center of the automatic doors wondering what to do first.

R.C., humming a tune, walked with purpose toward the ER when he arrived. As he passed under the awning, he was just about to sing out loud, "his name was Rico, he wore a diamond." At that moment he saw Ollie's face and the tune stuck in his throat.

"What's wrong, Chief?" he asked.

Ollie looked at R.C. and then down at the ground. "It's not Elizabeth."

"What? No way!"

"Go in there and find out who it is and what the hell's going on. I'll be right there. I want to talk to the Hale County boys first."

"Yes, sir!" R.C. turned and charged inside.

Ollie looked inside across the lobby to see Sheriff Marlow already in damage control mode with the editor of the Sumter County Journal. Marlow was at a loss for words, Ollie could tell.

"Sheriff?" Ollie asked, walking up to the pair.

"Excuse me, but I need to conference with Sheriff Ollie Landrum." Marlow was thankful to get away from the barrage of questions. This was not going as planned.

Ollie skillfully ushered Marlow and Lewis to a supply closet inside the hospital. Before Ollie went in, his eyes met Zach Beasley's and Steve Tillman's. "I'll be right back and we'll talk."

"What's going on, Ollie? You got missing girls all over this county!" Marlow demanded aggressively, in a transparent attempt to shift the focus of the situation.

"I don't know, Marlow, but I'm damn confused. I want to hear *his* story," he said, jerking his head toward Lewis, who began babbling about having a gut feeling and driving on up to the trailer to look around. Ollie glared at him. He knew a line of crap when he heard it. This wasn't making sense. Years of being around R.C. and Larson had fine-tuned Ollie's BS meter.

"Marlow, who tipped the newspaper?" he asked, clearly angered.

"I had to call them about something else and mentioned why I was in the county...that's all," Marlow explained.

"Look, fellas, I got a mess on my hands, and I need your help. I need some serious investigative work done. I need to know who that girl is and how she figures into this chaos, and then we have to start all over. Marlow, have your guys ready to go back out." Ollie ordered, taking charge.

Marlow sheepishly nodded.

Ollie opened the door, then hustled down the hall to find R.C. and the mysterious victim. As he passed, he asked the Beasleys to wait just a minute longer, he'd be right back. It didn't take long to find everyone. The hospital was small, and a crowd was gathered around the door to Exam Two. Ollie opened the door and saw Dr. Sarhan listening to the woman with his stethoscope. He saw the camo duct tape lying on the floor. R.C. was trying to ask questions of the medical staff but wasn't getting any answers.

"Let examination complete. You can ask question then." Dr. Sarhan said in a thick Indian accent to R.C. but looking up at Ollie.

Ollie understood and motioned to R.C. to stop. Ollie bent down and grabbed the pieces of duct tape. The woman appeared to be least thirty years old, maybe older. She was just waking up. He didn't recognize her.

"Please allow few minutes, Sheriff," Dr. Sarhan said.

"Come on, R.C." Ollie let out a deep breath and motioned R.C. out into the hall.

"Did you get anything?" Ollie asked R.C.

"Doc doesn't think she was raped. He was pissed that she was still taped up. He about bit my head off. What's up with that...what was that deputy thinking?"

"Youth," Ollie replied. "Anything else?"

"No, sir."

"You don't know her, do you?" Ollie asked rubbing his aching head without removing his hat.

"Never seen her before—and I think I would remember," R.C. replied, alluding to her good looks. "Want a Tums?" R.C. flipped one in his mouth and held the roll out.

"Yeah."

"Whaddaya need me to do?" R.C. asked as he handed the roll to Ollie.

Ollie saw the Beasleys charging up the hall straight to him. He knew he had stalled as long as he could.

"Call Miz Martha and bring her up to speed; then meet me right outside," Ollie instructed. "Have her call and wake up everybody available, including the county game warden. We're gonna need everybody."

"Ten-four," R.C. replied, reaching for his cell phone as he walked hurriedly toward the exit.

"Ollie, what the hell's going on? What are you doin' to find Elizabeth?" Zach launched into him.

"We are trying to determine where to concentrate our efforts right now. All this is very confusing. We all assumed that was Elizabeth." Ollie broke eye contact and looked at the floor. "Please give me a few minutes to determine who this woman is and how she fits into all this."

"Sheriff, you need some help. You should call in the FBI or something. This is serious. This is my daughter we are talking about," Zach Beasley said sternly.

"Yes, sir. I have…we are…just hang on for a minute," Ollie stuttered as he searched for the right words.

Zach didn't wait for Ollie to finish. He walked off to look for Sheriff Marlow.

Ollie raised his head to see R.C. hanging up his phone as he walked back into the hospital. He motioned to him; then the two of them went over to Steve Tillman.

"How's Tanner, sir?" Ollie asked, holding his hat in his hands.

"No change, but he is stable. I sure was shocked to see that wasn't Elizabeth, Sheriff."

"Yes, sir. Me too. Are you still willing to ride out to your property?"

"I'll do anything to help out, Ollie," and he meant it.

"R.C., Mr. Tillman owns some land on the Dummy Line. That may be where the kids were. Take Mr. Tillman and y'all go look around. Be careful. Call me if you see *anything*."

"Sure thing…let's go, Mr. Tillman."

"I have to tell my wife. I'll be right with you," Tillman said, walking away.

Ollie peered back in Exam Two. They were still working on the mystery woman. *Who the hell is she?* Then he watched R.C. walk out through the automatic doors as the Beasleys rounded the corner, about to explode. "Where's Sheriff Marlow?!"

Ollie only had to take a step toward the exit to see the television truck and the camera focused on Sheriff Marlow. "Damn it," he muttered under his breath and pointed toward the exit. Ollie turned back toward Exam Two as Dr. Sarhan waved him in.

"I think she will be fine…physically, but mentally she has been through much trauma."

"Has she been raped?" he asked softly.

"No, she has not. I see no signs of physical abuse." Dr. Sarhan pulled the latex gloves off and threw them in the trash.

"You can talk to her," he said as he walked out of the room.

Ollie was alone with the mystery woman. Their eyes met. He pulled out his notepad, sat down on the stool next to her bed, and smiled kindly, "Ma'am, I'm Sheriff Ollie Landrum. I need to know who you are and what happened?"

"Where am I?" she asked.

"You're at the hospital in Livingston."

"Livingston?...Alabama?"

"Yes, ma'am," he replied, noting her confusion, "Why don't you tell me who you are?"

"My name's Lindsay Littlepage. I live in West Point, Mississippi...I need to call my husband," she explained slowly.

West Point! He thought. He was certain that wasn't a coincidence. He thought about Mick and his friend.

"How did you get here? What happened?"

"My husband's out of town on business, and my kids were at a spend-the-night party, so I was home alone and this...this...this...." She was beginning to get emotional.

Ollie needed information. He would have to go slow. "It's all right, ma'am. Take your time, but you need to know that there may be more lives in danger. Do you understand?" he asked gently.

She nodded and continued, "This guy broke into our house and threatened me. He taped me up and put me in the back of his van, or maybe it was an SUV. He said my husband killed someone...and that...that makes no sense."

Ollie listened carefully and took notes.

"We drove for hours, and then he put me in a dark...a dark room." She was crying again. "I need to call my husband, *please*."

"Yes, ma'am, you will, I promise. I just need to know the rest first."

She wiped her eyes, and a nurse walked in to check on her. Ollie insisted she continue.

"Well, he left me and came back...and he said he was going to get his buddies...then he came back and he taped my eyes and told me to walk straight away and I would live. He insisted I walk straight away, but I couldn't see anything but a little bit of my feet. It was horrible."

"Yes, ma'am," Ollie responded.

She started crying again, "That's when the policeman found me. Please thank him for me."

"Do you know..." Ollie flipped back a few pages to make sure he had the right name. "Do you know Jake Crosby?"

Her eyes widened, and she said, "He's my next-door neighbor...he and my husband are good friends...they hunt together."

Ollie let out a deep breath. *Damn it,* he thought. *How could all this be connected?* He needed to call Mick.

"Mrs. Littlepage, why don't you rest now. I'll have a deputy come by to help you call your husband, okay? You said he was away on business...where is he?" he asked preparing to write down her answer.

"Biloxi. At a convention. He sells pharmaceuticals."

"Thank you, ma'am. I know you've been through a heck of an ordeal tonight. We'll help you get in touch with your husband, I promise."

Ollie stood up. He patted her hand gently to say everything is going to be all right and walked out as a nurse came in holding a small clear plastic cup containing little blue and peach colored pills.

Chapter 55

Reese felt something crawling on the back of his neck and reached for it. He found a small lump and pinched it. Holding it between his thumb and forefinger, he lit his cigarette lighter with the other hand to examine it.

"Damn tick," he said with disgust, then squished it between his fingers.

Wiping his hand on his blue jeans, he paused from his stalk to think. *That phone call's bugging me. Tiny lives with those two guys – that addict who's constantly gettin' busted and the drunk who fights everybody. There's always trouble with the cops at their house. It ain't no wonder that the sheriff picked up his phone. They probably raided the house and found it.*

"Those idiots!" Reese said a little louder than a mumble as he lit a cigarette.

Reese turned on his flashlight as he walked out into the old logging road. He checked his watch, looked-up at the clear night sky, and guessed that he had about two hours before daylight. He scanned back and forth searching for footprints. *He's gotta be on this side of the big creek. It's way too much water to cross. If I don't get you tonight, you sumbitch, I know who you are and where you live. I'll get you sooner or later.*

Reese could make out a shooting house on the ridge at the edge of a clear-cut. That would give him a vantage point with increased visibility. He ran to it and started to climb the ladder. The whole house shook as he climbed. When he reached the top, he felt for the door latch and flipped it up. Swinging the door open, Reese climbed in and quickly scanned the woods for any lights and listened for any sounds.

The predator was poised to strike.

Reese couldn't quit thinking about the sheriff's phone call. *He knows somethin',* he thought. He couldn't believe the sheriff had called him…or actually that the sheriff had called Johnny Lee.

After a few minutes of not seeing or hearing anything, Reese climbed down. He hit another logging road further south and started sweeping the flashlight back and forth. Twenty yards down the road Reese saw fresh footprints in the mud.

"Hot damn!" Reese exclaimed aloud.

He ran up to look closely. There were two distinct sets, a heavy boot track and a smaller track from tennis shoes. Reese grinned as he stalked his victims.

Chapter 56

Ollie stormed down the center hall of the ER. The automatic exit doors opened as he approached, and he charged through. Noticing the bright lights in the parking lot, he strained to see what was happening. Marlow's silhouette in front of the cameras was obvious. He was being interviewed by the CBS affiliate from Tuscaloosa.

"Shit!" Ollie said aloud.

"Sheriff Marlow, I need you!" Ollie hollered across the parking lot.

Sheriff Marlow looked over and nodded. He excitedly explained to the television crew that there must be a break in the case and promised to give them all the details as soon as he had them. He quickly unclipped his wireless microphone and handed it back to the news reporter.

Ollie stood impatiently waiting. He managed to keep his cool. When Marlow walked up, Ollie again escorted him straight to the supply closet. He was about to close the door when he caught Zach Beasley's eye. He held up one finger and mouthed, "Give me one minute." Zach nodded as if he were in a daze and about to melt down.

Ollie quickly closed the door and glared at Marlow.

"Marlow, what in the hell? Please, man, I need some help. I need a helicopter to search the woods at daylight. I'm gonna need every available officer to help search and secure a huge area. I'm going to set up a command post at my office and coordinate from there. We don't have time for the TV bullshit!" Ollie exploded.

"Calm down. Media management is part of the job. I'm trying to help you here, buddy, okay? I'll call the governor and get his helicopter. You can have all my men. What's the latest? Who's that woman?" Marlow asked calmly.

Ollie relaxed a bit; he needed to believe Marlow. He stared at him for a long moment then said, "Her name's Lindsay Littlepage. She's from West Point, Mississippi. Get a load of this…remember the guy I told you about that called on his cell phone and started all this confusion? She lives next door to him. That means he's out there somewhere too, I can feel it." Ollie let the information sink in and added, "Let's go to my office and get organized, but please, leave the media here."

"I'll do what I can…they smell a story," Marlow replied.

As they stepped out of the closet, Ollie said, "Well, keep 'em away from me. We have way too much to do." Ollie knew he couldn't manage everything, and he wasn't going to let the cameras distract him.

Sheriff Marlow headed out to tell the media that command central was going to be set up at the Sumter County Sheriff's Office. Ollie turned to address the Beasleys. He swallowed hard as he prepared an explanation of a situation that he didn't understand fully.

"I am so sorry for all this confusion. Let me tell you what we are doing. We are preparing to have a massive search at daylight, a helicopter, an army of men, road by road, house to house. I have my best deputy, R.C. Smithson, and Mr. Tillman headed to check out the Tillmans' property. All of our deputies and Hale County's are en route, and I even have the game warden coming in to help search. I'm going to my office to set up a command post there for coordinating everything." Ollie focused on making direct eye contact throughout the entire conversation.

"Ollie, what do you think happened?" Zach asked.

"I really don't know and I hate to speculate. But I can assure you of this, we have every asset at our disposal ready to be utilized."

"I...I...don't know what to think," Zach stammered. "I don't know what to do."

"Zach, y'all are welcome at my office. If you want to stay here, I can arrange a private room for you. I need to go...it's up to y'all."

"I'm coming with you," Zach instantly replied, then looked at his wife.

"I'm gonna stay here and pray Tanner wakes up and can talk," Olivia answered. She sniffled and shook her head, trying to regain her composure.

"You have a cell phone?" Ollie asked.

Olivia nodded and held it up to show him. "I'm hoping she'll call."

Ollie decided against telling Mrs. Beasley he had Elizabeth's cell phone. She needed hope.

"Good. We'll keep you up to date. Call us if Tanner wakes up. I need all my deputies right now."

Olivia grabbed Ollie's arm and looked him straight in the eyes. "Ollie, please find her...she's my life." Tears were rolling down her cheeks.

"Yes, ma'am. We will." This was his chance to really help someone—to make a difference. This was why he had gone into public office. He walked with a purpose through the automatic doors and never slowed when the television camera lights came up.

"No comment right now," he responded when asked what was going on.

"Sheriff, can you confirm that you have a missing teenager and that foul play is suspected?" The blond reporter asked.

"No comment," Ollie responded as he climbed into his Expedition and cranked up.

"One to Base," he radioed as he backed out of the ER driveway.

"Go ahead, Sheriff."

"I'm headed in to get organized. No TV crews inside. Got it?"

"Yes, sir. Sheriff Marlow just arrived and is in your office. I think he is talkin' to the governor."

"I hope so. Zach Beasley's right behind me. If any media show up, keep them away from that poor man."

Ollie switched on his blue lights and punched the gas.

Chapter 57

"You can relax, Mr. Tillman. I'm trained to handle a vehicle at high speeds." R.C. said, trying to be comforting. R.C. drove much faster than Tillman was accustomed to, but he hadn't said a word. He'd checked his seat belt several times, and R.C. had seen him once pressing the floorboard as if trying to push a nonexistent brake pedal.

"Don't worry about me; let's just get there and find Elizabeth," he replied, staring straight ahead.

"Do you think we can drive all the way through your property in this car?"

Tillman thought for a second, then said, "We can the front part for sure, but we can't get to the back forty."

"Yeah, we can. I've got the keys to Tanner's Jeep."

This caught Tillman by surprise. He realized that he didn't know any details about what had happened to Tanner. For the last thirty minutes he had been concentrating on Elizabeth.

"Where's the Jeep?" he finally asked.

"It's at the big yellow gate on the Dummy Line."

"R.C., what do you think happened?"

R.C. paused for a few moments. "I think they drove up on a drug deal or something like that. Methamphetamine's a huge problem all over west Alabama. We can't keep up. Meth labs are popping up everywhere…it's bad and getting worse. Tanner probably never knew what was going on."

R.C. whipped onto the gravel road. Tillman noticed the West Union Road sign when they turned. The land had been in his family for two generations. At one time the farm had been much larger, but years of bad crops and inheritance taxes had reduced it to only 160 acres. Eighteen years ago he had planted the entire property in pines. He planned to pay for Tanner's college by thinning them. He had many fond memories of hunting and fishing and horseback riding on this property. Now he was scared to death of what he might discover on the land he loved so much.

"Folks that do meth get addicted instantly. In short order, it ruins their lives," R.C. continued as he managed to insert a fresh dip at seventy miles an hour on the dirt road. Tillman tensed a bit more. "And none of 'em ever get rehabbed. I mean, it's unbelievably addictive. Meth heads get real paranoid too." Tillman just nodded, tightening his grip on the door handle.

"We had a guy last month that was convinced people were hiding in his appliances. He'd destroyed his oven, his microwave, the dryer, you should have seen his refrigerator, and—" R.C. was getting wound up.

"R.C., I really...can we concentrate on what we need to be doing?" Tillman said, cutting him off.

"Sure. No problem." R.C. spat into his green bottle. "But they are easy to spot...the addicts...they have sores on their legs, and their teeth rot out in the front."

"So you think they ran into somebody selling these drugs?" Tillman asked, resigned to the fact that R.C. was not going to stop rambling.

"Yeah...maybe, or there might be a lab out here if there are any old barns or buildings. It just wouldn't surprise me." R.C. slowed down and turned onto the Dummy Line.

R.C. kept up his speed until he saw reflections from Tanner's Jeep.

"The truck's gone!" R.C. screamed.

"What?" Tillman asked.

"There was a big blue Chevy pickup parked right there. I've got the keys to it in my pocket!"

"Whose is it?"

"We don't know for sure. Shit!" R.C. couldn't believe this. He knew he should radio in to report this, but he didn't want to take the time at that moment to call from his vehicle.

He parked his patrol car sideways across the road to prevent anyone from leaving and grabbed a handheld radio. They both got out, and he gave Tillman the keys to the Jeep.

"I like Tanner's Jeep," R.C. said as he climbed into the passenger's seat.

"Yeah, he does too," Tillman answered solemnly.

The Jeep cranked right up. Tillman backed up, and they started down the Dummy Line. R.C. powered up the handheld unit and pressed the Talk button.

"Miz Martha?"

"Go ahead, R.C."

"I'm mobile with Mr. Tillman, and I'll only have a handheld for a while."

"Ten-four. I'll tell the sheriff."

"Tell him the blue truck that was at the gate is gone."

"I will when he gets off the phone. Y'all be careful," she added, blowing smoke towards the ceiling.

"Let's go, Mr. Tillman."

CHAPTER 58

Marlow was sitting at Ollie's desk. As Ollie walked past Martha O'Brien, she gave him an understanding glance. He stopped to pour himself a cup of coffee. He could see Marlow in his office talking on the land-line. Zach Beasley walked in. Martha got up and hugged him. Martha had that uncanny knowledge of what to say and when to say it to make everyone feel better. She poured Zach a cup of coffee. Ollie could tell she was going to mother him.

Marlow motioned him to come in. Ollie hung up his cowboy hat, then sipped his coffee.

"That's right…there will be lots of media attention, and if your helicopter is being used, think of the positive PR that can come from this…you'll be the hero." Marlow winked at Ollie. He had opened a can of Vienna sausages and was busy dousing them with Tabasco while placing them on saltine crackers.

"Yes, sir…I'm telling you this is big enough the national media will pick it up…everybody from *USA Today* to CNN," he replied. He had started to take a bite of his snack when he gently placed the cracker on Ollie's desk and repositioned the pink weenie. "Okay. I'll keep that in mind…the beach tomorrow afternoon…no, Bill, I promise that won't happen again…it's not even deer season." Marlow laughed heartily. "Have him here as soon as you can. Have him land at the Livingston hospital…Yeah, they have a helipad. Thanks, governor, and good night," Marlow said with enthusiasm, then hung up.

Marlow leaned over Ollie's desk and beamed. "You've got your copter. It'll be here inside two hours."

"You know these things are good anytime," he added, proudly holding up the can of Vienna sausages. "You want one?"

Ollie ignored the offer, thinking about the helicopter. He was thrilled beyond words but wondered if Marlow was more interested in helping the governor's re-election efforts than he was in finding Elizabeth. "Thanks, Marlow. What was that about the beach?"

"He needs the helicopter back as soon as possible so he and his family can fly to their beach house on Ono Island…you know, down near Gulf Shores."

"Shit, Marlow, we don't know how long this is gonna take!" Ollie exclaimed.

"Relax…it'll all work out." Marlow stood up and offered Ollie his own chair.

"And what was that about deer season?" Ollie asked as he sat down and motioned Zach to come in.

"Oh, that…well, last year we went on a deer hunt down near Mobile and the governor had to be at a fundraiser in Montgomery by seven that night. It was cold and the bucks were chasing does hard. I killed a *huge* buck right before we had to leave. We didn't have time to clean it. He was *huge.* I didn't want to leave him, so I talked the governor into lettin' me load the whole thing, guts and all, in the helicopter and I'd get my trusties to clean it when we got home. Well, while we were flyin' a bunch of blood ran out and sprayed all over the underside of that white copter, and when we landed, the ground crew 'bout shit a purple snake thinkin' that gallons of hydraulic fluid had leaked out. He caught some grief about that, evidently. Son, that deer was *huge.*" Marlow laughed and stuffed his mouth.

Ollie stared at him. *Hunters are amazing. What they will do for a deer is unbelievable. Hell, it's insane.* Zach walked in, snapping him back to reality.

"Okay, okay, let's get organized." Ollie grabbed a sheet of paper and laid it next to a county map. He motioned for Zach to have a seat.

"No thanks, I'll stand." Zach couldn't be still.

Ollie nodded his understanding. "Here's what we know."

"The Tillman kid and Elizabeth went on a date and somehow ended up on this road. His family owns some land off that road…so that gives them a reason to be there…whatever they were doing…let's not worry about that right now. We found the boy, who had been beaten severely. There was another truck, but it didn't have a tag, and we confiscated the keys to it. Earlier, I'd been on a call to a hunting club located pretty close to all this. Some guy calls Mick Johnson from a cell phone telling him there's some kind of emergency, and when we get there we can't find him. The cell reception broke up, and we couldn't reestablish contact. We find some blood and later find a pistol. But we don't know anything else."

This was all news to Zach Beasley. He stood very still trying to process it. He was astonished.

"But get this: the guy who called Mick—his name's Jake Crosby—he's from West Point, Mississippi, and the woman they brought in tonight is his next-door neighbor."

"You think this Crosby fellow is behind all this?" Zach asked.

"No…I mean I don't know, but I don't think so. Marlow's deputy found the woman right after I had a phone conversation with Johnny Lee Glover. But he's definitely a person of *high* interest right now."

Marlow grunted when he heard Johnny Lee's name. "He's trouble with a capital T."

"We—R.C. and me—were standing at the truck I was telling y'all about and there's a radiophone that beeps and we hear a voice ask about a girl," Ollie continued, carefully choosing his words.

Zach's knees were getting weak. He couldn't believe all this.

"Well, we captured his name and number from Caller ID. It's Johnny Lee Glover. I called him from that phone and said I wanted to meet with him and that we wanted the girl back. I'd hoped to bargain and that he might betray his location. Of course, he played ignorant. Twenty minutes later, Marlow's deputy finds the woman from West Point at Johnny Lee's trailer. It may have been a coincidence, but I doubt it. There really aren't ever any coincidences."

Zach Beasley sat down and stared at the ceiling.

"You did the right thing, son," Marlow added, as much for Zach as for Ollie. "You've gotta push hunches to make things happen."

That made Ollie feel a little better about his gamble. He continued, looking at Zach, "So the call we overheard could have been referring to the Mississippi woman instead of your daughter. We just don't know."

Marlow stood up, anxious to offer his insight and wisdom. "What do you know about Crosby?"

Ollie answered, "Mick vouched for him. Said he was a good guy. We all know Mick...he's solid. I trust his judgment. Crosby's down here turkey hunting and I think—I'm not sure—but now I think he has a kid with him. At a camper where he was staying, there was a small sleeping bag and a stuffed animal and several books for young kids. I have an APB out on a vehicle that was seen at Johnny Lee's trailer just moments before we found the girl. It's a Tupelo registration."

Ollie looked up and saw several more of his off-duty deputies come in and talk to Martha. *Good, we need them,* Ollie thought. Behind him, Ollie could see the newspaper editor and two TV camera crews gathering.

"Your entourage is here, Marlow," Ollie said with a little attitude, referring to the media.

"They can help us, you know." He leaned forward and checked out who they were. "I'll handle the media for you. I have two more deputies that'll be here shortly."

"Mr. Beasley, I'm so sorry you had to hear all this but you need to know what we're up against…and it's mostly confusion. It just takes some time to sort through all the information," Ollie said compassionately.

Zach nodded, still deep in a trance, not taking his eyes off the ceiling.

"Zach, this is going to work out. You've got the best guys in west Alabama working on it, and the governor's personal helicopter will be here at dawn to help us search," Marlow added trying to reassure him.

Pointing at a map, Ollie commented, "This is the largest wilderness area in the county…miles of pine plantations and swamp. That's gonna make it tough to search…and we really don't know if that's where we need to be lookin'. But that's where we'll start. So, if y'all will excuse me, I need to call West Point to check out this Jake Crosby guy. Marlow, if you'll start laying out a search plan…don't forget your Tabasco." Ollie handed Marlow the small red bottle.

With that, Zach and Marlow walked out and shut Ollie's office door. Ollie stared at the chaos beginning in the outer room. He picked up the phone and dialed information.

Chapter 59

Lindsay Littlepage, assisted by Sumter County's only female deputy, Lakreshia Gibbons, tried to contact her husband, Scott. Lindsay called out his cell number to Lakreshia, who slowly dialed it. Once Lakreshia heard the first ring, she handed the phone to Lindsay.

Listening impatiently to the ringing, Lindsay started getting emotional. Finally she heard her husband answer sleepily, "Uh"—he cleared his throat—"hello?"

"Scott!...Scott!" She immediately started sobbing.

"Lindsay? Lindsay! What's the matter? Are you okay? Are the kids okay? Lindsay!" he said frantically. Scott had stayed out late gambling and drinking whiskey with several other pharmaceutical sales reps. His head was pounding.

When Lindsay heard her husband's voice, she couldn't speak. Lakreshia gently took the phone from her.

"Mr. Littlepage, I am Deputy Gibbons with the Sumter County Sheriff's Department, and we have your wife here in the hospital in Livingston. She's fine now. This is going to sound crazy, but we think she was kidnapped and somehow escaped."

"Kidnapped? Livingston? Alabama?" Scott was trying to force the thoughts to make sense.

"Yes, sir," the deputy responded.

"Is...is she okay?" Scott asked, sitting up and running his left hand through his hair.

"Yes, sir...I am looking at her right now. She's obviously tired and the doctors are checking her out."

"Wait...say all that again...I'm lost," Scott pleaded as he fumbled for the light on the nightstand.

"Sir, we don't have all the details. We do think that she was kidnapped sometime during the night. She escaped and was found by one of our deputies. We have her in the hospital and she is stable."

"Stable? She's okay?"

"Yes, sir."

"What about my kids!?"

"Apparently they were spending the night with some friends. We have officers checking that out...hold on...I think she can talk to you now—hang on."

"Scott, he said you killed somebody! Did you? What's going on? Who'd you kill? Please tell me you haven't killed somebody!" she begged, on the verge of hysterics.

Totally stunned by the head-on collision of events, Scott shook his head to try and make sense of Lindsay's babbling.

"Lindsay, I don't know what the hell you're talking about! I'm in Biloxi working. Who said that? I haven't killed anybody. Are you okay? This is crazy!" Scott exclaimed.

"Scott, please come get me. I'm scared," she pleaded.

"I will, honey. Don't be scared. Are you all right? What about the—"

"Yeah...yes, and the kids are safe, I'm sure. They spent the night with the Johnsons."

"Honey, I'm leaving right now, but it'll take me at least three hours to get there from Biloxi."

"Please hurry!"

"I'm on the way, baby," he promised. "Let me speak to the deputy again. I love you."

She handed the phone to Lakreshia and lay back down.

"Hello?" the officer said.

"Who kidnapped her?" Scott asked in disbelief.

"We don't know, sir." The deputy shrugged her shoulders.

"This is just crazy! Why?" Scott asked, obviously in shock.

"I don't know, sir, but we're working on getting answers to all these questions."

"Has she…has she been…was she…was she raped?"

"No, sir. There are no such indications," she replied and smiled kindly at Lindsay.

Scott's mind was whirling. "Hey, look, I have a friend, actually he's my next-door neighbor, who's at a hunting club ten miles or so from Livingston. His name's Jake Crosby, and the club's called the Bogue Chitto. I hunt there some with him. Can you have someone go out there and get him so he can stay with Lindsay? I'm sure he's at the camp house."

"Yes, sir. I'll see what I can do." Deputy Gibbons jotted down "Jake Crosby" in her notebook and took a stab at spelling "Bogue Chitto."

"Is there a number where I can call you back?" Scott asked. "I'm going to have a bunch of questions while I'm drivin'."

"Yes, sir." She gave Scott the hospital number and the sheriff's office number. He promised to be there as fast as he could. Scott hung up the phone and stared in disbelief at the hotel walls.

Lakreshia again smiled warmly at Lindsay and told her that her husband was on his way and had said to tell her that he loved her. Lindsay smiled weakly, closed her eyes, and allowed the Xanax to work its magic.

Lakreshia walked out and called Martha O'Brien with the details. When she mentioned the Jake Crosby connection, Martha immediately took the information to Ollie. At this point, Ollie believed Jake was one of the good guys, but he sure wanted to ask the man some questions. Ollie had just gotten off the phone with the sheriff's office in West Point. They really didn't know anything about Jake Crosby. They did know he had a perfectly clean record, and a deputy on duty knew Jake because Jake had coached his daughter's softball team two years earlier. The deputy didn't think Jake could be involved in anything this bizarre. West Point was dispatching units to the Johnsons' to check on the children and to the Littlepage and Crosby homes to investigate the kidnapping. The deputy promised to call him right back.

"Thank you, Miz Martha," Ollie said as he rubbed his head with both hands.

"You need anything, Sheriff?"

"Some fresh coffee please…if you don't mind."

"You got it." Martha turned to leave and stopped. "Do you think this Jake character kidnapped the woman from West Point?"

"I don't know what to think…common sense dictates we consider that angle, though," he responded.

"Nothing's ever as it seems; is it?"

"No, ma'am."

"I'll get your coffee; you're gonna need it."

Chapter 60

The head ICU nurse saw Tanner's right eye open slightly. He was blinking rapidly, trying to adjust to the bright lights. His left eye was swollen completely shut. She eased to his side, saying a few comforting words. When he seemed to relax a bit, she quietly left the room and paged Dr. Sarhan. She looked back into the room and noted that he had closed his eye.

The nurse walked across the hall to the waiting room to tell Mrs. Tillman that Tanner was waking and she would be allowed to see him soon. Olivia Beasley was there, wringing her hands. The two mothers hugged each other. The nurse's next duty was to call Martha O'Brien at the sheriff's office to alert her.

Dr. Sarhan walked very deliberately down the hall into the room and immediately checked the dilation in Tanner's right eye. "I am Doctor Sarhan. Tanner? You know where you are? What happened to you?"

Tanner's eye slowly rolled to the back of his head, then shut. Dr. Sarhan recognized the morphine fog in which Tanner's mind floated. "You been in bad accident. You serious injuries…but you be all right. You very lucky."

Tanner started to sit up and talk but couldn't. Dr. Sarhan placed both of his hands on Tanner's shoulders and gently forced him to lie still. Tanner was moaning. Dr. Sarhan looked up to check the morphine drip, then made a note on his chart. As soon as the doctor took his hand off him, Tanner tried to sit up again. He groped at the tube protruding from his mouth. Dr. Sarhan grabbed him. "Stop struggling, Tanner. You lie still…relax."

The doctor could clearly see the terror in Tanner's eye. "It's okay now. I promise. You safe. Nothing happen to you now," Dr. Sarhan explained in a soothing Indian accent.

Tanner tried to talk, but the tube down his throat prevented it. With his good eye he tried to communicate his urgency to the doctor. The doctor misinterpreted the look as pain, quickly ordering the nurse to increase the morphine drip. "Now!" he exclaimed.

As the nurse hurriedly approached she watched Tanner. Fifteen years as an ICU nurse had honed her clinical observation skills. She recognized Tanner's efforts.

"Dr. Sarhan, he's trying to speak!" She excitedly informed the doctor.

"What?" he replied looking up from the medical chart. "He can't talk. He is intubated."

"He sure is trying. Maybe he can write!" the nurse said as she rounded the bed, grabbed a notepad, and took a pen from the doctor's lab coat breast pocket. She placed the pen in Tanner's hand and wrapped his fingers around it. She guided his hand to the notepad.

"Write what you want, dear." She spoke slowly and deliberately. She could see Tanner's immediate relief. Dr. Sarhan also observed it.

Tanner was in a haze from the morphine, but all he could think about was Elizabeth. The image of her face was all he could see. He could hear her screaming. He fought to keep his mind clear. With great effort and concentration he finally scribbled Elizabeth's name then opened his eye wide with worry, waiting for the response.

"Elizabeth…he's asking about Elizabeth!" The nurse excitedly headed for the door. As she pushed it open, she saw Deputy Lakreshia Gibbons walking quickly toward the room.

"Lakreshia, come quickly! He just scribbled Elizabeth's name. He's asking about Elizabeth!"

Lakreshia knew they were searching for Elizabeth but didn't know any details. She rushed to Tanner's side. Dr. Sarhan, still concentrating on Tanner's injuries and pain level, reluctantly stepped back, out of her way.

Tanner had scribbled another note and was trying to give it to someone. She grabbed it and tried to read it.

"I can't read it," Lakreshia said in a frustrated tone, handing it to the nurse.

"I can't either," The nurse responded.

Lakreshia looked at him, concerned, and bluntly asked, "Where's Elizabeth? We can't find her. Tanner, where's Elizabeth? She's not at your Jeep."

Tanner's heart monitor started racing as he struggled to sit up. He was obviously very upset. He grabbed at the tube and the IV lines in his arms. He was trying with every fiber of his being to sit up when Dr. Sarhan pushed him back and ordered the nurse to immediately administer more sedative.

"Now!" he ordered. He watched her bypass the drip machine's settings, giving Tanner an immediate dose.

Tanner struggled to communicate. He couldn't speak. White-hot flashes of pain coursed through his body, taking away his breath. He couldn't make his hands move like he wanted. He could think clearly, but couldn't communicate.

"Everything okay. Pain will leave shortly." Dr. Sarhan said, not about to let the young man suffer.

In Tanner's mind, he was screaming *NO!* He couldn't keep his eye open. He wanted to find out more about Elizabeth! *Where was she! They had to find her!* The drugs were kicking in hard now. Everything became heavy and fuzzy—except for Elizabeth's image, which was crystal-clear.

Mrs. Tillman appeared in the edge of the door. Dr. Sarhan encouraged her to come in, thinking her presence might help calm Tanner.

Holding her hand over her mouth, she approached her son. Right behind her, Olivia Beasley came in, anxious to ask Tanner some questions.

Tanner could hear everything being said. "He not awake long," said Dr. Sarhan, stepping back to let the ladies get closer.

"Tanner, where's Elizabeth?" Mrs. Tillman asked.

Tanner's eye grew wider and then rolled back slightly. She could tell he wanted to talk but the morphine had a big grip on him.

"Tanner?" She asked, desperately trying to keep her emotions together. "Tanner?"

"He can't talk. He has tube. He in great pain."

"Yes...yes," Mrs. Tillman responded, trying to be upbeat, positive.

The nurse again handed Tanner the pen and replaced the notepad under his right hand.

"Tanner, can you write where Elizabeth is? There's a pen in your hand, sweetie. Just write down where she is. Tanner, are you with us?"

His eye rolled again. Mrs. Tillman thought he understood, but his hand never moved. Tanner couldn't stop the heavy curtain of drowsiness from being pulled closed. Elizabeth's image, every date, every kiss replayed in fast-forward. He silently screamed. The questions about Elizabeth hurt his soul. *No one knows where she is!*

"Tanner?! Please!" Olivia Beasley begged.

His hand slowly scribbled as everyone in the room watched intently. He desperately tried to write but couldn't.

"That's it, Tanner...just write it down!" his mother encouraged.

Tanner's hand twitched again, then his eye closed. It stayed closed.

"Sorry, ladies. He out now." Dr. Sarhan explained. His primary focus was on his patient.

"Who is Elizabeth?" Dr. Sarhan asked as an afterthought.

"She was with Tanner on a date, and now she's missing," Tanner's mother explained. "We don't have a clue where she is...the sheriff doesn't even know where to look." She began to sob.

"I see. I alert you when he wakes up," Dr. Sarhan said, preoccupied, looking down at Tanner's chart.

Dr. Sarhan had not been apprised of the circumstances surrounding Tanner's injuries. Had he been, he would not have ordered that last surge of morphine. He quietly left the room to search for Narcan to reverse the effects of the morphine. He didn't know if the hospital had any.

Tanner had heard every word.

Mrs. Tillman again covered her mouth while she looked at him. Her right hand brushed the hair over his forehead as tears streamed down her cheeks.

Olivia Beasley took the piece of paper but couldn't make out anything legible. *Maybe a "g" or a "9" and the second letter might be an "a,"* she thought. *Two letters...what were they?* She walked out of the room and stopped at the nurse's desk to study the scribbling. It didn't make any sense.

Chapter 61

A huge county map was spread on the table when Ollie walked in. Marlow had four Hale County deputies, three Sumter County deputies, the Sumter County game warden, and Zach Beasley all standing around the table. Ollie thanked everyone for being there, then quickly ran through the story, explaining in detail what they knew and what they theorized might have happened. He was careful not to paint a picture of Jake Crosby's innocence. The deputies were attentive, anxious. This was the rush for which they lived.

"What we want to do is contain this area around the gate, and then set up a perimeter that will stretch out to these points," Ollie explained, pointing to the map. "The good news is that there are only a few ways to exit the property by vehicle. The bad news is we have no idea if they are actually on it."

"That's a real problem," Marlow interjected. "And the guys we suspect are behind this, Johnny Lee Glover and crew, will damn sure be armed, and believe me, they are as crazy as car-struck dogs—really dangerous."

"That's right, so nobody try and be a hero. Get on the radio and get some backup, okay?" Ollie said, looked at each of them, then took a sip of coffee and continued. "We have a helicopter that will be here at daylight. That'll be a big help covering the area. Keep that in mind."

Ollie set his cup on the table, pulled out a chair, and sat down. Staring at each deputy again he said, "All right, everybody, before we make assignments, I wanna emphasize the importance of this search and ask that you stay away from the media. Don't let your excitement cloud your judgment or your training. There's an eighteen-year-old girl out there who needs us. Job One is to find her. Got it?"

Everyone nodded or said, "Yes, sir."

Ollie continued, "Miz Martha's prepared some fact sheets on Elizabeth. Grab one on your way out."

"Any questions?" Marlow interjected.

"It's turkey season...will there be other hunters in the area?" a deputy asked.

"I don't have a clue. It wouldn't surprise me," Ollie added.

"I vote we don't let 'em go in...if we run into any hunters wantin' to enter the property," the same deputy responded.

"Agreed. We don't need the added confusion," said Ollie. "Turn 'em around if any show up. But don't tell 'em anything."

The group nodded in unison.

"Good." Ollie continued, "One other thing: we just got word that Tanner Tillman woke up briefly; he couldn't speak, but when they asked where Elizabeth was, he scribbled what appeared to be a *G* and an *A* before he passed out again."

"That could mean 'gate,'" one deputy commented.

"And it could mean Gainesville," another added. "That's not but fifteen miles away."

"It could mean gang...or even garbage...you know the big dump is right up Highway Seventeen!" a deputy blurted excitedly.

"All true, but let's not let our imaginations run wild. This information is not really helpful at this point...it simply adds more confusion. I believe we will eventually determine that it means the gate," Ollie explained. He loved the group's enthusiasm but needed them to focus.

"Everyone knows R.C., right? He and Steve Tillman have gone to look around on the property where we believe the kids were tonight.

If we hear anything, we'll pass it along. I expect a report from them soon," Ollie added as he stood.

"One last thing…I have a man named Mick Johnson that may show up to help. He knows Crosby, and he knows the property, so let him through," Ollie explained, watching them all write down the name.

"Zach, do you have anything?" Ollie asked kindly.

This caught Zach by surprise. He wasn't prepared to talk. The group watched him with compassion. Ollie hoped to inspire the group with Zach's presence.

"Please find my daughter. Please find her and bring her home," he said with a quiver in his voice. The group was clearly touched by his emotion.

"All right, gentlemen. Here's what I want everyone to do." Ollie ran his hand over the map and began laying out his plan. The group listened to every word. Even Sheriff Marlow paid attention. For Ollie, it was like his football days when he would take over the defensive huddle and rally the team for a fourth-quarter, red-zone stand.

Chapter 62

Jake stopped to check his map when they came up to an intersection of two logging roads. He was out of breath. He knelt down, letting Katy slide off his back. He hid the light as he got his bearings. He now knew for certain where they were. The field was not very far. He clicked off the light and looked at the girls.

Elizabeth was trying to catch her breath. Katy simply studied Elizabeth.

"Okay, ladies, we don't have much farther. There's a perfect place for us to hide and rest. Can y'all make it for ten more minutes?" he whispered.

They both nodded. Jake could tell Elizabeth was numb, mentally and physically. Katy was subdued but definitely more upbeat since her focus and concerns were now on Elizabeth. *Thank God she doesn't understand how serious all this is,* Jake thought. He gently rubbed the top of her head reassuringly before he picked her up, grunting lightly.

Jake consciously thought about where to walk in an effort to leave the least amount of tracks. He even thought of splitting up, but that was no good. Jake didn't want the guys chasing Elizabeth by herself and they might not ever be able to get back together. No, they were a group and needed to stay a group, he decided. He had to take care of her as well. *It's my fault she's in this mess.* Jake decided to stay on this higher ground, in the pines, and hope for the best as he made his way toward the field.

"Katy, you've turned into a chunk. How much do you weigh, girl?" he whispered, readjusting her weight.

"Only fifty-two pounds, Dad. Less than the dog," she whispered back.

"I think you've put on some weight in the last few hours," he quietly grunted.

"Dad, I'll walk…let me walk."

"No, no. It's muddy and there are sharp sticks and pine cones. This is better, trust me. I'm fine. Just don't ever let me forget your boots again, okay?"

"Okay," she giggled.

"You still have Cheddar?"

"Oh, yeah." She held the Beanie Baby in front of his eyes, temporarily blocking his vision.

"Good. I don't wanna have to go back and look for him somewhere."

"And I'd make you," Katy said smartly, momentarily forgetting their circumstances.

"I know you would," Jake replied.

She grabbed his head and put her lips right next to his ear and said, "I'm gonna give him to Elizabeth when we get outta here. He's a good-luck charm. I think she needs some good luck."

"That's a great idea," he whispered as he snaked his way through the dense trees. Glancing over his shoulder, he could see Elizabeth with her crude crutch and that the cushion was still on the bottom of the gun barrel.

Jake tried to think through potential outcomes to their situation. He wondered if Mick had understood his call for help. He reached into his vest for his cell phone, found it and punched a key to light it. *No Service. Damn it,* he thought. He hated cell phones. He jammed it back in his pocket and kept walking. *I should've tried to call back from that same spot,* he thought, cursing himself. *I panicked.* Even if Mick didn't hear enough of Jake's call to alert the authorities, surely some-body would miss Elizabeth and her boyfriend. *They aren't old enough to stay out all night. Would their folks even know where to look? Probably not,* he realized. *Just keep walking; it'll come to you,* he told himself.

Chapter 63

Scott Littlepage called the bell captain and had his Toyota Land Cruiser brought up from the parking garage. He was standing outside waiting when it arrived. Throwing the luggage in the back, he left the Beau Rivage Resort & Casino without even checking out. He was in shock, stunned. *Kidnapped?* he wondered. He still had too much whiskey in his system.

Plugging his cell phone into the cigarette lighter, he thought about whom he should call. *I need to check on the kids, I should try Jake, and I need to call the hospital back to check on Lindsay. I probably oughta call Lindsay's mother, too – but what do I tell her? I'll wait until I know more before I call her.*

"This is just un-freakin'-believable! Kidnapped?" he said aloud as he clicked on the emergency flashers and punched the gas. Heading west on Interstate 10, Scott drove as fast as he ever had in his life. He then turned north on Highway 49 and into the rolling timberlands of southern Mississippi. He'd be there in a few hours. If he got stopped, he could explain—they could verify his story—he prayed.

After calling information for the number, Scott confirmed that his kids were safe and sound asleep. He apologized, without explaining, for calling at this ungodly hour. *That's a relief.* Then he dialed Jake's cell number from his phone book. "Come on, Jake," he said aloud, hoping that he had his cell with him in the camper. "The subscriber you have called has traveled out of the calling area. Please try your call again later," the automated message replied. "Shit," Scott said, remembering that cell service at the hunting camp sucked. He thought for a second, then dialed the Crosby house.

"Hello?" Morgan replied groggily after four rings.

"Morgan, this is Scott…is Jake there?"

"No…no…he and Katy went hunting. What time is it?" she replied as she sat up in the bed.

"Morgan, Lindsay was kidnapped. I know this sounds crazy, but I just got a call and she's in the hospital in Livingston…she somehow got away!"

"What? Who called you?" she asked, jolted awake.

"The Sumter County Sheriff's office. I don't know any details. I'm on my way to the hospital. I was in Biloxi when they called me."

"You?…what?…she?…Where are your kids?"

"They spent the night with some friends. They're safe," he replied. "I may need you to pick them up this morning."

"Sure. What the…I…just…hang on. I think there's someone outside," she explained.

Morgan had suddenly become aware that Scout was barking more excitedly than usual. She heard a vehicle pulling up in their driveway and saw the flash of lights through the bedroom window.

"Morgan? They kidnapped her from our house, so be careful. I'm gonna try and catch up with Jake and get him to go to the hospital until I can get there."

"What? Scott, I'm sorry…I didn't hear what you said…hold on…someone just drove up," Morgan replied, trying to figure out just what was going on.

"Morgan! They kidnapped her from our house! Be careful!" he screamed, but she didn't hear him.

Morgan was already setting down the phone. "Hold on!" she yelled, running to a window at the front of the house.

Morgan saw two cars in her driveway. Scout was going wild,

barking as fast as she could. *What's going on?!* she thought. Running back into the bedroom, she reached under the mattress and grabbed Jake's pistol. She pulled the gun from its holster. It felt alien. She didn't know if it was loaded or even how to check.

A sudden loud banging came from the front door. She jumped and screamed. She could hear voices, but Scout's barking was so intense she couldn't understand their words. She quickly grabbed her robe, wrapping it around herself. She peeked around the corner of the bedroom door. Looking down the hall, she could see through the leaded-glass front door. Someone was standing in the shadows. Holding the pistol level in front of her, she crept down the hallway, sliding along the wall. As she got to the foyer, she reached around the corner and flipped on the front porch lights.

"Sheriff's Department! Don't shoot!" the deputies yelled, holding up their badges and looking at the pistol pointing at them.

"Please, put the gun down!" they shouted. "Put it down, ma'am!" they screamed with their hands on their holstered pistols. Scout was in a total frenzy.

"Ma'am...we're from the sheriff's office, and we need to ask you some questions!" one deputy yelled over the dog's barking. He watched her lower the pistol.

Reaching for the deadbolt, Morgan took a deep breath and unlocked it.

"Ma'am, can we come in please?" the deputy asked, keeping one eye on the fat black Lab growling at his side.

She looked at both of them, recognizing the one furthest away. His daughter had been on one of Katy's softball teams.

"Come in...what's going on?" she replied. "Scout, hush...Scout!" Reaching out to reassure her with a head rub, "Good girl," she said and then stepped back to allow the deputies inside.

The two deputies were clearly relieved to be out of Scout's reach. They took off their hats and apologized for scaring her.

"Mrs. Crosby, would you mind doing something with that pistol? It makes us real nervous," asked the tall deputy—the one she knew.

"I...I'm sorry. I just didn't have a clue what was going on...and still don't." She placed the pistol on a shelf in the bookcase, next to Jake's collection of African hunting novels.

"Where's Jake right now?" the tallest one asked.

"He's turkey huntin'. He and my daughter—Katy—left last night. Why?" she asked, sitting down on the leather ottoman.

"I can see he hunts," the deputy said, looking around at the mounts.

"What's goin' on. Why are you here? This is weird. I just got a call from Scott Littlepage saying Lindsay had been kidnapped," she added, furrowing her brow.

The deputies looked at each other. *So much for surprises,* they thought.

"Yes, ma'am, we have a unit over there right now. How would you describe Jake's relationship with Mrs. Littlepage?"

"Kidnapped? Are you serious? This is like a bad dream."

"Yes ma'am. Now, how would you describe their relationship?"

"Huh? Relationship? Um...he...well...she's our next-door neighbor. I think she aggravates him some, or more like he aggravates her. She's always complaining about something. You know, typical neighbor stuff. Jake comes and goes at all hours, and she complains about him waking her up, but wait...I don't understand what this has to do with anything," Morgan rambled.

"We don't either. We do know that she was kidnapped tonight and somehow got away from her abductors. She was rescued by a deputy in Sumter County, Alabama."

"Really kidnapped?"

"Yes, ma'am."

"Do you think she would have gone to the hunting club with Jake for any reason?" the short pudgy deputy asked, watching her body language.

The thought had never crossed Morgan's mind and then she quickly dismissed it. Shaking her head, she decreed, "No. Absolutely not. I know my husband and I know her. No. No way."

Morgan didn't know exactly where Jake was, and before tonight she had never heard of Sumter County. She looked blankly at the deputies, "Sumter County…and that's in Alabama, right?"

"Isn't that where your husband hunts?" asked the stocky one, with no small amount of derision.

"I don't know. Maybe…it's a few hours from here. Scott's in the same hunting club. Crap, I still have him on the phone!" She ran back to the bedroom and grabbed the phone. The line was disconnected. "He hung up," she called to the deputies.

Walking back down the hallway with the portable phone in hand, she said, "This is crazy. You think Jake kidnapped her? You're crazy. What about Lindsay, is she all right?"

"Yes, ma'am, she is. We know something has occurred, we can't say what exactly. We're just trying to gather information for the sheriff down there."

"Let me try Jake." She dialed while they studied her. The phone rang and she stared at them. "He's out of the coverage area…but I never can call him when he's down there. Jake says it's pretty much a dead cell area."

"Look, we have a lot to do. We need to go and secure the Littlepages' residence. We need you to help. If Jake calls, we need to talk to him immediately, okay?" The tall deputy handed her his card.

"Yes, sure, of course. Whatever I can do. I can't believe this has happened!" she exclaimed. "So, Jake's *not* at the camp house?"

"No, ma'am, and we sure wanna talk to him. I'm sure you do too," said Chubby with a sneer.

"What time is it?" she asked, glancing at the clock on the wall. "He may already be in the woods hunting…he leaves so early…I just don't know what—"

"That's right. So don't jump to any conclusions," the friendly deputy responded.

"Jump to any conclusions?! You tell me my neighbor has been kidnapped, she turns up in Wherever, Alabama, where my husband and my daughter are hunting, and you're asking questions about him! You can't find him! What am I *supposed* to think?" she said, exasperated.

"Please, Mrs. Crosby, calm down. We don't know anything, and we aren't suggesting anything. I'm sure you're right. He and your daughter are probably getting ready to set up on an old gobbler right now as we speak."

"It's Sumter County, Alabama," said the fat deputy.

"Whatever," she responded, folding her arms. She was beginning to fume. "And what about Tate Newsom?"

"Who?" the tall deputy asked curiously.

"Tate Newsom…he lives in Columbus. He's down there with them."

The deputies looked at each other. They didn't know what to say. This was the first they heard of Tate Newsom.

"I'm calling his wife…maybe she's heard from him," Morgan replied, grabbing the cordless telephone. She walked into the kitchen to look in the phone book for his number.

Morgan came back into the den with the phone next to her ear. She watched the deputies' faces while the phone rang. She rubbed her face with her free hand.

"Tate?" she said, surprised. "Tate, this is Morgan Crosby, I thought you went huntin' with Jake?" she asked and then listened. The two deputies tried in vain to overhear his reply.

"Okay. Listen. Something terrible has happened. Lindsay Littlepage was kidnapped and found down near y'all's huntin' camp. They can't find Jake, and Katy is with him…Yes, I swear! Tate, I need you to come get me, we've got to go find Katy and Jake."

"Whoa, no way…we can't let…I need to speak to him," the tall deputy immediately interrupted. Morgan handed him the phone.

"Mr. Newsom, I'm Deputy Franks of Clay County. I really need to talk to you in person. Please, this is very important. Can you come over here? Yes, sir. How fast can you be here? Thank you, sir." And with that he handed the phone back to Morgan.

"Tate, please hurry," she pleaded and hung up.

"Why didn't he go hunting?" the heavy deputy asked.

"He said he got a 'better offer.' I think that's man code for sex," Morgan explained, rolling her eyes. "He just got married."

"I'm sorry for all this, but please stay around here and keep your phone line open. Please call us immediately if you hear from Jake. We need to call in to report and make sure the Littlepages' house is secure. We'll be back before Mr. Newsom gets here," Deputy Franks said compassionately.

"Sure," she replied, not really knowing what else to say. "I'll do whatever you need me to. Can I come over there?" She asked looking out the window at all the flashing lights from the police cars that had pulled into the Littlepages'.

"There's nothin' to see. Stay here by the phone," snapped Pudgy.

"Okay…fine," she replied, sitting on the edge of the chair, nervously running her hands through her hair.

"Thank you, ma'am. We'll be right back," Deputy Franks replied as he moved toward the front door.

Scout started barking again as the door opened. Morgan yelled, "Hush, Scout! Get in here." The deputies stepped back to let Scout in, then left as fast as they could.

Morgan jumped at the phone ringing in her hand. She answered it on the first ring. It was Scott Littlepage again. He was a basket case. Morgan promised to take care of their kids and explained the little that she learned from the deputies and the Tate Newsom situation. Scott promised to call back if he learned anything new.

"Hurry up, Scott. They can't find Jake, and Katy's with him," she pleaded.

"He's probably already in the woods waitin' on daylight," he said trying to reassure her.

"I hope so," Morgan said, and then hung up.

Morgan sat down and stared at the walls, trying to clear her thoughts. What should she do? She needed to talk to Jake, and she wanted Katy safely tucked in her own bed. There was no way Jake could be involved in this. As she looked around the "trophy room" she suddenly, for the first time in several years, missed Jake.

CHAPTER 64

R.C. and Steve Tillman drove silently along the Dummy Line. R.C. checked the handheld radio once to make certain it was working properly. Tillman slowed the Jeep.

"What the heck's that?" Tillman asked, the headlights illuminating something odd-looking in the middle of the road.

"I don't know. Let's check it out," R.C. replied.

Tillman stopped ten feet in front of the unknown object. They both got out and slowly walked toward it.

"It's a fleece jacket," R.C. said as he laid down the radio on a hard, dry spot and picked up the jacket by the edge of a sleeve. "Oh shit, it's bloody and almost ripped in two!" he blurted out.

"Oh, my God! How can you rip fleece?" Tillman exclaimed, his eyes wide from fear.

R.C. held it to his nose and breathed deeply. "It smells of perfume...my favorite ex-girlfriend wears this brand."

"It's Elizabeth's," Tillman groaned. "It's her cheerleading jacket," he said in shock. They both stared at each other. R.C. looked around and noticed a shooting house on the side of the road. The door was wide open. As he slowly approached it, with one hand on his holstered pistol, the other holding a Maglight, he saw blood on the third and fourth steps. R.C. let out a deep breath.

"What do you think this means?" asked Tillman, staring at the blood.

"I hope we aren't too late. I mean...I hope whoever has Elizabeth didn't leave in that truck when we went back to town," R.C. said, staring at the old wooden structure. "We better keep going just to be sure," he added, nodding down the Dummy Line into the darkness.

Tillman agreed. R.C. carefully laid the jacket on the back seat while Tillman put the Jeep in gear and revved the engine. R.C. began searching for the handheld radio as Tillman let out the clutch and began rolling. They both heard a plastic crunch. Tillman stopped. R.C. immediately knew what it was.

"Shit! Ollie's gonna kill me!" R.C. cried out.

"What was it?" Tillman asked, puzzled.

"The radio," R.C. said glumly as he slid out of the Jeep. He reached under it. He held up the flattened radio for Tillman to see and got back in. "Drive on…we gotta find her."

CHAPTER 65

In the moonlight, Jake could make out Little Buck Field. It looked to be about two hundred yards long and about seventy-five yards wide. Without using the flashlight, he searched in vain for the telltale outline of the shooting house. He waited for Elizabeth to catch up, then bent over close to her ear.

"You two stay here for just a second. I'm gonna walk down this field to look for something," he said as he slid Katy off of his shoulders. He stretched as he stood up.

"Dad…no!" Katy cried.

"Katy, listen. I'm not even gonna be out of sight…just right down there," he said, pointing toward the end of the field. "I'll be right back. I promise. Okay?"

"Okay," she replied.

Jake looked at each of the girls, saying, "Y'all have to be real quiet. Not a word, okay? Just sit right here and don't move. I'll be right back."

The girls nodded. He turned to walk down the field. His neck and shoulders were aching, but they had made it. The shooting house, if he could find it, would be their sanctuary until daylight and help arrived. Jake realized he had walked out into the field without thinking and was probably leaving footprints. The clover was thick and would make it tough to follow his tracks. Tough, but not impossible. He moved back to the field's edge.

The shooting house wasn't on the east side of the field. He had started up the west side when he saw it. *Yes!* he said to himself and ran back to the girls.

"Come on. I found it!" he said excitedly. "Let's go."

Jake grabbed Katy and helped her climb up his back. Her arms squeezed around his neck. He could make it for two more minutes, he thought. Elizabeth struggled to keep up with them. The shooting house was about fifteen feet off the ground and appeared to be large enough for the three of them. It was made of plywood and had a wooden ladder leading up to it. It was just what he wanted.

"No!" Elizabeth suddenly blurted out when she caught up.

Jake was startled. "What? What's wrong?" Trying to keep his voice low.

"No…he caught me in one of these!" she said staring up at it.

"Elizabeth, I have a gun. I can protect us. It's okay. Everything's gonna be okay," he said reassuringly.

"No…no. I can't."

"Listen to me, Elizabeth. It's the safest place we've got. I can protect us."

Katy put an arm around Elizabeth and said reassuringly, "Elizabeth, we'll protect you."

Elizabeth looked at Jake and then at Katy. She closed her eyes and took a deep breath. "All right," she said, her voice weak and trailing off. She squeezed her eyes shut.

Jake could only imagine what she was trying to block out of her mind. He put his hand on her shoulder and said, "You're safe now."

"Okay, girls, let me check it out first," he said, and he started climbing up the ladder. The door opened easily. He briefly shined his light inside. Remnants of a bird's nest were on the floor, along with a few empty aluminum cans and a folding chair. There was a ten-inch-high opening all the way around the box for a hunter to see and shoot through. Jake quickly climbed back down.

"Katy, climb up and get in the far corner," Jake said quietly.

"Yes, sir."

"I don't know if I can climb," Elizabeth said dolefully. "I can hardly stand."

Jake thought for a second. He took a hard look at her. He figured she weighed maybe a hundred pounds. He leaned the shotgun against the legs of the shooting house and with no warning bent over and picked her up like a sack of seed. "I'll carry you up."

"Hang on," he said. She was heavier than he had thought, but he felt like he could do it. One step at a time, he went up the ladder. Elizabeth was hanging almost upside-down, but she trusted Jake and held on tightly. As they neared the top he was straining to balance and hold onto her.

At the top step he stopped, "Elizabeth, ease your feet down and try to stand up. You can crawl in from here."

"Be careful, Elizabeth," Katy said, grabbing the sleeve of her shirt to help pull her in.

After some straining and twisting, Elizabeth slowly slid into the house, crawled to a corner, and sat with her legs out in front of her.

Once she was safely inside, Jake climbed down. He quickly grabbed the shotgun and cut off the parachute cord holding the cushion in place. He reached in his vest, grabbed the two remaining shotguns shells, and quietly loaded them into his gun. He worked the pump action, feeding one into the chamber. He checked the safety and took a deep breath. He searched the darkness for their stalker and then looked up the ladder at his sanctuary.

As Jake reached the top of the ladder, he could see the girls each sitting in a corner. He crawled inside, latched the door, and sat on the floor. There wasn't room for another person inside the box. For the first time in several hours Jake felt somewhat safe.

"Turn the flashlight on, Dad." Katy whispered.

"No, baby, we need to keep it off so nobody will see us."

"But Elizabeth's shaking," Katy said caringly.

Jake had been so preoccupied with getting himself settled, he hadn't noticed.

"Elizabeth, we're safe now. Try to relax and rest. We're okay," Jake said with as much confidence as he could muster.

Jake knew she had been traumatized, but he didn't know what else he could do for her. She couldn't walk much further, and this shooting house was safe and dry. He hit the light button on his Timex: 4:43. *Another hour or so and daylight'll be breakin'.*

"All right now, y'all close your eyes and rest. I'll be the lookout," Jake explained as he leaned back. "Here's a cushion…who needs it?"

"Give it to Elizabeth, Dad." Katy said.

Jake handed her the cushion, and she thanked Katy. *Elizabeth's settling down some,* Jake thought as he leaned back against the wall to consider what daylight would bring. It was silent outside. Inside everybody rested.

CHAPTER 66

Martha O'Brien was draining another cup of coffee when a call came in from the Clay County, Mississippi, Sheriff's Department. Holding her hand over the receiver, she whistled loudly. Ollie looked up from the map. She frantically pointed at the phone. Ollie quickly went into his office to take the call. Sheriff Marlow grinned at Martha's enthusiasm—it was time to update the media. Marlow went to the restroom to check his hair and then to gather the media outside.

"Sheriff Landrum," said Ollie when he picked up the telephone.

"Sheriff, we have been to the Littlepages' house. We found the telephone lines cut, the glass on their front door broken by a pro, and there's evidence of a struggle in the master bedroom. Sometime later this morning, we'll have a crew there to dust for prints. That's about it," the officer explained.

"Thank you. What about the Crosbys?"

"As you know, they live right next door...actually, it's about a hundred and fifty yards away. The Crosby lady was talking on the phone to Scott Littlepage when we arrived. She was obviously shocked by what all was going on."

"Had she spoken to her husband?"

"No. She tried to call him while we were there. He's at his hunting club with their nine-year-old daughter. Turkey huntin'."

That confirmed Ollie's suspicions. This was getting worse. *A nine-year-old little girl,* Ollie thought and grunted his displeasure into the phone.

"Both families are solid members of the community. They have never had any issues at all."

"Yeah, I understand...but there's got to be a connection somehow."

"I understand that Scott Littlepage is en route, but it will be a few hours before he arrives."

"That's right. I need you to do something for me. Don't let Mrs. Crosby come down here yet...she'll probably want to, but don't let her. Tell her that we need her at home, in case her husband calls. I have my hands full as it is, and she'll do us more good staying at home. I'll keep you informed. What's your cell phone number?"

Ollie promised to keep the officer up to speed and hung up, more worried than ever. *I've got to notify everyone that there's a child involved. Involved in what, though? I don't have a clue what's really goin' on. I need to talk to R.C. to see what they've found.*

"Miz Martha?"

"Yes, Sheriff."

"Please get R.C. on the radio for me."

Ollie leaned back in his chair. This was a disaster. He jotted down the details for Martha to relay to the officers in the field. He would also ask her for the latest on the APB for the Tupelo fellow. After checking the accuracy of the note, he walked to the front of the office and gave it to Martha.

"Make sure everyone gets this info please."

"Yes, sir. I can't raise R.C. on the radio. I know he's on the handheld. He may be down in a low spot or something."

"Keep tryin'." Ollie thought about this for a second and decided not to worry about R.C. right now. There would be no simple explanation for his not returning the radio call. R.C. always had the most outlandish excuses.

Ollie went back to his office to call Mick Johnson. Mick answered on the third ring.

"It's okay. I wasn't sleeping," Mick said in response to Ollie's apology for calling so early in the morning. "I was just puttin' my boots on to go huntin'. I overslept. Any word on Jake?" Mick continued.

"Mick, there may be more to the phone call you received than we thought. I may need your help searching. Elizabeth Beasley, an eighteen-year-old girl from around here, is missing and a lady from West Point named Littlepage was found out in the county. She'd been kidnapped."

"Littlepage? I've met Scott Littlepage. Jake introduced me to him—he's in the same club!"

"It was his wife who was abducted, but she escaped. It's all really confusing. Can you come down here?"

"Sure. I'll be right there, Sheriff," Mick replied.

"Thanks." Ollie hung up and stared at the phone. He pressed Martha's extension.

"Have you heard from R.C.?"

"No, sir."

"Damn."

Ollie looked up when he heard the front door open. Sheriff Marlow came in laughing loudly about something.

"Hey, Ollie, we need a podium. Can someone from the college here in town bring one over?"

"We don't need a podium. We need to find some missing girls!" Ollie fumed, then looked at Zach Beasley and back at Marlow. Ollie really wanted to punch Marlow in the throat.

"*Girls?* As in plural?"

"Yes. I just found out for sure that Jake Crosby, the guy from the hunting club, has his nine-year-old daughter with him."

"Jeez um...well, that helicopter will be here in an hour. That's our best hope. By the way, CNN and FOX are sending crews."

"What? Why?" Ollie asked incredulously. He could understand the local media's interest, but CNN?

"Well, since the governor's helicopter is being used for the search, they picked up on it."

Ollie glared at Marlow, then walked away.

Before he went into his office, he stopped and turned. "Marlow, it's way more important to rescue those kids than it is to reelect the governor."

Ollie couldn't believe he had said it. But he had. He'd just blurted it out. He let out a deep breath, turned around, walked into his office, and slammed the door.

Marlow didn't know what to say. He glanced furtively around the room. Everybody turned away to act busy. His face flushed red with anger. He decided to go update the media, saying defiantly, to no one in particular, "Obviously, nobody around here understands what it takes to be a twenty-first-century law enforcement officer."

CHAPTER 67

The helicopter pilot, retired Army Captain Joe Wilson, arrived at Dannelly Field in Montgomery, Alabama, forty-five minutes after receiving the call. The hangar was void of any personnel who could assist him in preparing for the flight. If Jeffrey, his ground crew, did not arrive soon, he would have to do it all himself. This life was almost as bad as being a corporate pilot but not as dreadful as being a flight instructor. Wilson had retired three years earlier as a helicopter pilot instructor at Fort Rucker, Alabama. The current governor, a close friend, had hired him immediately to pilot his new Bell Ranger. It was state-of-the-art, with lots of luxuries. Since it could land almost anywhere, it was perfect for hopping to events all over the region.

Captain Wilson knew this call was much more important than flying the governor and his kids to the beach. He wasn't a fan of Sheriff Marlow, because of the deer incident a few years ago, but he craved a crisis. Wilson was military to the core and he was bored with civilian flying.

"Come on, Jeffrey. Where the hell are you? Get your ass moving," Wilson said aloud to no one as he loosened the tie-down straps, then climbed in. The bird was full of fuel. He checked all the instruments and electronics. Finally, he sat down to study the flight map to Livingston. *Due west, basically,* he noted. *Should be easy.* He punched the coordinates into the GPS. *Simple.*

"Jeffrey, you incompetent, worthless piece of....," Wilson muttered as he fired up the Ranger and the rotors slowly started turning. He needed someone to know his flight plan, and it never hurt to have a second set of eyes look over everything. He tightened the chin strap on his helmet and buckled himself to the seat. When he looked up, Jeffrey was running toward him, his hair flying in the wind of the rotors.

"Whaddaya want me to do?" he yelled.

"File a flight plan to Livingston, Alabama! Do a quick visual! Hurry up!" he yelled back.

Jeffery ran around the machine and looked at everything in thirty seconds. Wilson just shook his head. *What kind of inspection was that? This kid would never make it in the military. Screw it. It'll have to do.* When Jeffrey got back to the window, he gave him the thumbs up sign.

"File that flight plan, now. I'll be doing search and rescue operations, so don't let them call me back for any bullshit!"

"Yes, sir!" Jeffrey mouthed with a mock salute, crouching as he backed away from the bird.

The powerful helicopter revved up as Wilson did one last quick instrument check. He gave a thumbs up and slowly lifted off the ground. He felt more alive than he had in twenty years. *Finally a worthwhile mission.*

Jeffrey stood in the rotor wash wondering why he'd had to get out of bed so early on his day off.

Chapter 68

Reese was on his hands and knees trying to discern the tracks in the pine needles. Most of the time the trail was obvious. The recent rain helped. The frequent logging roads crisscrossing the property also assisted him. Twice he had lost the trail in the thick pines, to pick it back up again once his quarry hit the logging roads.

Reese stood, stretched his back, and looked at his watch. He had about an hour and a half until daylight. He leaned his rifle against a giant oak tree and retrieved Johnny Lee's radiophone from his pocket.

Beep-beep. "Yo," he whispered.

Beep-beep. "I'm here...but dude, the cops are all over me, man."

Beep-beep. "Where are you?"

Beep-beep. "I'm south of Livingston a few miles. I finally shook the deputy off my tail. This thing's way too dangerous for me, man."

Beep-beep. "Look, I need you bad. There's an old road on Seventeen around mile marker one-fifty-four called Brown Chapel Road. It's pretty easy to find. Go hide there. Wait for me to beep you. We'll only be a few miles apart."

Beep-beep. "Brown Chapel Road at mile one-fifty-four. Got it. Hurry up, dude, we gotta get the hell outta here before daylight."

Beep-beep. "I know...just hang on, bro."

Reese folded the phone and stuck it in his pocket. He knelt back down to search for the trail. He picked it up and, like a bloodhound, followed the footprints twenty-five solid minutes without letting up. He knew he was getting close. Once, when he crossed a small creek, Reese could easily see the damp leaves where they had stepped and the mud had not settled back down in the still waters.

Reese quit using the flashlight, depending on his hearing as much as his eyes. At the edge of a big field, Reese stood silently to listen. A deer was snorting off in the woods ahead of him, maybe three hundred yards away. Something had startled it. Reese blew out a breath to check the wind—to determine whether the deer could possibly smell him. Just as he thought, the wind was blowing his scent away from the alarmed deer. *There was no way that deer smelled me. Johnny Lee's killer musta spooked it.* Reese's prey was closer than he expected.

Chapter 69

Sitting in total darkness, Jake and the girls had been silent for twenty minutes. Katy was tired but couldn't sleep. She had laid her head in Jake's lap, and he was gently rubbing her back. Elizabeth occasionally sobbed, wiping her nose on her shirt-sleeve. Jake was exhausted. His adrenaline rush was starting to play out, making his muscles ache. Every few minutes he leaned up without disturbing Katy to look out the shooting slits—each time silently praying he wouldn't see anything.

"Dad, if you could go anyplace in the whole world, where would you wanna go?" Katy whispered.

"You mean besides *home* right this minute? I don't know…there's a lot I've always wanted to do…hunt Africa for sure, Canada maybe, and stay at this castle called Banff. It's near a huge lake called Lake Louise—I think Mom would like that, too. What about you?"

"I'd like to meet Mary Kate and Ashley and go horseback riding. They've got a stable, you know."

"That sounds like fun," he replied, stroking her hair.

"What about you, Elizabeth?" Katy whispered.

Silence.

Finally, Elizabeth quietly answered, "Actually, this is gonna sound crazy, but I think…I wanna go to Auburn this fall so I can be with my boyfriend, Tanner."

"Why's that crazy?" Jake asked.

"Yeah?" Katy wondered.

"Well, my dad's a huge Alabama fan, and he'd probably disown me if he knew I was even *thinking* of going to Auburn. My mom wants me to go the University of Virginia—Dad hates that, but he finally agreed to it."

Jake laughed quietly, remembering the tough decisions facing high school grads. *Had it really been twenty years ago that he was having the same anxieties?* he thought. *These decisions will affect the rest of their lives.*

"Just take your time. Think everything through. You've got the rest of your life to be an adult."

"I'm serious. Until tonight, I…I never really knew what I wanted. But now I do. Tanner was fighting for my life. I could see how scared he was…and he was scared for me." She added, "Now I realize how much…how much I love him." The words were barely out of her mouth before she broke down sobbing again.

This serious tone hung in the air. Jake rubbed Katy's back. He was about to tell Elizabeth that life was too short, and too long, not to do what *she* wanted when Katy screamed, "AAAAAHHH! There's a spider on me!" as she kicked her legs. "Get it off!"

Jake put his hand over her mouth, a split-second too slow. The scream pierced the darkness. Katy was deathly afraid of spiders. Jake tried to calm her and keep her quiet. Finally, he clicked on the flashlight.

"Where is it?" he whispered, agitated.

"It was on my leg. I could feel it!"

"Katy, be quiet…we have to be quiet," Jake whispered.

He saw a small brown wood roach and quickly brushed it off her leg, then crushed it with his boot. He immediately clicked off the flashlight and was about to tell Katy not to scream anymore when wood chips flew through the air and a loud whacking sound enveloped the box, followed instantly by the booming report from a high-powered rifle.

"Get down! Is anyone hurt!?" he screamed, quickly lying on top of Katy. Jake rubbed his hands all over Katy. He didn't feel anything that felt like a bullet wound. His heart was pounding.

"No!" Elizabeth answered immediately. She was covered in tiny wood splinters.

"Katy, are you hurt?!"

"No! What was that?! Dad, I'm scared!"

Jake burst open the door. "Come on—we've gotta get out!" Grabbing Katy around the waist, he started down the ladder. When he was five feet from the ground he slid her down his body, held on to her arms, then dropped her. Katy grunted when she hit the ground and stood up quickly. Immediately he was back up the ladder. He reached in and grabbed the shotgun, putting it over his shoulder. Elizabeth was waiting for help.

"Here, lean out over my shoulder. I'll carry you down. Hurry up!" he yelled.

Another shot whizzed by, striking the wood just above their heads—*KABAM!* The thundering report was almost instantaneous. Jake hesitated for a fraction of a second.

"Dad, what's going on!?" Katy yelled.

The sound of Katy's voice snapped Jake back to reality. Darkness was Jake's only ally. He could tell the shots were at least two hundred yards away and knew it would be hard to hit a specific target in the dark. *We gotta get into the woods fast,* he thought.

When he hit the ground, he grabbed Katy and threw her over his left shoulder. He had Katy on one shoulder, Elizabeth on the other. The two of them were too heavy to run with, so he settled into a slow, awkward trot. Jake was really straining under the load and was scared to death. He was making a significant amount of noise plowing through the thick brush, but he had no other options. "Shit!" he exclaimed, huffing and puffing his way through the woods. He tried to look behind him several times, but couldn't. He couldn't see or hear anything.

Slowly the realization hit him that he was going to have to be proactive if they were to survive. These guys were only a few hundred yards behind them with a high-powered rifle. They had been tracking him every step of the way. Jake could only think of one option, and he didn't much like it. Jake prayed that his tactic would work.

A couple of hundred yards behind Jake and the girls, Reese was struggling to see and hear. The muzzle flash and report had briefly blinded and deafened him. When Reese first heard the screams and then saw the light in the elevated house, he had gotten excited and shot too fast. He cursed himself for not being patient. He should have found something to support the rifle on. Two hundred yards was too far to shoot offhand. *I could have snuck right up on the shooting house and executed all of them.*

After rubbing his eyes, he was ready. He'd take it slow. He knew he had the advantage. There was no way the girl he had heard scream was going to keep quiet now. They'd be running scared, making mistakes. The thought of catching Johnny Lee's killer and the girl aroused a prurient interest in Reese. *This ain't just for you anymore, Johnny Lee,* Reese thought, as a sinister grin spread across his face.

Chapter 70

R.C. and Steve Tillman had just gotten out of the Jeep when they heard the first rifle shot. They had followed Tanner's tire tracks to an opening in the middle of the property. It was the end of the road. It appeared they had pulled in and stopped before turning around and leaving.

"That's got to be them!" R.C. exclaimed after the shot. He let out a deep breath. He had been looking around where the Jeep was parked.

"How far away was that?" Tillman asked.

"Not more than a mile," R.C. said, as he stared in the direction of the shot, "but it's hard to be sure. It may be closer."

"Is there a road that will take us closer?" he asked excitedly after the second shot. He took a directional reading from the compass on his watch.

"No, not that I'm aware of," Tillman replied after a moment.

"I'm going on…you need to stay here," R.C. said in a very serious voice. "It could be dangerous."

"Whoa, whoa, I'm going with you. You're not leaving me."

R.C. was checking his pistol and his flashlight. Patting his belt, he felt the additional rounds of ammunition and the absence of his radio. He fully realized that protocol dictated that he back off and call in support, but R.C. knew he didn't have time to go all the way back to his cruiser.

Tillman continued, "Tanner was responsible for Elizabeth's safety. I'm going with you, R.C."

R.C. stopped to listen to Tillman. He could hear the determination in his voice, and he really didn't want to chase these guys alone.

"Okay, but you have to do exactly what I say," R.C. insisted.

"No problem. I know you're doing what you think is right, and I agree with you."

"You sure?" R.C. asked, as he reached down and took a small revolver from his ankle holster. He checked it, then gave it to Tillman. Taking a deep breath, Tillman gripped it tightly.

"I can use it if I have to," he said calmly.

R.C. nodded, then clicked on his flashlight, "Let's go get to the bottom of all this mess!"

Chapter 71

Ollie opened his office door. He glanced around the room at everybody diligently working. There were a few new faces in the crowd.

"Miz Martha, have you gotten in touch with R.C.?" Ollie asked.

"No, sir." She sighed with frustration.

Ollie stood thinking. *That piece of property's very remote, or maybe his handheld just wasn't working. The battery could be drained. He probably didn't even have it turned on – which would be typical of R.C.*

"Have Ricky go and check on him. I'm sure in all his years of game wardening he knows the lay of that land. Tell him to just look for R.C. and report in. No hero crap."

"Yes, sir. Sheriff, the helicopter will be here in about twenty minutes."

"Does it have a searchlight?"

"No one's mentioned one. I don't think so."

"Me either…so we'll have to wait until it's daylight," he said, looking at his watch. "At least an hour I'd guess. I just don't know. I don't ever get up this early."

"That's about right," Martha confirmed. She knew exactly when daylight occurred.

Glancing up, Ollie saw Zach Beasley talking firmly to someone on his cell phone. He turned back to Martha.

"Have you heard from the hospital?" Ollie asked, sipping his coffee.

"Tanner hasn't changed. He's stable, and the Mississippi lady's doin' better," she explained.

"Mick will be here soon. I think he knows everybody mixed up in this," Ollie said with a tone of exasperation.

Martha reached for the ringing phone. Ollie watched Zach pacing back and forth like a caged animal; he was off the phone. The front door opened and Marlow strutted back in after copping his media fix. He went straight for the coffeepot and a day-old doughnut. Ollie glanced back at Martha. He could tell from her tone that it was an important call. She started waving at him as he headed back to his office.

Ollie's phone beeped. He picked up the receiver as he sat down.

"Sheriff Landrum," he answered.

"Sheriff, this is Bill Bracker from the Alabama Bureau of Investigation. I met a guy through a friend a few years ago—I hardly remember him; I spoke to the Rotary Club there—and anyway he just called me. A Mr. Zach Beasley. He's worked up something fierce. What's going on over there? Anything I can help with?" he asked with a thick Southern accent.

Ollie could tell that he was very genuine in his concern. So he gave Bracker the story from the start and explained the dragnet that they were throwing over the area. Ollie knew that Bill Bracker could lend some serious manpower, and he needed it. It didn't bother him at all that Zach had called Bracker.

"Sheriff, if you don't mind, I'm gonna send you some men from our Tuscaloosa and Birmingham offices. I could have sent some guys from Montgomery on the helicopter if I had known. It sounds like you have a good plan, and I don't want to usurp your authority. When my guys arrive, you deploy them however you see fit. I'll keep in touch. The Bureau will be glad to assist any way it can," he offered sincerely.

"Thank you, sir. I *really* appreciate it."

"Since Marlow's there, I'm sure the TV crews are on site already," Bracker added and then chuckled.

"Oh, yeah."

"Yeah, well, that old goat loves the cameras, but you don't need that distraction right now. *You* especially don't need the media scrutiny. Stay focused; my boys are en route. I'm a phone call away. Here's my home number. Please keep me posted."

"Yes, sir. And thanks again," Ollie replied as he jotted down the ABI chief's home phone number.

"No problem. Good luck, Sheriff."

Chapter 72

Ollie walked out of his office straight to the big table with the county topographic map. While he studied it, Marlow walked up and set down his cup of coffee, spilling some on the wooden table. He stretched and coughed. Ollie never looked up.

"We haven't heard from R.C. in a while. I sent him with Steve Tillman to check out Tillman's property. We think that's where the kids may have been."

"You worried?" Marlow asked, sipping his coffee loudly.

"Hell yeah. This ain't good. ABI called. They're sending some men."

"Bill Bracker?"

"Yeah."

"That's good, that's real good." Marlow knew the ABI involvement would raise the media's interest.

"What are we missing, Marlow?" Ollie asked, staring at the map. He wanted to make sure he had all the bases covered—those he could reach.

"Let's walk through it. Tell me where you have everybody," Marlow said, pulling out a chair to sit down.

Ollie leaned over the table and sighed. He pointed toward the gate on the Dummy Line. "All right, your superstar Deputy Lewis is stationed there."

"I'm securing the junction of these two county roads. I have a man heading down into here to check on R.C. and Steve Tillman, and I sent Larson down this road here that runs past the camp house. Your other deputy—I can't remember his name—is on this county road."

"That's Conner. He's a good man," Marlow added.

"I have two Livingston policemen searching Johnny Lee's trailer. Judge Cross didn't hesitate to sign the search warrant."

"We need more judges like him. He appreciates good police work," Marlow said.

"And Elizabeth is his niece," Ollie added. "Lakreshia is here to help Miz Martha with the APBs and other details. I'm going up with the helicopter when it gets here." Ollie stared at the expanse of river swamp shaking his head. He knew it would be a hard search. "Hell, they could be a hundred miles from here by now…that's why I hate to commit everything to one area."

"Ollie, we just need it to get daylight. That helicopter will speed everything up."

"I figured you would handle the media," Ollie said sarcastically.

"Yeah, sure; I'll do that for you," Marlow responded, not catching Ollie's tone. "You're doing all you can do. We just need a little luck," Marlow continued, taking a sip of coffee.

"Mr. Littlepage from West Point will be at the hospital in a few hours."

"I can't wait to hear how all this fits together," Marlow said.

"I just wanna find Elizabeth and the Crosbys," Ollie said as he stood up straight, then glanced at the clock on the wall.

Chapter 73

Larson and Shug were assigned to search the camp house and the road that left the camp leading into the heart of the property. Larson could tell Ollie was steaming mad at him for losing the tail on the Mississippi thug and knew that he would catch hell when this was all over. He needed to redeem himself. *We'll do a thorough search of the camp house and trailer, then move on down that road. Last time we just stopped searching. There could be more evidence,* Larson thought, then said to Shug, "We gotta find something else, big boy. Come on!"

Their subsequent search of the camp turned up nothing of any value—to the investigation. Larson, however, duly noted the life-size Faith Hill poster adorning one wall of the camp house. Shug paid more attention to the pantry. Something was driving Shug crazy. Larson allowed time to investigate. It turned out to be a giant bag of dried pig ears.

"Achtung, Shug!" Larson said as he eyed the disgusting dog treats. He thought they were dog treats. He hoped they were dog treats. "Let's go to the camper."

The grass surrounding the camper yielded only one possible clue. A freshly fired black Winchester three-inch magnum shotgun shell. At first Larson got excited; then he realized it was a turkey load, during turkey season, and he was standing in a hunting camp. He placed it in his pocket anyway, then looked at the open camper door. He quickly scanned the interior and then carefully stepped further inside. Larson noticed the heater glowing in the corner. As he walked towards the sleeping area the alarm clock sounded. Larson jumped straight up.

"Sonofabitch!" Larson found the alarm button and punched it off. He took a deep breath and continued his search, checking behind him for his faithful companion.

"Leave that alone, Shug. No. Nein!" Larson said to Shug, raising his voice an octave with each command. Shug wanted to play with the Beanie Baby lying on the camper floor. Larson's wife collected the small Ty toys, so he bent down to check it out. It was a black Labrador named Lucky. "She's got that one," he said, dropping it on the counter.

The interior looked pretty standard for a hunting camper. A bunch of camo clothes, boots, turkey calls, a gray T-shirt, Honey Buns, and a camo fleece blanket. *What's the use of a camo blanket?* he thought, shaking his head. Larson picked up a magazine from the couch. Turning it over, he noticed the small white label and read aloud, "Scott Littlepage, 304 Magnolia Blossom Court, West Point, Mississippi." Dropping the magazine back on the couch, he whistled for Shug and headed to the police cruiser. He wanted to ease down the muddy logging road as far as he could.

Larson listened to lots of chatter on the police radio as deputies dispersed and reported back to the command post. Nobody had found anything, and almost everyone was in place to secure his respective area. Shug settled comfortably on the back seat and resumed his grooming. Larson began to feel a knot in his stomach from the roller coaster ride from hero to goat. *I can't believe it. That lady had to have been there while I was talkin' to that Mississippi redneck. I missed my chance. But maybe I should be thankful. It coulda gotten deadly, for me.*

The first couple hundred yards of the old logging road had enough gravel that tracks were not obvious. Now that the road had turned to red clay, the tire tracks were plain as day. Larson struggled on the slippery mud to keep the cruiser headed straight. Just as he was about to request that someone bring in a four-wheeler or a four-wheel drive truck, his headlights illuminated the taillights of a parked pickup.

Larson stopped and got out. He clicked on his Maglight and unsnapped his holstered Glock 9mm pistol.

"Come on, Shug," he said. Shug eased out of the back seat and sat down by the car.

Pulling Shug by the search leash, Larson slowly approached the black truck. He recognized it as Johnny Lee Glover's. Then Shug perked up and proceeded to go berserk, smelling something dripping out of the back of the pickup. Goose bumps covered Larson's neck and arms as he took deliberate steps closer to the truck—a flashlight in one hand under his drawn pistol in the other.

Larson eased up to within reach of the truck. Shug tensed, the fur on his back rising. Larson shined the light into the back of the truck. A body was covered from the chest up in an old hunting jacket. Larson's hands shook as he reached in to remove the jacket. He dry-heaved when he saw Johnny Lee's ashen face, his right eye partially open, looking at him. The body was caked in blood.

Without calling Shug, Larson raced back to the cruiser to report what he had found.

Chapter 74

R.C. pushed to cover as much ground as possible. He stopped on some high ground. He didn't want to run right into the middle of a dangerous scene. He needed the element of surprise. Tillman caught up with him, cussing his shoes. R.C. was wearing work boots. Tillman had on some type of fancy dress shoes. They were ruined. R.C. turned off the flashlight and listened.

"Do you hear anything?" Tillman whispered between breaths.

"No, not yet," R.C. answered. "How far is Seventeen?"

"Maybe two miles; a little less as the crow flies," Tillman answered, trying to catch his breath.

R.C. thumped his can of Copenhagen, reached in, and pinched a dip. His lip pouched out as he stood thinking.

"You think whoever fired those shots has Elizabeth?" Tillman asked.

"I don't know with that pickup gone. There are several ways that truck coulda gone. And, as I think about it, we don't even know how people or vehicles are involved. Elizabeth might have been taken away in another truck when I found Tanner," R.C. said, then spat and continued, "If Tanner had been there for two hours before I found him, then Elizabeth could be in Birmingham by now."

Tillman sighed and looked off into the woods.

R.C. continued, "But those shots are giving me the chills. Nobody should be shootin' a high-powered rifle this time of year, at this hour. I feel it in my bones, that it's all some how connected."

"Yeah, I agree."

"Come on. Let's go," R.C. said, checking his compass.

They started off again in the direction of the shots, limbs slapping their faces as they hustled through the dense underbrush. R.C. was pleased that Tillman was keeping up. They picked up the pace when they entered an open hardwood bottom.

Chapter 75

Drenched in sweat and nearing exhaustion, Jake stopped, then eased both girls down to the ground. Every muscle in his body burned and ached. He had run half a mile through the thickest woods he had ever seen. He couldn't hear anything over the pounding of his heart in his ears. He thought he was going to have a heart attack. Jake stood bent over with his hands on his knees looking behind them.

He was still mulling over the plan—the inspiration of which was his favorite African hunting story. He didn't know if the story was even true, but it was the best idea he could come up with. He also knew that if he made a mistake in executing this plan, it would have deadly consequences for all of them.

"Elizabeth, can you walk some without the crutch?" he asked.

"I'll try," she said.

"You can lean on me," Jake offered.

"I'll do my best."

"Listen, I have a plan but y'all are gonna have to do exactly what I say when the time comes…no arguin', okay?" Jake looked at each of them. They both nodded in agreement.

"Come on," he said, picking up Katy and holding out his arm for Elizabeth.

They took off down a logging road, purposely leaving tracks a blind man could follow. Jake moved as fast as he could while he searched the woods for the right tree. *They're all too small*, he thought. While they struggled deeper into the swamp, Jake continued to think through his plan. *I've only got two shells. Two opportunities. I have to be close. Are there more than two guys after us?* He wondered. It would be just like calling in two big old gobblers—letting them walk in as close as possible. Jake had done it before. His toughest challenge was to remain unseen.

After another three hundred yards of hobbling down the logging road, laying tracks, Jake saw *the* tree—a giant water oak with large limbs and a huge canopy. It was enormous. It had to be over a hundred years old. The tree had just started to put out new leaves and the massive limbs hung level over the road. Jake kept Elizabeth moving past the tree for another hundred yards or so before he stopped and put Katy down. He looked back in the direction of the giant tree. *This should be far enough,* he hoped.

"Okay, y'all listen and no arguments. I want y'all to hide behind those trees right over there. Sit on the other side. Take my flashlight, but do *not* and I mean do *not,* turn it on unless it is absolutely necessary. If you hear a shot, don't run unless you hear me yell at you to run and then run that way," he said pointing in the direction they were facing. "Highway Seventeen can't be much farther. Run until you hit it." The girls didn't say a word; so, he continued, "Y'all sit still. I'm gonna get these guys. I need to hurry and I need y'all to sit quiet and wait on me, okay?"

"Dad?" Katy was tearing up.

"No, Katy, I need you to be a big girl and help Elizabeth. Please. I know what I'm doing," Jake cut in before she could finish. He was about to choke up himself.

"Elizabeth, please watch her. Y'all stay together. Don't freak out if you hear shootin', all right? In fact, expect it. I'm going to get us out of here one way or another."

"Yes, sir." Elizabeth could see how serious he was and she could hear it in his voice. She also could tell he was scared.

Jake grabbed Katy and hugged her as hard as he ever had in his life. "I love you, Katy." He wanted to say more but couldn't. He swallowed hard. "I'll...I'll be back in...one hour at the most. Please be quiet—just like when we deer hunt. Okay?"

Katy couldn't speak.

"You gotta take care of Elizabeth now. Okay? She needs your help." He winked at Elizabeth. She smiled understandingly. He knew Katy liked to feel needed, to have a purpose, "You're in charge now."

Katy wouldn't let go. "Come on, Katy, please." She finally loosened her grip.

"I love you, Dad."

"I love you too, sweetheart."

Jake watched them walk away. He knew they would hide in the right spot. Katy was great at hiding. He turned off the logging road, walked about twenty feet out into the woods, and then he hurriedly made his way back to the giant tree, staying off the logging road. He thought of Peter Capstick's story about the leopard waiting in the tree over his tracks for the unsuspecting hunter. That was Jake's plan.

The stalkers would be looking for them on the ground. Jake would surprise them, but they had to be close. His white arms and face would stand out, almost glowing, in dark woods, so at a mud puddle he rubbed sludge on his exposed skin. When he arrived at the giant oak, he saw that he was going to have problems reaching the first limb. Other than that, the tree was perfect. He listened for sounds of them approaching. Satisfied that he had some time, he silently unloaded his shotgun.

Jake held the two remaining shotgun shells in his hand, thinking. They were both three-inch magnum turkey loads filled with number 4 shot. Maximum killing range on a man would be thirty yards. He had a trick that he'd seen once. He took out his pocketknife. Placing the blade against the plastic just above the brass rim, he slowly cut around the diameter of each shell, taking great care not to cut into the wadding. Jake knew that by rimming the shells, when he shot, the whole wad and pellets would stay together as a large mass in the plastic of the shell casing. This might stretch his effective killing range to fifty yards.

Jake unscrewed the extra-full choke from the barrel and dropped it in his vest, fearing it might constrict the modified shotgun shell too much, limiting his killing distance. He carefully loaded the shells back into the gun, then slung it over his shoulder. Jake took a quick look down the logging road. He didn't see anything. He was sweating more now than before. He grabbed the side of the tree like Spiderman and tried to shimmy up. He struggled for a while then finally dropped to the ground. "SHIT!" he said under his breath.

He tried again with a slightly different technique. He finally got a hand over the lowest limb. Ever so slowly, Jake used all his remaining strength to pull himself up onto the limb. He was quivering from the effort. He reached up to the next limb. It leaned out over the road. He slowly crawled out on it. Once he was over the road, he pulled the shotgun from his shoulder and clicked off the safety. He was strategically balanced twenty feet in the air, right over the center of the road. *They'll never look up,* he thought hopefully.

Jake tried to get comfortable, but there was absolutely no way. He was covered in perspiration. He couldn't stay very long in this position, and he started to rethink the notion of sitting on the ground. At least he would be comfortable, but it was too late…he was too committed. Jake let out a deep breath, gritted his teeth, and stared down the logging road into the darkness.

Chapter 76

Without totally regaining his vision, Reese ran as fast as he could down the field toward the shooting house. When he was thirty yards away he stopped to listen and to watch for any movement. He walked closer, the rifle held ready at his hip. At the base of the ladder, he clicked on his flashlight to look for blood. He found none, but to make sure, he climbed up the ladder to look inside. He saw where one of his shots had ripped through the house. No blood, just small wood splinters everywhere.

"Dammit!" he said out loud as he climbed down.

Working the action on his Browning rifle, Reese unloaded it. He had three cartridges left. He couldn't take any more wild shots. He had to concentrate; he had to make each shot count. Searching around with the flashlight, he found the footprints of one obviously very heavy person running off towards the southeast. The killer's trail was taking Reese closer to Highway 17—that made all this easier for him and Moon Pie. Reese now knew the guy was carrying the kid, and this would slow him down.

Reese reloaded the rifle and dialed down the scope's magnification to 4, giving him greater field of vision in the low light. He started following the tracks, edgy for more action. Like a bloodhound, he stayed right on the trail. When he couldn't see footprints, he found broken sticks and branches. Reese smiled thinking about his prey running through the woods, scared to death.

Reese sensed that his quarry was just ahead. He needed to kill the guy quickly. Daylight wasn't far off. He made better time by guessing the direction and only checking for tracks every twenty yards or so. The signs were always easy to find. *This guy's freakin' out. He ain't even trying to hide 'em,* Reese thought.

The logging road turned hard to the left. Reese could see foot steps in the soft mud for fifteen to twenty yards. He moved to the far side of the road where the ground was harder. He quietly picked up his pace.

After a few hundred yards, Reese slowed down. He had an eerie feeling. The trees had gotten considerably larger. It would be easy to get ambushed. But the tracks continued straight down the road—tracks don't lie. Obviously they were fresh, so he continued the pursuit. *This stupid sumbitch is runnin' scared,* he told himself.

Chapter 77

About eighty yards back down the logging road, Jake could barely make out movement. His heart rate doubled. *This is it. They're taking the bait,* he thought. Now all he had to do was be patient—let them get within fifteen yards and he'd kill the first one. He prayed that he'd have time to shoot the second goon before he got shot himself. Sweat began to bead on him again. *I gotta concentrate. If I miss, they'll kill me, and then God knows what they'll do to Katy and Elizabeth.*

Jake couldn't believe that for the third time tonight he was preparing to kill someone. He took a long deep breath then slowly let it out. The movement was now at about fifty yards, approaching rapidly. Jake took another deep breath, held it for a moment, then slowly exhaled. He started shaking. Images of Katy hugging him and of Elizabeth about to be raped flashed through his mind. He shook his head slightly, trying to clear it. The movement was at forty yards. In his mind, he saw Katy's face and heard her giggling.

Slowly he raised the gun, pointing in the direction of his target. Occasionally he could hear a stick snap. Jake's mind was liquid with fear. He forced himself to take another deep breath. There was only one guy. *Where's the other one?!* he screamed in his mind. He wanted both. He had to end this right here, right now. Jake looked behind the first guy, who was twenty yards away, watching for any other movement. Glancing back to the only man visible, Jake recognized him as one of the gang members. He quickly looked back up the logging road. *Damn it!* He was only ten yards away now—he had let him get too close. Jake looked at him and then back up the road one last time.

No one else was coming...that he could see. *Damn it!* he silently screamed.

The gangster slowed his pace. He was directly underneath Jake. With one hand, Jake simply pointed the shotgun straight down. He held onto the tree limb with the other. Jake's desire to kill both gangsters had allowed the guy to get too close. He quickly considered allowing him to walk by a few yards, to make for a larger, better target. *To hell with it!* he thought, taking another deep breath as he aimed the shotgun at the gangster's head—twelve short feet away. Jake had him.

Just as Jake's mind told his finger to squeeze the trigger, he felt a huge sweat bead roll off his nose. He watched it drop in slow motion straight down, landing on the side of the gangster's face. The gangster instantly looked up at Jake and jumped back. Still holding the shotgun with one hand, Jake squeezed the trigger. *BOOM!* Almost instantaneously there was another gunshot. *KABAM!* The gangster had shot up at him. Jake felt a hard punch in his chest. He blinked several times trying to clear the blindness from the muzzle flash. The gangster aimed at him again. Jake had missed! He immediately pumped the last shell into the chamber as he swung the shotgun at the thug. *BOOM!* Jake fell out of the tree, landing hard on his side.

Jake slowly staggered to his feet. He struggled over to the gangster. Jake Crosby was mortified at what he saw. The thug had a hole in his chest big enough to drop a softball clean through. He was sprawled on his back, spread eagle, not moving a muscle. The rimmed three-inch magnum had gone straight through him. It was the goriest thing Jake had ever seen. He stood hyperventilating for several moments. Finally regaining his composure, he looked at the guy's rifle lying next to him. As soon as Jake touched it he knew it was useless. Part of the receiver was bent. The sulfurous odor of blood made him want to puke.

Quickly looking around for any sign of other pursuers, Jake did not see anything. Nothing. No movement anywhere. Then he felt his own chest. *No blood.* Jake looked up at his perch. He could see the white, freshly exposed wood where the rifle shot had hit. *I was lying on that limb.* A chill went down his spine. Jake had been within mere inches of catching a high-powered rifle bullet in the chest. Thinking of it caused him to dry-heave. After salvaging what little remained of his self-control, he ran wildly toward the girls.

When he was near, Jake started calling, "Katy! Katy! Where are you!?"

"Over here, Dad!"

"Over here!" added Elizabeth.

They were right where they were supposed to be. Jake hugged Katy, then Elizabeth.

"What happened?" Katy asked, her voice quivering more than ever.

"We gotta keep movin', I got one of 'em. I got the one that shot at us. He may be the only bad guy left. But I'm not sure," Jake said, the image of the guy who had killed Elizabeth's attacker coming to his mind.

"You shot him?" Elizabeth asked in disbelief.

"Dad!" Katy was shocked.

"I had to. He was gonna kill us. Come on, let's get goin'." Jake thought he heard road noise just to the southwest. If they could get to the highway, they'd be able to flag down some help.

"Here, Elizabeth. Use this as a crutch." he said, handing her the shotgun.

"What about the cushion?"

"It doesn't matter. I don't have any more shells."

Jake picked up Katy. He held her close. Her warm little body felt so good to him. Katy squeezed him back. Jake kissed her cheek and said, "You're safe, baby. Quit shaking."

Katy squeezed even harder. "That's you, Dad."

Chapter 78

Sheriff, Lakreshia's back with the pilot." Martha spoke into Ollie's speakerphone.

"Okay. Send him back," Ollie instructed, rubbing his scalp as he glanced up at the wall clock. They had an hour before they could get airborne.

"Ollie Landrum," Ollie said standing with an outstretched hand.

"Joe Wilson, sir. I'm your copter pilot," he said shaking hands firmly.

"Thanks for comin'. I really appreciate it. I'm the Sumter County sheriff. You probably saw Sheriff Marlow outside."

"Yes, sir. I'd just as soon stay out of the spotlight, sir."

"I know the feeling. I'll be going up with you. I have a fair knowledge of the area. We've got a missing eighteen-year-old girl and a thirty-something adult male along with his nine-year-old daughter. We don't know how they're connected. We suspect serious foul play because—."

"Do you get airsick, sir?" Wilson interrupted bluntly. "Because when we're doing back-and-forth ground sweeps, it can be pretty rough on your stomach, sir." The last thing Wilson wanted was someone puking up coffee and doughnuts all over his helicopter.

"I'll be fine," Ollie said, not totally convinced. "And please cut out the 'sir' business...this ain't the Army. I appreciate it and all, but it's not necessary."

"Yes, sir. Sorry, sir. It's a hard habit to break, sir."

"Since we've got a little time, I want to brief you on the terrain.

It's an immense area of pine plantations and hardwood swamps."

"Good. Thanks. It's gonna be foggy in the low areas. That'll hurt our vis."

"Let me ask you something. Are you leaving at eight o'clock to fly the governor to the beach?"

"No, sir. I'm yours...as long as you can keep me topped off with fuel. This mission is *Priority One*...for me. It's the first real mission I've had in quite a while. But just in case, tell the governor that you can't get in touch with me. He can be a bit overbearing."

Ollie smiled approvingly at him. He could tell Wilson wanted to help. His military background might be useful too.

"Sir...Sheriff, I really enjoyed watching you play football. It's a real pleasure to work with you," Wilson said.

Ollie smiled and shook his hand again. "Thanks for being here. Let's go look at those maps. Need some coffee?"

"I'd love some," Wilson replied.

"Lakreshia?" Ollie asked turning to her.

"I'll get it," she responded.

"I like mine *black*," he said, smiling boldly at Lakreshia.

Lakreshia glared at him as she walked away. Ollie chuckled to himself. He liked Joe Wilson.

Chapter 79

Now that's close," R.C. said. Tillman and R.C. froze when they heard the gunshots. "A shotgun blast, then a high-powered rifle shot, then another shotgun round!" R.C. continued, his police skills beginning to show. R.C. coursed the shots with his compass. They listened. Nothing.

"Come on!" R.C. said, taking off through the woods.

Limbs slapped R.C. in the face. Tillman's shoe came off in the mud, but he quickly caught up when R.C. stopped again to listen.

"I just heard a man yelling somethin'!" R.C. whispered excitedly. With his hands on his knees, R.C. was trying to catch his breath. His left side was hurting. He wasn't used to much physical exertion. Tillman was even more winded.

R.C. took off again. The woods had become dense. The timber changed from pines to hardwoods. The ground was soggy, which slowed them a bit. R.C. could see a logging road off to his right. He let Tillman catch up. They stood still for about thirty seconds to catch their breath and listen.

R.C. pointed at the old logging road, "We can travel easier on that," he whispered.

As soon as they stepped onto the logging road, R.C. spotted fresh footprints. He clicked on his flashlight and kneeled down for a closer look.

"Look at this. I'd say that's a man's boot, and that's probably a female's print, maybe Elizabeth's," he said, then looked up at Tillman.

"What about those?" Tillman, asked pointing out the tracks off to the side.

"I don't know…definitely male," R.C. shook his head, continuing, "and very fresh."

R.C. clicked off his flashlight and stood.

"Come on."

They had gone another seventy-five yards or so down the logging road when R.C. noticed something out of place ahead of him. He clicked on his flashlight. He couldn't quite make out what it was. They slowly approached.

"What the hell is it?" Mr. Tillman whispered.

"I don't know," R.C. responded, easing his pistol out of its holster. The hair on the back of his neck was beginning to stand up. Something wasn't right.

"Holy shit!" he exclaimed as he recognized that the form was actually a body.

"Who is it?" Tillman asked, putting his hand over his mouth. The gore shocked him.

"I'm not sure. Man, I've never seen a hole that size. There's blood everywhere. He musta been shot with a grenade launcher. Be careful where you step."

R.C. felt in the corpse's pockets. He found a new 9mm pistol, a cell phone, and a wallet. He stuck the pistol in his back pocket, then opened the wallet. Shining his flashlight on the driver's license, R.C. nodded.

"Reese Turner," R.C. reported. "That makes some sense. He runs with Johnny Lee Glover. Didn't recognize him." R.C. quickly flipped open the phone and looked at the call history. "This will be enlightening," he quipped with a nod and slid the phone in his pocket.

"Shine around and see if anybody else is here," Tillman suggested.

"Okay," R.C. said as he put the wallet in his pocket. He quickly shined the light around the perimeter. "I don't see anybody else."

"What's that?" Tillman asked, pointing up at a bright white spot on the dark oak tree limb above them.

"Looks like something blew the bark off that limb...had to be a gunshot."

R.C. started shining his light around and under the canopy of the big tree. "Look at this shotgun shell," R.C. said, holding the brass of a shell under the light. "Have you ever seen one do that?

"No. It looks like it was cut...the plastic's gone," he commented.

"It's been rimmed. That's gotta be what happened to our buddy here," R.C. said, pointing at Reese's body.

"I thought a shotgun would be enough..."

"A rimmed twelve-gauge would be like a mortar round, ten times the knockdown power. Instant death," R.C. replied.

R.C. swung the light to illuminate the tracks going down the logging road. "Let's keep going," R.C. said.

After they had walked only a few yards, Tillman stopped. "Am I seeing things, or are there more tracks now?" Tillman asked.

"No you're right. There's one more pair of tracks, but these tracks are identical to the ones we've been following. It's the same guy. He doubled back and tricked ole Reese here into a close encounter," R.C. said, pointing out the tracks' similarities with his flashlight. "It's the shooter. And I'd say he's pretty slick," R.C. continued, shining the flashlight back at the tree limb, then down at the body, and then holding up the rimmed shotgun shell.

CHAPTER 80

Jake stopped cold. He had caught a glimpse of a flashlight beam through the woods. Then he heard distant voices. His heart raced even more. *How many more of them were there?* He had no ammunition. This was not good. He knew they would catch up with them before he got to the highway.

"Girls, we gotta cover a lot of ground quickly. The ground slopes that way...there has to be some kinda creek down there. Hurry. We need to cross it."

Both the girls nodded.

"Let me help," Jake whispered to Elizabeth.

Jake was shaking again. His shotgun was useless, except as a crutch. All he had resembling a weapon was a pocketknife. He was trying to come up with a plan. *Think. THINK!* He kept screaming to himself.

When Jake saw the creek he knew what he had to do. As soon as they crossed it, Jake set Katy down on a log and pulled Elizabeth over so she could hear. He paused for a second. He hated what he was about to do.

"Okay, girls. The highway's right through there. It's not very far. There are at least two guys tracking us. I'm gonna stay here to distract them while y'all run to the highway. Flag down the first car you see and make them take you straight to the sheriff's office in Livingston."

"No, Dad!" Katy cried out.

"Mr. Crosby, I don't wanna leave you."

"Listen to me. I'll be fine. You have to help each other. Promise me you will," he said, looking Katy in the eyes. "We don't have time to argue. Promise?"

"But Dad!" she whined.

"Katy, honey, we don't have time," Jake pleaded. "Please take care of her," he said calmly to Elizabeth.

They both started crying. Jake told them to stop. Jake hugged Katy for as long as he dared and afterward looked up at Elizabeth. She looked worn out. He prayed that she had another mile in her. Jake looked down at Katy's feet, covered only by a pair of cotton camo gloves.

He stepped out of his boots saying, "Wear these, Katy. It's better than nothin'."

She slipped them on. She wore them around the house when she had to feed the animals.

"I'll catch up. Okay? Elizabeth, I need to keep the gun. Now y'all go."

Jake watched them walking away, realizing that might be the last time he saw Katy. It hurt down to the bone. He dreaded what he was about to do.

He hurriedly took out his pocketknife, opened it, and locked the blade. He tried to slip the handle into the gun barrel but it was slightly too big. He jabbed the blade into the log lying at his feet. Then he slid the end of the barrel onto the handle and with all his weight, forced the barrel a few inches over the knife handle. He now had a new weapon and a chance to attack the remaining thugs.

Jake had purposely crossed the creek beside a large oak. Squatting down on the bank, he rubbed mud all over his arms, chest, neck and more on his face. Then he leaned up against the back side of the huge old tree. When the thugs were crossing the deepest part, he would charge with his Remington model 870 bayonet.

He could hear them closing in. Each step sent Jake's heart into another gear. The intensity was overwhelming. Sweat was pouring off him. Vapor from his breath was pluming out into the night. Jake concentrated on reducing his breathing so as not to compromise his location.

"There they go...they're gonna cross the creek," he heard one say and another one grunted in agreement. They approached cautiously, but Jake could hear every step. Visions of his beautiful daughter, and the wife that he so often disappointed, and even Elizabeth, whose life depended on him, were flying through his mind. His decision to come hunting had forever changed the lives of countless people and set in motion an unfathomable sequence of events.

Jake took a deep breath and tightened his grip on his bayonet. He waited to hear the sound of the rednecks sloshing in the creek. He was determined to kill both of them.

CHAPTER 81

Katy and Elizabeth were moving slowly through the swamp. The mud kept pulling off Katy's boots. Elizabeth was in excruciating pain. They held hands, and Katy tried her best to help support Elizabeth. Both girls were sobbing.

Elizabeth understood the danger that Jake faced and the sacrifice he was making. She knew why he was doing it. Elizabeth also knew that he was counting on her to get Katy to safety. A vision of Tanner's fight flashed through her mind and then an image of her attacker—it was so vivid she could smell him. *Walk. Just keep walking,* she told herself.

Both girls heard a big truck cross the Noxubee River Bridge, the sound echoing across the swamp. They could almost feel the vibrations. They looked at each other and smiled knowingly. Elizabeth noted that it was still pretty far away because she couldn't see any lights, but at least she knew they were headed in the right direction.

After sloshing through the mud for a hundred yards or so, Elizabeth saw a log that they would have to cross or go around. Pointing at it, she asked Katy, "You wanna sit a minute?"

"Yes," Katy whispered.

The moment they sat down for a much-needed rest, a gray fox jumped from a hole in the ground at their feet, ran between them, then headed deep into the swamp.

"AAAAAHHHHHHHHHH!" they both yelled at the top of their lungs. Elizabeth's long scream matched Katy's. As fast as it happened, it was over.

Elizabeth realized that they had betrayed their location. She instantly grabbed Katy by the hand and they took off running for the highway. Elizabeth fell down. Katy helped her get up. They were both in a panic.

Chapter 82

Jake could tell that his pursuers were hesitating at the edge of the creek. *Come on. Just a few more feet,* he thought. He gritted his teeth, listening intently, waiting for the sounds of them wading into the water.

Katy and Elizabeth's scream of terror pierced the silence. He tensed and turned to look in their direction. The dense swamp was coal-black. He couldn't see anything. Jake heard one of the thugs mumble something, then walk into the water. Jake had them where he wanted them, but Katy was in danger. *Katy! What the hell's goin' on? What are they screaming at?* Jake's mind raced immediately to a vision of Katy and Elizabeth being caught by those maniacs. But *these* monsters were less than twenty feet away from him. Right now. He was shaking so hard he knew the thugs could hear—even over the sloshing sounds they made. The instant before Jake attacked, a graphic image of Katy in the hands of those fiends seared his brain. Jake bolted toward the girls, never looking back. He ran with all his might.

"SHIT! Who is that! Hey, come back here!" Jake heard an incredulous voice yell. As he was running, Jake could hear obvious confusion—shouting and the thrashing of water.

"Elizabeth! Elizabeth!" a man screamed as Jake plowed through vines and limbs in the direction of the girls, "Elizabeth! It's Steve Tillman!"

"Mr. Tillman? Is that you?" Elizabeth yelled in response.

"Yes! Yes! We're coming, Elizabeth!"

Jake stopped. He couldn't hear clearly over the ringing in his ears from the pounding of his heart. He tried to make sense of it. Elizabeth seemed to recognize one of the voices coming from behind him. He cupped his hands and hollered, "Elizabeth do you know him?'"

"Yes! It's my boyfriend's dad!" she yelled with excitement.

After a moment, Jake heard the girls crashing toward him through the undergrowth. "Is Katy all right?"

"Yes, sir!" Elizabeth shouted back. Jake felt a wave of relief rush over him.

"Elizabeth, we're coming. Stay where you are!" Tillman yelled.

Jake was stunned and exhausted. Everybody was yelling at once.

R.C. drew down on Jake's chest when he saw him. Jake was totally covered in mud, barefooted, and carrying a shotgun with a knife jutting out of the end of the barrel—all very *Apocalypse Now*. "Deputy Sheriff! Deputy Sheriff! Drop it! Drop the gun! Drop it, NOW!" R.C. screamed. "Put your hands in the air!"

Jake let go of the shotgun and raised his hands. He then dropped to his knees, locking his fingers across the top of his head. He could stand no longer although the weight of the world had just been lifted from his shoulders.

"Man, I'm glad to see you," Jake said with relief.

R.C. didn't respond. He kept his pistol trained on Jake as he slowly approached the shotgun. He picked it up and leaned it against a tree out of Jake's reach.

Steve Tillman was out of sight heading toward Elizabeth. Jake could hear Katy running back toward him and yelling, "Dad! Dad!"

When R.C. saw the little girl run to the muddy man and hug him, he dropped his pistol to his side. R.C. listened to Steve Tillman talking excitedly to Elizabeth Beasley.

"Is Elizabeth okay?" R.C. yelled.

"Yes!"

"Who are you?" R.C. turned to Jake.

"I'm Jake Crosby. I'm...I'm in a huntin' club back that direction, somewhere. Bogue Chitto. This is my daughter, Katy," Jake continued, "You won't believe what we've been through tonight."

R.C. began connecting the dots. He holstered his weapon, then walked closer.

"And who are you?" Katy asked bluntly before R.C. could ask another question.

R.C. smiled. "R.C. Smithson, young lady. I'm a deputy sheriff."

"R.C.? Well, what took you so long to get here!?" Katy exclaimed with a very serious look, catching R.C. off guard.

"I thought y'all were part of that gang of rednecks tryin' to kill us," Jake explained to the deputy, as Elizabeth, with Tillman's help, walked up.

"You scared the shit outta me when you took off runnin'. Oh. Uh...excuse me, Miss Katy," R.C. said.

"That's okay. My dad's said that a bunch tonight," Katy said brightly.

"I bet he did." R.C. smiled at Jake.

"Mr. Tillman, these are the people I was tellin' you about—they saved my life," Elizabeth explained as they approached Jake, Katy, and the deputy. She was giddy with relief, thinking she was out of danger.

Steve Tillman shook Jake's hand. "Pleased to meet you. I'm Steve Tillman. I don't know what all y'all have been through tonight, but thank you so much for taking care of her."

"Jake Crosby. This is my daughter, Katy," Jake said, beginning to get choked up.

"Mr. Tillman said Tanner's in the hospital and is stable...which means he's going to be all right!" Elizabeth said joyously.

"That's great news," Jake responded, slowly looking at everyone. He couldn't believe what he had done tonight. "I almost killed one of y'all," he said reflectively to R.C. and Steve Tillman.

"Yeah, that was close," R.C. replied stoically, eyeing the modified shotgun. "We saw some of your handiwork back there," R.C. continued, then looked at Jake in the flashlight beam.

Jake replied simply, "He deserved it," with no hint of contrition. "And there's still one more out here somewhere. A great big fat guy," he added.

"I think he's left the area. I'm dying to know all the details but we really need to get y'all outta here," R.C. said, noticing Elizabeth's swollen ankle. Then, looking at Jake, he continued, "and get y'all cleaned up. The sheriff will have tons of questions."

There was so much to say, but Jake knew the deputy was right. They needed to get to safety. Jake couldn't relax fully until they were out of these woods.

"My truck's miles back that way," Jake said pointing northwest.

"Our Jeep's a good two miles that way, so I think we walk out to the highway and hitch a ride to town," R.C. said to the group. He noticed Steve Tillman giving Elizabeth his jacket. He looked at Jake slowly getting up, covered in mud and sweat, then with a laugh said to Jake, "I'd give you mine but I'm probably wetter than you right now. When you took off runnin' you scared me so bad, I fell in the creek face first!"

"That's okay...why don't you carry the shotgun. I'll carry Katy Bug here—been doin' it all night anyway," he said affectionately.

Jake watched Tillman pick up Elizabeth. He turned to pick up Katy. They followed R.C.'s big flashlight beam toward the highway.

"My mom's gonna kill Dad when we get home!" Katy exclaimed.

Everyone laughed. Even Jake mustered an exhausted smile.

"Don't you have a radio?" Jake asked R.C.

"It's a long story; the Jeep crushed it," R.C. said sheepishly. "It's gonna be a tough one to explain."

Before Jake knew it, they were crawling up the steep side of the highway. When Jake got up on the road, R.C. was already looking back and forth to see if any vehicles were coming. They all huddled in the middle of the road. Steve Tillman returned the pistol to R.C. when no one was looking.

After a few minutes they could see headlights approaching. R.C. started flashing his light and waving his arms. The vehicle came to a stop a hundred yards away. Its lights switched to high beam. After ten seconds, the vehicle slowly backed up, turned around, and drove off at a high rate of speed.

"That was weird. Whoever's driving that SUV acted scared of us," R.C. stated.

"Well, yeah, take a closer look," Tillman said, laughing.

"Right. I might pick *them* up," R.C. said, pointing at the girls, "but I definitely wouldn't pick up old Jake there…not on a bet." Everyone laughed.

"I wouldn't pick me up either," Jake added, wiping some mud off his forehead.

"There are plenty folks in this part of the world that would think you were some kinda swamp haint," R.C. added, grinning.

Eventually, another vehicle approached. An eighteen-wheeler. The giant white truck slowed down as R.C. stood in the center of the road waving his flashlight and arms, directing him to stop. The truck driver was obviously nervous. He stared in disbelief at the group standing in his headlights' beams. Jake smiled and shook his head when he saw it was a Wal-Mart truck. *They're everywhere,* he thought.

Shining his light on his uniform, R.C. said, "Sir, I'm Deputy

Sheriff Smithson. This is an emergency. We need a ride to Livingston."

The truck driver looked at everyone, then back at R.C.'s badge, and said, "Sure, Officer...y'all jump in."

"Thank you, sir. Just drop us off at the hospital. I'll show you where it is," R.C. said.

"Are you folks okay?" the truck driver asked, watching the mixed group crawl up into his truck. "Just crawl in the back, sweetheart," he said to Katy.

"It's been a long night," Jake answered back. "Can we all get in here?" he asked as he climbed up.

"Sure—cram in," R.C. replied as he shook hands with the truck driver. "We really appreciate the lift."

"No problem. I was just a little shocked. I thought y'all were hijackers."

Jake, Katy, and R.C. climbed into the sleeper. Tillman and Elizabeth shared the front seat. Katy was excited to be in a big truck.

"I'm definitely adding Wal-Mart stock to my Buy List," Jake said aloud to no one in particular.

The driver was old-school. He couldn't have been nicer. He never asked a question, he simply kept his mouth shut. He spent only brief moments looking inquisitively at his passengers.

"I buy all my stuff at Wal-Mart," R.C. added, trying to make conversation. "Whatcha hauling?"

"Televisions," the driver answered politely.

"Hey, do you have a cell phone?" R.C. asked.

"Yeah, sure," he said, handing it to R.C. It was red, white, and blue.

"No service," R.C. reported.

"Tell me about it. This area needs another tower real bad," Jake replied.

"When we get closer to Livingston, we'll have service," R.C. explained. Then, looking at Jake, he said, "I can't wait to hear *your* story."

Chapter 83

"Shit! Shit! Shit!" screamed Moon Pie, pounding on the steering wheel. He had just realized that the shadowy figure in the middle of the highway waving a flashlight wasn't Reese—it was a cop. *This is bad. Really bad.*

"I gotta get the hell outta here!" he said aloud. Slamming the Tahoe into reverse, he whipped around and burned rubber heading north. His mind raced as he tried unsuccessfully to reach Reese. Moon Pie hated to breach the buddy code and leave Reese in limbo, but he sensed this place was about to be crawling with cops, and they were going to be looking for the whole crew. *It's just dumb luck that I got away from Deputy Dawg back in Livingston. They got my name, my tag number, and they're probably gonna be waitin' for my stupid ass when I pull up to my crib. Dammit!*

Trying to return a favor for a buddy, Moon Pie had gotten himself into a neck-deep pile of trouble. His gut was telling him to run.

Ethan "Moon Pie" Daniels sped away from his planned rendezvous with Reese, thinking he would head straight to Memphis, and then on up to Missouri to a remote fishing camp deep in the Ozarks. He could lie low. Nobody would be suspicious. He'd be just another eccentric fly-fisherman. He had about four grand in cash on him and enough weed to raise maybe another twenty. The hillbillies would buy it all, including the seeds. The Ozarks are the perfect hideout. He could catch some trout and hang until he knew exactly what was going down. *I can be there in six hours. Maybe seven. And my old lady won't even miss me, as long as she's got Internet access. Or, maybe I'll just...*, he thought, considering all his options.

By the time Moon Pie reached Macon, Mississippi, his mind was made up.

Chapter 84

Ollie and Joe Wilson were headed out the front door when Martha screamed and jumped up and down like she had just won the lottery.

"What the hell?" Ollie said with his hand on the front door.

"R.C. has them all. Elizabeth and the guy from West Point and his daughter! He's got 'em all!" she said excitedly.

"Where are they?" he asked after he let out a deep breath of relief.

"They're on their way to the hospital. They'll be there in a few minutes."

"Let's go!" Ollie said to everyone. The entire Sumter County Sheriff's staff began racing for the door. Nobody thought to tell Marlow. He was in the bathroom tucking in his shirttail, which had pulled out while he was setting up the official podium.

"Damn it, R.C. Answer me!" Ollie finally said after three unsuccessful attempts to contact the deputy via radio. There were several questions he needed answered immediately.

When Ollie turned the corner to the ER entrance, he did not see R.C.'s cruiser in the parking lot. He could see TV camera crews sitting on the ground resting. They obviously did not know what was about to happen, but they would react quickly. Parking on the side of the building, Ollie glanced back down the road. Several cars were approaching at high rates of speed. R.C. was not one of them. He folded his arms and waited.

Martha O'Brien screeched her car to a stop and sprinted by him without a glance, headed inside to spread the news to Mrs. Tillman and Mrs. Beasley. Ollie smiled. He noticed the camera crews were staring at him. One female reporter was approaching to ask a question. While the reporter was walking toward him, Ollie noticed Zach Beasley drive up and scurry into the hospital.

"What's going on, deputy? Where's Sheriff Marlow?" asked the reporter insolently.

The question burned Ollie. He counted to five before responding sternly, "I am Sumter County Sheriff Ollie Landrum. Sheriff Marlow is either at *my* office or on his way here."

"Sorry, Sheriff. What's going on?" asked the vacuous, perfectly groomed blond reporter.

"You'll know in a few minutes," he said, looking up the road for blue lights. He wanted to preserve the illusion that he knew what was going on. *This was classic R.C.... keep everybody in the dark,* Ollie thought. The reporter started frantically waving at her cameraman to get ready.

Suddenly, the ER's automatic doors opened. Nurses, orderlies, and all manner of hospital personnel came running out with wheelchairs and stretchers. Ollie observed the enthusiasm of a small town in a crisis. He noticed Martha and Olivia Beasley in the crowd and another woman who had to be Mrs. Tillman.

A car screeched to a stop by the ER. Its passengers—a young lady and man—raced across the parking lot straight to Mrs. Tillman. *Must be Tanner's sister and brother-in-law.* Ollie couldn't hear what they were saying. Their hugs and tears spoke volumes.

Looking back up the road, Ollie couldn't see any blue lights. He did see an eighteen-wheeler making the turn. Ollie spun around to look at the crowd. Anticipation was running high. It was similar to a high school football team returning from a big victory—except for the wheelchairs and gurneys.

When the big diesel started to pull into the ER, Ollie almost ran out to stop him. But something told him to wait. Then he saw Steve Tillman's smiling face in the passenger's side window. He immediately hurried to help open the door before the truck stopped.

"We found them, Ollie!" Tillman exclaimed and then turned to start climbing down. "Elizabeth has a hurt ankle, but other than that, I think she's fine!" he said loudly over the idling diesel engine. "We'll have to help her out."

Ollie was so relieved to see Elizabeth Beasley's smiling face. He helped Tillman assist her in climbing down. They set her in a waiting wheelchair. The television camera lights were blinding. Everybody was talking excitedly and asking questions. Elizabeth was covered in mud. Her ankle was swollen, but she was smiling and asking about Tanner. She was going to be just fine. Behind her came R.C., grinning. Ollie hugged him when he climbed down.

"Look who else I found, Chief!" he said and pointed up.

A man in muddy wet jeans and a camo hunting vest climbed down. His back was to Ollie. On the seat was a cute little blond-headed girl dressed from head to toe in camouflage. She was waiting for the man to climb out so she could follow. Ollie allowed him to help her down and then placed his hand on his shoulder.

"Jake Crosby?" Ollie asked.

"Yes, sir," Jake said, trying to tell the orderly that he didn't need a wheelchair.

"We've been wonderin' about you all night."

"I'm sure glad to be out of those woods. I've got a lot to tell you."

"I want to hear—" Ollie said before he was interrupted.

"Jake. Jake!" Mick Johnson called out as he pushed his way through the crowd.

"Mick! Did you get my message?"

"Kinda. We didn't really know what it meant...what's with all the blood at your camper?" he asked before Ollie could cut him off.

R.C. picked Katy up and said, "I'll take her in and get her warmed up." Jake nodded his understanding. R.C. avoided the cameras like someone in a witness protection program.

"Sheriff, I killed two men, but they had every intention of killing us, I swear," Jake said soberly, looking Ollie straight in the eyes.

Two men! Shit! Ollie thought. This was way too much to discuss in the parking lot. But before he could tell Jake to wait, the muddy man added, pointing at Elizabeth, "and I witnessed one of the gang members killing another gangster who was about to rape her." The TV reporters and the mass of spectators went wild. Jake hadn't even noticed the reporters or anyone in the crowd before he started the pandemonium.

Ollie grabbed Jake by the arm, "We need to get outta here. Do you need medical attention?"

"No. I'm okay!" Jake shouted over the reporter's questions. "But my little girl just got taken inside. I don't wanna leave her!"

"You need to call your wife. She's worried," Ollie added.

"She knows?" Jake asked confused.

"Yes. We have a lot to talk about, Mr. Crosby," Ollie answered, putting his arm around Jake and guiding him toward the ER entrance. Mick followed. Out of the corner of his eye, Ollie saw Marlow drive up. Marlow's face was the picture of jealousy. The deputies cleared a path through the sea of people so Ollie and Jake could go through the automatic doors. Ollie wanted to get Jake into a quiet room and make sure there wasn't anybody else out there that needed rescuing.

"Damn fine job on the recovery, Marlow" Joe Wilson said sarcastically.

Sheriff Marlow glared at him, then turned to follow the group inside. *Maybe I can salvage a photo op inside,* he thought.

Jake saw Elizabeth hugging her mother and father. When she saw him, she immediately pointed at him. Her mother turned to look. Tears were flowing as she mouthed the words "Thank you."

Jake smiled and nodded.

Chapter 85

Just as Elizabeth rounded the corner of the intensive care unit, the nurses caught up with her. The head nurse was filling out paperwork when the rowdy group suddenly appeared. She stepped in front of the door to Tanner's room. "Whoa…you can't go in there, dear. You need to get cleaned up," she said, looking at the dried blood and mud all over Elizabeth. "You can visit him later. He's heavily sedated now, anyway."

"I'm going in! You can't stop me!" Elizabeth said defiantly, and several nurses grabbed her. "Please…please, I have to see him," she pleaded as tears rolled down her cheeks.

"Let her in," Dr. Sarhan responded to everyone's surprise as he stepped out from behind a curtain cleaning his glasses.

Elizabeth gathered her composure. Dr. Sarhan stepped in front of her. "He is sedated. He will not know you here. He has a tube down his throat to help him breathe. He has terrible trauma. Do not be surprised at what you see," Dr. Sarhan explained calmly, hoping to prepare her.

"I know, I was there," Elizabeth replied, pushing her hair behind her ears. She pushed open the door and limped slowly into the dark room. Only Dr. Sarhan followed her. Everyone else watched. The Beasleys hugged each other. Then Tanner's family began asking Steve Tillman questions faster than he could answer.

Inside the room Elizabeth saw a myriad of lights, gauges, and several pieces of sophisticated pieces of equipment all dedicated to monitoring Tanner, who was lying flat on his back, eyes closed. Elizabeth fought hard to keep from sobbing when she saw his badly swollen and bruised face. She used the backs of her hands to dry her tears, then slowly limped to the side of his bed. Grabbing his right hand, she held it tight. With her left, she gently touched his face.

"Tanner?" She asked softly. A tear fell, landing on their hands. "Tanner…sweetheart, it's me. I'm here. I'm here for you. Oh, God, Tanner. I love you so much," she couldn't hold back the sobs anymore. Kissing his hand, she tried to dry the tears again. "Tanner, I'm okay…I'm all right, thanks to you."

Dr. Sarhan watched Tanner's heart monitor begin to race, yet no outward physical response was detectable. The doctor wondered if he could hear Elizabeth.

"It's been an awful night, but I'm here now and I'll be here for you as long as it takes for you to get better. I'm so glad to see you…you look so good to me," she said, barely audible. Her tears were now flowing faster than she could wipe them away.

Tanner could hear every word she said. He could smell her hair. He recognized her gentle touch. He wanted to shout, he wanted to scream with joy. For the first time tonight he relaxed. Her presence, her voice, was the best medicine he could receive.

"Oh, Tanner…we have so much to talk about. I'm just so thankful you're alive. I have…I've been so worried about you," she said, sitting down on the edge on the bed, never letting go of his hand. "I've decided that I don't care where I go to college as long as it's with you. I don't care what my parents say…I never want to be separated from you again, Tanner Tillman."

Elizabeth kissed his cheek and noticed that tears were flowing out of the corners of his eyes. She smiled and kissed him again. She knew he could hear her.

"I love you, Tanner."

"I not know he can hear you, young lady. We need to check you.

Let him rest," Dr. Sarhan said as he looked at her swollen ankle. "He awake in a few hours. You talk then."

"He *can* hear me," she replied, looking at Tanner's face. "I *know* he can."

"Tanner, I need to go get cleaned up; then I'll be right back. Everything's gonna be better than ever," she said and then tenderly kissed his cheek as she whispered, "and I get to pick the parking place next time."

Elizabeth stood up, reached into her pocket, and pulled out the tiny Beanie Baby that Katy had given her in the truck. She carefully placed it right next to Tanner's head and wiped away another round of her tears. Elizabeth smiled and kissed him one more time, gently wiping away his tears that told her everything she needed to know.

Chapter 86

"And you're not married...so what's wrong with you?" Jake heard Katy ask R.C., cocking her head to one side. She said it with the tone and inflection conveying her belief that every adult was supposed to be married. They were sharing a handful of M&M's, obviously having an in-depth conversation about R.C.'s life. Katy loved to meddle.

"No, but I have a trophy girlfriend. She's...how can I put this, she's a professional dancer and—" But before R.C. could complete the sentence, Ollie laid a firm hand on his shoulder. R.C. knew better than to provide any more details.

"A dancer...eeeww...I took dancing lessons and hated it. So what does R.C. stand for?" she innocently asked.

"Well...um...it stands for Ralph Carmelo," he said shyly. He really didn't want to tell her.

"I like R.C. better," she replied instantly. Everybody within hearing range laughed out loud.

With that exchange, Jake knew that Katy was all right. He let out a deep sigh of relief, then looked around the ER. All this was the consequence of his decision to use deadly force to protect her. The bloody image of the shooting at the camper flashed through his mind, followed by the vision of Elizabeth's attacker, then the horrifying sight of the dead stalker he had left in the swamp. Jake knew many new nightmares were ahead. He wondered if he would ever be able to go into dark woods again. He started to question having killed the first guy. He'd always second-guess that decision. Jake's mind was spinning out of control. He stared blankly across the room.

"Hey, are you okay?" Ollie asked, grabbing Jake's arm.

"Yeah, yeah...I'm sorry. What was I saying? I'm just totally exhausted." Jake started shaking and rubbing his forehead with his right hand.

Ollie opened the supply closet door and led Jake inside. Ollie wanted to debrief him—to make certain there was nobody else out there and he was anxious to hear Jake's version of the events.

Something in Jake's vest hit the doorjamb as he entered. He reached into his pocket; feeling his cell phone, he shook his head. He checked it. Twenty-one missed calls. The last twelve were from his home. He smiled. For the first time in years, Jake really wanted to talk with Morgan. In fact, he yearned to see her.

"Hey, Sheriff, can I please have a minute to call my wife?" Jake begged. He knew the sheriff needed to question him, but he had to talk with Morgan.

Ollie understood.

The sheriff's attention shifted briefly to Marlow, who could be seen through the glass ER doors waving his arms in front of a television camera. *What an idiot.* "Sure...take your time. I'll be out here," Ollie replied as he turned over a cleaning bucket to make a seat for Jake. "Everybody gets one phone call," he chuckled, closing the closet door behind him.

Acknowledgements

I owe my wife, Melissa, and daughter, Jessi, the deepest heartfelt gratitude for allowing me to slip away countless nights and weekends to write. Thanks also to the many friends and family who read the manuscript along the way and kept me motivated. I also want to thank my Mossy Oak®, BioLogic®, and Alabama Farmers Coop families for being supportive of this whole process. And I can't forget Joe Bush, who worked miracles on a regular basis retrieving "lost" chapters from the mysterious place that I would accidentally save them.

Paul Brown was always ready to hand out publishing advice and in fact, introduced me to Kyle Jennings, of Bad Dog Management, who acted as agent, editor and ultimately got *The Dummy Line* published.

Kyle deserves special thanks for seeing the story as worthy and spending countless hours editing. And I do mean countless.

Jill Conner Browne's belief and support of my writings and her up-grades to this story and its flow are greatly appreciated. Her perfectly timed wit made us all smile when we wanted to scream and probably prevented a brutal homicide—mine.

A very special thanks to Suzanne Barnhill whose keen eye and wise counsel in all things English is unparalleled. I am quite certain that I challenged her skills and patience.

Many times I have wished that my good friend Bob Dixon could have read this story. Bob loved a good book almost as much as he loved to hunt. Turkey season isn't the same without him.

Living in Mississippi for the past 13 years has been a blessing. I certainly haven't traveled all over the world, but I have yet to find a place that appreciates a good story like the folks of my adopted home. I hope this one finds favor.

All errors and omissions are mine.